*Little Town*

of

Deathlehem

Little Town

of

Deathlehem

Edited by
Michael J. Evans
and
Harrison Graves

A
Grinning Skull Press
Publication

O Little Town of Deathlehem
Compilation Copyright © 2013 Grinning Skull Press

The Skull logo with stylized lettering and ghoulish garland was created for Grinning Skull Press by Dan Moran, http://dan-moran-art.com/.
Cover designed by Jeffrey Kosh, http://jeffreykosh.wix.com/jeffreykoshgraphics.

ISBN: 0989026949 (paperback)
ISBN-13: 978-0-9890269-4-9 (paperback)
ISBN: 978-0-9890269-5-6 (e-book)

DEDICATION

This time it's personal. To my mother and father, Eileen and Frank, my sister and brother, Susan and Roy, and my grandparents, Emily and Roy, it's not Christmas without you. Love and miss you all.

TABLE OF CONTENTS

ACKNOWLEDGMENTS

We would like to thank Michael R. Danaitis, Jr. and Theresa Dooley. All your hard work is greatly appreciated. We would also to like thank Dan Moran for his generous donation of the interior artwork, and Jeffrey Kosh for an amazing job on the cover design. Huge thanks also go out to Jessica McHugh for coming up with the title. And lastly, to all the authors who submitted to this anthology, you made it such a joy, it actually felt a little like Christmas.

S*EASON'S S*CREAMINGS

Merry Christmas!, *Happy Holidays!*, *Season's Greetings!*, and all that other happy crappy holiday stuff.

To that, I say, "BAH! HUMBUG!"

Yeah, that's my typical response lately to all the holiday greetings I get, which is really a shame. I wasn't always an Ebenezer; as a kid, I enjoyed the holiday season and did the usual kid things at Christmas, including leaving cookies and milk out for Santa, falling asleep on the stairs while waiting for the jolly old elf to arrive, and sneaking peeks at Christmas gifts weeks before it was time. The tree went up on Christmas Eve and we would put some ornaments on it. Not all, mind you, but some. The lights, tinsel, garland, and the rest of the ornaments "magically" appeared after we went to bed. A "gift" from Santa to the family. Imagine, through the eyes of a child, the wonder of going to bed to a semi-naked tree and waking up to find one done up in all her holiday glory. And the presents! So many presents packed under that artificial tree! More than we deserved, really, but who were we to question. There were the usual ones from mom and dad, my brothers and sister, and my grandparents, but the best ones were always the ones from Santa. Well, from mom and dad and Santa because those were the gifts you really *wanted*, not the ones you *needed*. Never mind the fact that the lettering on the gift tags was identical, something my older brothers were all too eager to point out. They tried everything they could think of to get me to say that Santa wasn't real because mom always said, "The minute you stop believing, there'll be no more gifts for you under the tree." I guess they figured that would mean more presents for them.

The memories, as you can see, are happy ones, even with the conspiring evil brothers. So you might find yourself asking, "What changed?" And my answer to that question is, "I don't know." I've tried to figure it out, but for the life of me, I haven't been able to pinpoint when or why it happened. Maybe it has to do with the commercialism of the holiday, and the fact that the stores have all the Christmas decorations and candy on display in July. At least around here they do. So Christmas is right there alongside the jack o'lanterns, trick-or-treat buckets, latex masks, and candy corn, and by the time the actual holiday rolls around, I'm sick of it.

More recently, however, even my Ebenezer attitude has fizzled, and I don't even want to acknowledge the holidays. Too much personal loss has caused dark clouds to amass half way through November, and they don't dissipate until March. This deeply saddens me, and I mean that with all sincerity. Yeah, I used to laugh at people's reactions when I tossed out a "Bah! Humbug!" to their holiday wishes, but the loss of the holiday spirit is more heart-breaking because Christmas meant so much to the people I miss the most around this time of year. Especially to my mother and sister. Friends have told me I should celebrate if for no other reason than to keep the spirit of the holiday alive in honor of them, but it's easier said than done. But I told them I would try.

And that's where this anthology comes in.

It might sound strange to put together a collection of Christmas horror stories, but it's a melding of the thing I love with the holiday the people I love cherished. And holding with the spirit of the season—and because mama always told us when we were kids that it is better to give than receive—it was decided that this would be a charity anthology benefiting the Elizabeth Glaser Pediatric AIDS Foundation.

As with any anthology, I never know what to expect when the call for submissions goes out. Given the holiday theme, I was expecting stories with happily-ever-after endings. I mean, after all, it is Christmas, and you can't have a story about Christmas that doesn't end on a cheerful note, right?

Wrong. Oh so wrong.

The stories you are about to read are dark, some humorously so (at least I got a chuckle out of them), but dark nevertheless. In fact, the closest we get to a happy ending comes from Catherine Grant, who opens this collection. Her tale, *One of His Own*, shows us that even Krampus, surprisingly enough, has a softer side. Even more surprising, though, is Simon Bradley's *Special Delivery*, who lets us know that jolly old Saint Nicholas isn't as saintly as his name implies. You might just find yourself stoking up the fire in the ol' fireplace with the hopes that Santa will think twice before sliding down your chimney on Christmas Eve.

But Santa and Krampus aside (yeah, I know some of you don't believe), the holidays, especially Christmas, are about spending time with family—unless, of course, your family is like the ones that appear in D. Alexander Ward's *Home for the Holidays* and JP Behrens' *A Christmas to Remember*. With folks like these, maybe it would be better to forego the relatives and spend the day curled up on the sofa by yourself and admire the tree you laboriously decorated. Then again, maybe that's not such a good idea, not after reading Christopher Miron's *Ornaments* and Jeff C. Carter's *With Their Eyes All Aglow*. That pre-lit fiber optic tree you paid a fortune for just might end up at curbside, decorations and all. But such is Christmas in Deathlehem.

Deathlehem, where the simple act of believing in Santa and Christmas miracles helps keep the horrors alive and prolong the suffering of others. Don't believe me? Just check out Peter White's *Saint Nick Sticks* or Mark Onspaugh's *You'd Better Watch Out*.

Deathlehem, where Christmas miracles comes with a price and family gatherings and office parties more often than not turn deadly. Need a last-minute gift? Why not check out Professor LaGungo's place just down the road—the gift selection there is to die for.

Welcome to Deathlehem…

Michal J. Evans
and the staff at
Grinning Skull Press,
Best Wishes for a very scary Christmas
and a frightful New Year!

❄One of His Own❄
Catherine Grant

Krampus and Sinterklaas winked into the apartment early Christmas morning. They stood on a floor coated in excrement and cockroaches that moved in the dark, the faint moonlight glittering off the vermin's forewings. There was dirty laundry in every corner, as well as dishes coated in grime and mold. Any decorations that would indicate it was the holiday season were absent. There was no evergreen tree, no twinkling lights, no cookies and milk left for Sinterklaas or carrots for the reindeer.

The smell hit them both immediately: a stench of decay, bodily fluids, and cigarettes. Sinterklaas gagged and one brown mitten went to his face.

"I'm getting the fuck out of here," he mumbled from behind hand and beard.

He was about to hit the button on his doeskin belt and open the portal when Krampus lay a hand on his forearm, stilling him. "There's supposed to be a child here. We can't just leave."

The fat man pointed around them. "Do you see a tree? Presents?"

"You know that doesn't mean anything."

Sinterklaaus rolled his eyes. He refused to move from where he stood and venture into the apartment, or remove his gloved hand from his face. His blue eyes twinkled, and then teared up.

"Well, there's obviously nothing here for *me*. Oh, God, I think I'm going to throw up."

Krampus held up his hand. "I hear something rustling." He cocked his horned head toward the hallway, which was obstructed with bags of garbage and more laundry.

"There are at least five cats in this apartment. That's probably what you're hearing. It's certainly what I'm smelling."

"No, it's human. I can sense it, even over your groaning." He took a few steps into the center of the living room and roaches crunched under his hooves.

"Whatever child is here, they're certainly one of your own. You go fetch it if you want it so badly. I'll be outside waiting." Sinterklaas hit the button on his belt and disappeared in a flash of brilliant rainbow light.

Krampus narrowed his eyes at his elf half-brother's fading impression, just an outline of the robust man's body left by temporal distortion. He uttered a low growl and swung one clawed hand through the space, scattering the particles like glitter. It was wholly unsatisfying.

He turned his attention back to the hallway, which led to three doors. Krampus pushed his way through piles of garbage and laundry streaked with shit and grime, kicking a pizza box across the room with one cloven hoof. He opened the first door and what he saw inside made his lips curl. His demon eyes adjusted to the darkness and there was a woman, half-naked, passed out on a stained, bare mattress on the floor, a belt still wrapped around her arm. Her body was covered in bruises, and she smelled like vinegar and disease. Her mind was asleep, but dreamless, formless, and dark.

He closed the door and went to the next room, which was filled top to bottom with boxes and bags of garbage and laundry. He didn't know how someone so visibly poor could afford so many clothes, but the room was a mountain of fabric. A legion of cockroaches scurried out and Krampus slammed the door, cursing Sinterklaas for making him search the home alone after such a painfully uneventful Yule. The night was almost over and he hadn't found a single child that was his, not even a hint of one. His stomach ached with hunger and his throat cried out for hot blood and fear. Then he smelled what he'd come for, like a faint perfume.

The door behind him creaked open. A tiny face peered out from the darkness of the third room, pale and dirty. He could sense it was a girl, maybe a little older than three, though small. She had large brown eyes that looked at him with interest rather than fear, and burning in her mind like a bonfire was a singular instinct—*hunger*. She opened the door a bit more and he saw she was wearing a sagging diaper and nothing else. Her long brown hair was greasy and matted.

The room she'd been in was a bathroom, smeared and over-flowing with filth. She stepped into the hallway and looked up at Krampus, who towered above her at almost seven feet tall from the tip of his horns to his hooves. Moonlight came in from a window at the end of the hall and she could see him, a hulking, horned beast with sharp teeth and eyes like drops of onyx. She walked up to him on shaky legs and put a hand on his knee, which, like the rest of his body, was covered in thick gray fur. She liked the feel of it, and she reached out and wrapped her body around his calf. The girl child didn't cry or even speak. She just clung to him and placed her tiny feet against his hooves.

Krampus reached down and picked up the girl child in his arms. Her diaper was full and oozed its foulness onto his fur. She was malnourished, probably dehydrated as well. Her cheeks and eyes were sunken and dark. She smiled and buried herself in his arms and sighed, releasing a burden that Krampus couldn't name. He'd never felt such an emotion in a child before, and it was not easy to decipher unfamiliar thoughts. Emotions came to him in bursts of color and light. The thoughts from the little girl, under the bonfire of hunger, were dark and thick, like oil. When she buried her face in his fur, it was like someone poured cool, clean water into her subconscious. She began to fall asleep in his arms, a sense of happy, pink contentment diluting the foulness further.

A groan came from the first room. "Lydia!" Krampus heard the flicking sound of a lighter. "Lydia, bring Momma a Mountain Dew from the fridge."

The little girl tensed and the blackness began to creep back in, poisoning the spring and drowning her pink happiness in gray. She looked up at Krampus with her large brown eyes, and although she didn't make a sound, he knew she was pleading with him. His own black eyes looked into hers, through to her soul. What he saw made him still. The little girl had no fear to give him. She had already seen horrors that eclipsed even the appearance of a horned demon in her living room. The memories she allowed him to see made Krampus sick with revulsion. Without hesitation, he pushed the button on his belt and the portal enveloped them both, sending them outside. The rush of cool, clean air was immediate, and Krampus drank it in. The little girl breathed deeply and was soon back to sleep.

He looked down at the bundle in his arms. The twinkling of the multicolored lights in the courtyard trees danced on her skin and gave the illusion of health. After a few moments, her breathing slowed and her thoughts stilled. The inky dark drifted away, leaving only calm waters of blue.

A scream of anguish erupted from the apartment and the girl tensed again. Krampus pulled her tighter to him and she relaxed and fell back to sleep. He found his basket and placed her inside, then took out his brass looking glass and held it against the wall.

It fascinated Krampus how upset the mother became when she realized her daughter was gone. How much could one miss a demanding, dirty bundle of flesh? He watched with puzzlement as the waifish woman with blonde hair chain-smoked and paced the floor in her bathrobe, telling the officer on the other end of the phone that her *baby* was stolen, screaming every other word for emphasis. She was crying so hard she shook, although he couldn't tell if her arm trembled from emotion or withdrawal every time she took a puff of her stale cigarette. As soon as she hung up the phone, the woman went back into the room she'd been sleeping in and slammed the door. Krampus sensed she was worried about the girl, but she was also afraid: not that her *baby* was gone as she said, but that she herself would get in trouble. He saw her leave the bedroom with a box, and head toward the small room where he'd found the child.

Krampus had never understood human attachment to their young, but the woman stumbling around her apartment was an anathema. He felt good about taking the little girl and assumed the mother would get over her bout of conscience and move on with her life, thankful that some kind stranger had relieved her of her obligation to clothe and feed a tiny person. Truthfully, she was doing a terrible job to begin with. She looked through stacks of garbage for what should have been her most valuable possession.

As he watched her through the small brass ring of enchanted crystal, Krampus realized that he wanted the woman's life. It was a purely irrational desire. He could claw open her throat and lick the hot blood as it pooled on her chest, but it wouldn't satiate his hunger. She was too old and her fear would taste like ashes. Eating corrupted flesh would also make him more ravenous, and the thirst for pure blood would drive him mad. He rubbed his bearded chin and flicked off the looking glass.

Krampus lifted the basket with the sleeping child onto his shoulders and hit the wink button again, this time for home, knowing that it meant he would go hungry for another year. Sinterklaas would most likely stay out 'til dawn, eating cookies and gobbling joy like he did every Christmas Eve night. Then he would stumble home, his belly stretched tight from feeding, and rub it in with a smug arrogance he knew drove his demon half-brother to rage.

It didn't matter. Next year, Krampus would hunt better with two sets of eyes.

❄ ❄ ❄

He called her Etta, little one, and she would become his Child of Yule.

Sinterklaas had first objected to the presence of a human child at the North Pole. "Are you mad?" He belched, and the smell of gingerbread filled the air. He went to the cupboard and took out a bottle of Christmas wine and poured the contents into a horned cup. "Or are you keeping it as a snack for later?" He wrinkled his nose in disgust at the basket. "It smells like that dwelling. Even humans wash their livestock before eating them, so I suppose that's civilized."

Krampus growled and snatched the basket away. "You disgust me. I'm not eating the child." He sighed. "It would do me no good, she's not afraid of me. From what I can see inside her thoughts, she isn't afraid of anything anymore." He went to his room and placed the basket inside. The little girl had been asleep for hours, a deep, peaceful slumber that Krampus didn't want to disturb.

Sinterklaas laughed until his belly shook. He belched again and sat down on a sofa in the inner common room. The two bachelor brothers shared a modest cabin of gleaming hardwood, swept and kept clean by the house elves. The furniture was comfortable, overstuffed red couches covered with furs. Although the elf and demon did not eat regular food, the house elves did, so the air was filled with the smells of honey and baking bread.

Sinterklaas sighed and drank deeply from the horn. The hearth crackled, and from its center a fire sprite giggled and swam in the flames. Krampus wouldn't sit with his brother—his fur was still soiled. He stood in front of the fire, his arms crossed.

"I want to keep the child with us," Krampus said. "I could use some help hunting on Yule."

"You're a sentimental fool," said Sinterklaas. "Do what you will, just don't come to me when your pet becomes more of a burden than you bargained for."

"I wasn't asking your permission, brother."

Krampus turned and stalked away, toward the baths. After he was done washing the stink of the human world from his fur, he turned to Nixie, the bath sprite, and asked her to take care of the girl in his chambers and make sure she had proper clothes, but only after she'd awoken.

When Etta rolled out of the basket more than twelve hours later, she was hungry and cranky. Nixie made no haste in finding the child and pulling her toward the baths. The girl's eyes were transfixed on the blue-skinned sprite with almond soap eyes and hair of foam. One of the house elves helped to get the diaper off, frowning in distaste at the contents, and Etta was unceremoniously pushed into the hot, frothing water and scrubbed until her skin was pink. The little girl appeared quite angry at the bath sprite, enough so that Krampus quickly dismissed Nixie once Etta was groomed and dressed in a modest shift and fitted with doeskin booties.

Sinterklaas was kinder to the girl once her hair was brushed out and she smelled of peppermint, but he still cast a skeptical eye toward Krampus and grunted, waving the girl away from him when she tried to poke his enormous girth. He sighed, resigning himself to the new houseguest, and stumbled toward his chambers, his belly full of mulled wine and sugar. For him, Christmas was over, but to Krampus the year had just begun.

Etta was much older than Krampus thought; maybe five instead of two or three. When he began to feed her properly, she grew tall and strong, although she never learned to speak. She communicated with Krampus and Sinterklaas through her thoughts, which ebbed and flowed between the innocent thoughts of a child and the murky darkness of her memories.

When she was seven, Etta began helping Krampus on Yule night. Although she couldn't fully read the thoughts of other humans, her proximity to the demon and half-elf for extended periods gave her the ability to sense strong emotions such as lust and hate.

The first year, she led Krampus to the home of a ten-year-old boy who liked to torture and skin neighborhood dogs. The second year, Etta pointed to one house where a little girl not much older than she was planning to murder her baby sister. Sinterklaas was no longer able to boast that he gorged on joy while his brother starved most years. In fact, he seemed to be a bit jealous of his brother's protégée and good fortune. Krampus ate well from then forward, and rewarded Etta with whatever her heart desired. Usually her requests were simple—dolls or sweets—and she was given all that and more in abundance.

When Etta was eleven, she asked Krampus for a different gift. She wanted a dagger. He commissioned a dwarf craftsman renowned for his skill and the beauty of his wares. The blade was sheathed in ornately carved silver, the hilt decorated with a ruby that shone like a drop of blood. When Krampus gave it to her, Etta's thoughts were a well-spring of green and blue, the closest thing that she would ever say to *I love you*. She hugged him, burying her face in his fur. The next twelve months were consumed with how to use the small weapon, much to the dismay of the house elves who sanded and re-painted much of the hardwood in the house that year.

The year afterward, Etta approached Krampus on Yule's Eve while he was in the sitting room reading a worn copy of *Nibelungenlied*. She wore a homespun dress of purple linen and doeskin boots bound in rabbit furs. Nixie had combed her auburn brown hair and made a single braid down both sides that tucked behind her ears. Despite how much the girl protested and rolled her eyes, Krampus knew that Etta liked the attention from the bath sprite, even if she pretended not to and pouted the whole time. When she was younger, she never acted in such a way. He found the girl's recent change of mood to be both confusing and troubling.

Krampus looked up from his book at Etta, his eyebrow

arched. She was staring at her feet, biting her lip as she always did when she was anxious. He put down the tome and waited.

I want to find my mother.

Etta's thoughts were clear to him now. It took almost no effort to decipher the complex bursts of color and texture. He saw that she indeed wanted to find her mother, but not for the reasons he feared for so long after he took her. For years, he'd wondered if Etta would want to go back home, to live among her own kind and make friends with other children. Sinterklaas had only stoked his anxiety by muttering occasionally that he couldn't keep the girl in the North Pole forever, only going out on Yule Eve to be among her own kind, and even then it was not to play with children. After a time, that fear passed as Etta became content.

Now, she expressed in color and jagged ripples that she did indeed want to visit the woman who gave birth to her, to kill her.

Krampus still saw the murky black of Etta's old memories, but only on the outlying edges of her subconscious. After years of nightmares and pain, she was able to cope with the memories of abuse. She'd controlled her anger and bitterness, but only through focusing on one thought—someday, she would return and kill the waifish, blonde woman who had once called herself "mother." Krampus hadn't discouraged it. He himself had felt the urge that first night to end the woman's life and drink from her flesh. Etta's desire to kill the woman she called Mara, or "nightmare," was as thick and velvety as a red rose. When she had those thoughts, Krampus tended to withdraw from her and let her be. She would come to him afterward and they would sit together, speaking their silent language of comfort and love.

Etta sat down on the sofa, the worn copy of *Nibelungenlied* between them, and Krampus didn't sense that deep vengeance within her now. She was calm, emotionless.

We will go tonight, he told her.

Etta nodded and went back to her rooms to prepare. She emerged hours later wearing a pair of slacks, a loose-fitting shirt, and her doeskin boots. The dagger was sheathed and tucked into her belt. Krampus handed Etta her coat, lined with furs to keep warm, and then the wink button. She'd gotten too big for them to use one button together, so Krampus and Sinterklaas made the decision to trust her with one of her own. She placed it on her belt, next to the dagger, and nodded.

Krampus hefted the basket onto his shoulders and placed one hand on Etta's face. Her emotions were almost absent, which struck him as odd. He dismissed the concern as Sinterklaas entered the room.

"You two are thick as thieves," he bellowed, and then slapped his brother on the arm.

Krampus growled and rubbed the spot. "Etta and I are going our own way tonight." He glanced toward the girl, who only nodded. "Don't wait up for us. Not that I expected it."

Sinterklaas frowned and looked toward Etta, who betrayed nothing with her demeanor. He shrugged and pushed the wink button, the glittery temporal distortion appearing as he vanished. Krampus took Etta's hand and they hit their own buttons simultaneously.

They were transported to a dark, snowy street lined with businesses and offices. The building closest to them was a hospital, and it smelled of fear, piss, and rubbing alcohol, even from a distance. Krampus looked toward Etta, who narrowed her eyes and marched forward. She entered the hospital with her wink button and he came in close behind, looking about to make sure they weren't discovered. Etta seemed to know where to go, and they navigated the dark, sterile hallways in what seemed like a maze of identical corridors. Even the residents looked the same: old and frail and wrinkly. They came to another wing of the hospital and Etta pushed through a double door. The people in this section seemed less frail, but more lost. Krampus passed rooms with patients strapped to beds. Others seemed trapped in their own minds and drowned in a fog of sedatives. They reached the end of the hall, and Etta turned and opened a door.

The room was dark, lit only by moonlight. Lying in the bed was a skeleton with stringy blonde hair and sunken eyes. Time had not been kind to Mara. *Mara* had not been kind to Mara. Her skin was pocked with red, crusting sores, most of them on her face. Although time passed more harshly in the human world, the woman looked twenty years older, closer to fifty than thirty.

Mara's eyes fluttered open and Krampus made himself dim, hiding his form from view. Her eyes caught the outline of a giant, horned beast in her room, and she breathed in to scream until her gaze fell on Etta, sitting on the side of the bed. The resemblance between the two, even in Mara's ruined state, was undeniable. She reached out for her daughter and then began to cry.

"My baby," she whispered. "You've come back to me. I don't know how, but you came back to me."

Etta shuffled forward and took Mara's hand. She reached out to hold her daughter, but Etta wouldn't go to her.

"Come give your Mamma a hug." She licked her cracked lips and stared forward, the smile dying. Krampus could sense a strong desire for a cigarette. "Hey sweetie, do you think you could get me a Mountain Dew from the machine outside?"

Etta froze, then slowly reached to her belt for the dagger. As the blade was unsheathed, something inside the little girl spilled out, a malformed horror in the dark places of her mind that she'd kept buried there. Krampus gasped as he saw the monster emerge from hiding. The anger and fear inside Etta was a dark, snarling beast of murder and rage that flew from the pool of her subconscious like a dragon, dripping with blood and gore. The velvet rose of bitterness was gone. It had been masquerading as pain, but was really a vicious animal waiting to devour. Etta's revenge was a sticky, deadly pool of hate that terrified even Etta herself. It was evil, and for the first time Krampus could smell her fear. She was one of the bad children, and to him she smelled as divine as a Christmas roast.

His eyes glowed yellow with the thirst. *Stop it, Etta.* He whispered to her, using every ounce of willpower not to step forward and snatch her up. *This woman is no threat to anyone. She's going to die here, you know that. There's nothing for us here.*

He felt Etta pull back, her hand hovering over the dagger. The blood dragon screamed and rolled in the thick, oxblood water, and Etta pulled the dagger out of its sheath.

She deserves pain. Etta held the blade against her body, hiding it. She wanted to push it into Mara's ribs, into her heart. The desire fed the blood dragon more and Krampus growled in frustration, feeling his control shrink as Etta gave in to her hate.

I love you. He knelt on the ground and closed his eyes, feeling his composure slip away inch by inch. Etta's fear would taste so delicious; it would be hot and bitter in his mouth. Afterward, he would weep for her and Sinterklaas would only shake his head in pity. He would mutter as he drank his mead that it was bound to happen. Krampus growled and his jaw opened and he began to pant like a dog, his tongue lolling out and nearly touching the floor.

My little one, he said. He repeated it over and over, like a mantra.

Etta watched him as he struggled, although to her mother it seemed like she was staring at nothing.

"You stupid or somethin', kid?" Mara barked. "You gonna get me a Mountain Dew or not?"

Etta wouldn't look at her. She stood and the dagger dropped from her hand and clattered to the floor. She went to Krampus and threw her arms around his neck, burying her face in the fur. The blood dragon in her subconscious melted away like wax, and in its place was the pink calm, the place of belonging and acceptance that had been so hard for Krampus to identify that first night Etta came to him. His bloodlust faded as her hot tears fell onto his fur. He looked into Etta's eyes, her brown eyes that were so open to him, and he did not see even the velvet rose.

She smiled and wiped her tears. *Leave?*

Krampus nodded. *Go ahead. I have something to do.*

Etta pushed her button, leaving a small cloud of glitter. Mara stared at the empty space, her eyes wide.

Krampus stood back on his feet and stalked across the room. He bent down and picked up the tiny dagger, no more than a toothpick in his hand. He made himself visible to the human and a scream caught itself in Mara's throat. She put her hand to her chest, and Krampus cocked his horned head and listened. Her heart was weak, the heartbeat irregular and slowing. He bent down and smiled, his grin yellow and terrible, and grasped Mara's wrist.

"We can't have this happen again, so I'm going to be merciful. Your heart is failing, but the doctors could come in and revive you. They could prolong your miserable, selfish life. Is that what you want?" He lifted the blade, the point hovering over her wrist.

Mara's eyes shifted back and forth, and then closed. A single tear fell down her cheek and she shook her head, then lifted her wrist upward. Surprisingly to Krampus, she had no fear. He ran the dagger down the inside of her arm from wrist to elbow, trying not to gag at the smell of her tainted blood as it spilled onto the off-white industrial sheets. She lifted her other arm to him and he did the same, the thin blade easily slicing through the skin. Mara lay down and closed her eyes, the sheets around her blooming red like a velvet rose. Soon she was still and white. Krampus closed her eyes and hit the button, transporting himself outside the hospital. He left the dagger on her nightstand.

Etta waited for him. Her eyes were glossy with tears and she began to apologize immediately in bursts of blue bubbles that floated over the surface of the pink water. Krampus shook his head, indicating there was no need. He did, however, plead that they move on, and quickly. He was still hungry, and the willpower he'd expended had taxed him sorely. Besides, the night was almost over and they would have to hurry if they wanted to catch up with Sinterklaas.

Etta nodded, and they hit their wink buttons again. She led Krampus to a suburb in London, to a house where an eleven-year-old girl named Mary lived with her parents. Mary had already murdered a little boy, strangled him and carved her initials in his stomach with a pair of scissors. When they winked into her room, it was clean and orderly. The girl slept peacefully in a white canopy bed with pink curtains that matched her carpet. On the desk there was a note, written in crayon that read,

I murder so that I may come back.

Krampus ate well that night, even better than his brother, and when Sinterklaas came home, reeking of tinsel and evergreen and with dog poop on one boot, Etta and Krampus laughed at him. They boasted of their meal over cups of hot chocolate, rubbing it in until the elf stormed away in a huff, belching gingerbread and clouds of joy as insubstantial as cotton candy.

Christmas Wine
Matt Cowan

Cindy stared out the frost-hazed front window at the ornamental congregation across the street as plump snowflakes drifted down to accumulate on her grandmother's lawn. The air was heavy with the scent of pine from the Christmas tree. A smiling Santa on his sleigh urging reindeer forward was surrounded by a rock garden full of gnomish statuettes wearing conical hats. Cindy assumed they were meant to serve as stand-ins for Santa's elves, but found their crafty expressions unsettling. In the far corner of the yard stood the frailest snowman Cindy had ever seen, far too thin to withstand the day's strong winds. A station wagon moved into view, blocking the scene as it pulled into the driveway. "Uncle Winston's here!" Cindy yelled, turning away from the window and racing toward the door.

Uncle Winston was a large, grey-bearded man. Cindy loved to listen to him talk, particularly on late Christmas Eve nights when she was supposed to be asleep; rather than stay beneath the covers and await the arrival of morning so she could open presents, she would sneak to the door and listen as he told ghost stories to the grown-ups. Cindy looked forward to them almost as much as opening packages on Christmas morning.

Icy wind swept into the room as Grandma opened the door for Uncle Winston, who carried a large bag over his shoulder.

"You've brought the elements with you," Grandma laughed.

"If that's the worst that follows me this year, it'll be a jolly holiday indeed," he said, dropping the bag by the tree, and giving Cindy a wink as he did so. "How's my favorite niece?"

Cindy beamed back at him. "Great, now that you're here! I was worried you weren't coming."

Uncle Winston's broad smile faltered. "Yes, I was a bit... delayed this year. Couldn't be avoided," he said, shifting his eyes to the window. "What say you join me for some eggnog?"

As Uncle Winston moved inside, Cindy caught sight of the house across the street again. The slender snowman she glimpsed earlier was gone.

❄ ❄ ❄

Later that evening, Uncle Winston entered the packed front room dressed as Santa Claus. Cindy's younger cousins stared at him in wide-eyed amazement as he bellowed "Ho, ho, ho!" in his deep voice. She'd learned the truth about Santa two years ago, but didn't mind pretending for the others, especially since it made her feel she was helping sell his performance. He placed his bag in the center of the room and began his speech. "Hello, and Merry Christmas, my fine friends. I hold in my hand a bag of gifts for some special boys and girls here tonight."

The children smiled with unconcealed joy.

"However, I can only give them to those who have been good," he continued, pausing to regard each of them. "So, if you have been bad, please raise your hand."

Several of the kids looked worried, but no hands rose.

Uncle Winston rubbed his chin. "All been good, huh? Well, if any of you know of one here who has been not been good, please point them out now."

Several of the giggling children motioned toward each other. Cindy remembered her cousin Greg pointing her out every year because she wouldn't play guns with him. The recollection stopped when she noticed Uncle Winston's suddenly pale appearance. He was facing the Christmas tree, but seemed focused on something outside. Cindy followed his gaze. A mini-vortex of snow wavered upright a moment before being swept away.

"Something wrong, Santa?" one of the adults asked.

Cindy turned to her uncle again.

"No... no, of course not. Let's get these presents delivered, shall we?" he said unsteadily.

Cindy looked out the window again, but saw nothing besides the ugly gnome statues across the street, illuminated by the glowing Santa.

That night Cindy lay awake an hour before hearing the adults return to the front room. She moved silently to the door, opening it just enough to listen as Uncle Winston spoke.

"Have any of you heard the legend that claims water stored in stone jugs turns to wine between the hour of 11:00 and midnight on Christmas Eve?"

A few jokes were cracked, but none had heard of it.

"Well, you may remember I wasn't here last year because I was visiting my friend Arthur Wooldridge in Minnesota. He was in poor health, and I wanted to see him while I still could. He told me of the legend, and as he had some stone jugs, we decided to put it to the test."

"Too cheap to buy your own wine, Winston?" Cindy's father quipped.

"Not at all. It was an experiment. Anyway, we filled two quart-sized stone jugs with tap water, then sat before the fireplace regaling each other with tales from our adventure-some youth until the clock chimed eleven. Arthur retrieved one of the jugs, dipped his finger in, then tasted it. 'By George, it's happened,' he said. 'It's the best I've ever tasted.' I imme-diately tried my own jug, and he was correct. Never will you find a more exquisite wine."

"You should've saved some for the rest of us," Cindy's father laughed.

Uncle Winston's voice took on a somber tone when he replied, "Yes, we had the same idea, which is what started the whole mess. We'd already consumed a good bit of the stuff and wanted to save the rest, but feared it might revert back to water. We thought perhaps we could keep it wine by freezing it, so we stored it in his deep freeze and retired for the evening. The next morning, sure enough, we found the jugs contained frozen wine. We decided to keep it that way until the following Christmas Eve, and if he was well enough, we would meet again to defrost and drink it before setting up to make more. When I departed a few days later, he sent me off with a jug. Our contact was sporadic throughout the year, but he seemed to make an astounding recovery from his ill health, so we planned to meet again at the same time this year."

"Since you're here, I'm guessing something went wrong," Cindy's father noted.

"Unfortunately, it did. I got a call from him two weeks ago. He told me his condition had worsened, and his doctor didn't believe he would survive the month. I expressed my dismay, and that's when he told me his plan. He believed the Christmas wine had healing properties because his earlier miraculous recovery occurred after drinking it. He said he was going to finish the remainder of his before our scheduled meeting in hopes it would extend his life enough to gain a larger supply. I told him I understood, and I would send him mine if he thought it would help, but he declined, not trusting it to survive the shipping process. I told him I would bring it on my visit. He contacted me last week to tell me his wine had turned bitter, and his health had become suddenly worse. He warned me to dispose of mine, saying he was convinced the Christmas wine was not meant to be consumed after its allotted hour."

"What became of yours?" Cindy's grandmother asked.

Uncle Winston sighed. "I took his advice and poured it out. I was cautious about it since I thought it may have turned toxic. I didn't want to throw it out with the garbage or pour it down a drain. Instead, I defrosted it and took it to the vacant wooden shed across the street. It'd been rotting there unused for the past 50 years, so I felt no harm would be done. I poured it onto the snowy ground behind the shed. The acidic stench it gave off caused my eyes to burn. Then I tossed the jug beside the shed and returned home."

Cindy's knees ached from kneeling on the hardwood floor, but she wasn't about to allow creaking floorboards to give her away as she focused in on Uncle Winston's words.

"The next morning I learned Arthur had passed. I attended his funeral two days ago. To my surprise it was a closed casket. When I asked why, I was told the disease had metastasized, covering his body in hideous boils. His doctors had no explanation for it. Returning home, I noticed someone lurking about behind the empty shack across from my house, keeping to the shadows. I couldn't make out much besides an emaciated form. I assumed it must be one of the teenagers from down the street sneaking a smoke away from his parents. That night I was awakened near midnight by a furious rapping at my front door. I ignored it and went back to sleep. The next morning when I went to retrieve my paper, I found the empty stone jug smashed to pieces on my porch. No one could have known it was mine. I thought of the scraggly fellow from the previous day and felt an unreasonable fear that he, whoever *he* was, had been the one knocking."

A spray of ice tapped against Cindy's window. When she turned to look, she thought she saw a hollow-eyed, white face pressed against the glass until a gust of wind struck the pane, disintegrating it into disjointed bits of snow that trailed off into the night. She told herself it was nothing more than a trick of poor lighting and bad weather, but it still took her a moment to regain her composure.

"I had no choice," Uncle Winston was saying when she returned to listening. "I went across the street to the spot I'd seen the figure. A large patch of snow had melted away where I'd poured out the wine."

"Are you trying to say some ghost rose up to return your jug?" Cindy's father asked mirthfully. "Perhaps the old property owner's ghost didn't take kindly to your littering on his property."

Some of the grown-ups chuckled, but Uncle Winston's voice remained serious. "All I know is Arthur and I tried to cheat something we didn't understand. We assumed there would be no consequences. I fear we were wrong. Something has followed me since that evening I poured out the wine. The whole trip here I've caught glimpses of it, hovering at the periphery just enough to let me know it's there... that it's coming."

No one said anything, then someone began to clap. The others joined in.

"Another excellent story, Winston," Cindy's father said. "You never fail to entertain us."

Uncle Winston cleared his throat. "Yes, of course, I hope you all enjoyed it. Now, I believe I'll retire for the night. The journey here was more... stressful than expected." She heard most of her relatives saying goodbye and rousing their sleeping children to return home until only her parents, her grandmother, and Uncle Winston remained in the house with her. Cindy returned to bed trying not to think about the thin snowman she'd seen across the street when Uncle Winston first arrived.

❄ ❄ ❄

Cindy still couldn't sleep when the grandfather clock chimed midnight. The tapping at her window had returned, only to move on to the next room. She held her breath, listening to it systematically circle the house, rattling the front door, then shaking the large picture window. Cindy reminded herself that ghosts weren't real, and if they were, they had no body with which to hurt her. She counted the seconds, wondering how long it would take the tapping to loop back around to her room. The thought spurred her from bed.

She followed the festive glow of lights down the long hall to the front room. The tree shimmered, casting its array of fairy lights upon darkened walls. Through the picture window she could see that snow continued to add to already impressive mounds. Across the street, the gnomes were buried waist deep, their smiles now resembling nervous fear.

The tapping had stopped; the house stilled. Maybe whatever it was had given up. Feeling more at ease, she knelt before the tree to look over the presents. She was lifting one with her name on it when she noticed something on the adjacent dining room floor. It glistened, reflecting the light from the tree topper. Returning the present, Cindy moved slowly toward the glimmer. Small pools of water were spaced out on the linoleum. She let out a sigh and started back when more caught her eye. Several of the splotches trailed through the kitchen, as though snow had been tracked in from outside.

A creak sounded behind her, followed by a blast of cold air that raised goose bumps on her arms. The back door swayed open, pushed by a frigid winter wind. She clamped it shut and locked it before returning to follow the water spots through the archway into the TV room. Multicolored lights draped across the ceiling gave the room a prismatic glow. A thick sheen of frost coated the windows from inside. Something shifted beside the recliner. Cindy held her breath and took a tentative step forward.

Uncle Winston lay in a crumpled heap on the floor, eyes bulging, tongue flopped onto his beard. A thin, white shape crouched above him. It turned a crumbling head of packed snow toward her. Its black-pool eyes contrasted against the crystallizing white of its gaunt cheeks.

Cindy screamed and ran until her parents and grand-mother caught her in the hall. She tried to tell them about

Uncle Winston, but the words wouldn't form. Instead, she led them to the TV room. Her father dropped to his knees to feel for Uncle Winston's pulse while Cindy's mother grabbed the phone off the wall to call 9-1-1. "He's ice cold," her father whispered.

"Why is there so much snow around him?" her grandma asked.

From the back door in the kitchen, Cindy's mother screamed.

They ran to her side. Footprints dotted the snow from the house to the pair of long, spindly legs attached to a vague, amorphous white shape moving across the backyard toward the tree line. Cindy's father took off after it.

"The police are on their way!" her mother called out after him, as the clock chimed one. At the same time, a wave of snow and ice swept across the yard, making it difficult to see. Her father appeared to have caught up to the intruder when it promptly collapsed to the snow beneath them.

A minute later, Cindy's shivering father returned to the house alone.

"What happened?" her mother asked breathlessly.

He shook his head. "I don't know. I reached out to grab him when he fell and just... disappeared. I don't understand how he got away."

❄ ❄ ❄

Thirty years later, Cindy stood beside her father's hospital bed and touched his arm.

"Linda?" he said, groggy from sleep.

"No, it's Cindy."

"Oh, sorry dear. Where's your mother?"

Cindy paused before answering. "It's just us these days,

Daddy."

He looked confused a moment. "What time is it?"

"Eleven o'clock," she said, moving from the bed. "In an hour it'll be Christmas."

Her father shifted in his bed with a groan. "Afraid I'm not up to celebrating this year."

Cindy returned to his side with a Styrofoam cup. "We'll worry about that later. Right now you need to drink this."

He leaned forward, taking the bendy straw between chapped lips, then smiled at her. "What is that?"

"It's going to make you better."

"I guess I'd better have some more then," he said with a weak chuckle.

Cindy smiled. "You should drink as much as you can before midnight."

With another sip, a little color returned to his cheeks. "Why before midnight?"

Cindy took the cup and refilled it from the jug she'd brought with her. Holding the straw to him again, she watched the snow falling outside his window. "Because it isn't safe."

Home for the Holidays

D. Alexander Ward

Once upon a time, Mummy had raised hunting dogs and sold them off to all the raw-boned boys in the area for use in their pursuits of duck and pheasant. But that was a long time ago, in Mummy's old life. Henry trekked out to the outbuilding—for it would have been too kind to call it a proper barn—where she had kept the hounds. He did this twice a day no matter the season, though as it was winter now, he did so in the freezing cold that swept across the flatlands surrounding the house.

"Supper time!" he announced as he plucked the lock free and opened the doors. He reached up and tugged on the pull chain for the light bulb and the shack was suddenly flooded with a warm glow. He juggled the three metal dishes filled with chunks of overcooked meat and a careless slop of instant grits.

"Who's hungry?" he teased as he raked the toe of his

31

boot across the iron bars of the cages.

Were it the old days before he came along, Henry might have been greeted with the enthusiastic scrabble and baying of dogs at the announcement of their meal, but now he was regarded with dreadful looks from the quarry kept locked in the old shack. He wasn't raising dogs for Mummy. No, indeed. He was raising a family.

He dropped two of the dishes and slid one through the slot at the bottom of the cage where he kept the blond one that he called Squirrel. She hugged the far corner of her cage and glanced warily at him from the shadows with her bright, blue eyes. He had named her Squirrel because that thick patch of wild hair over her lady parts reminded him of a joke he had once heard but could not quite remember now, though it had something to do with the cracking of nuts. Not literal nuts, though. Something else that he just didn't quite grasp. Maybe that was why Henry had such a hard time recalling the joke.

"Come on now," he entreated. "Girl's gotta eat, right?"

She nodded and scurried toward the dish, the stinking rags that she wore hanging from her like the chains of a ghost. She dug her fingers into the mess and began shoveling it into her mouth in a ravenous way.

Henry smiled.

Squirrel was just his type. Not as young, no, but blond and pretty, and she had what Mummy called moxie. Back in the day, he would have made her his own. But Mummy had broken him of those ways during the dreaming times and had helped him to see the error of his ways. It wasn't the innocents he sought out anymore. It was the bad meat, the rotten meat. The ones who had already spoiled long ago. Besides, Squirrel wasn't meant for him. She was for the family.

He turned and slid the second dish into the cage opposite her's, where he kept the wiry, gray-haired one he called Wolfie, who was his favorite of the pair.

"I got extra," Henry said, holding the third dish aloft, "for whoever deserves it most."

He grinned and winked at the gray-haired man.

Wolfie glared at him from between the bars and made no move toward his dish.

"You ain't hungry?"

The man snarled at him with his old, yellowed teeth.

"Fuck you, cyclops!"

Henry was taken aback. This kind of thing from his favorite of the pair left him feeling disappointed, and the words had hurt even more. Reflexively, his hand went to touch the black-painted swimming goggle that he wore like a patch over what used to be his eye. Henry's own mother had burned that orb out long ago with a hot poker from the fireplace, declaring that it was punishment for the profane way he had always leered at his sister.

He stood and fetched the cow prod from the hook. Sliding the third dish over to Squirrel, Henry bent and undid the lock on Wolfie's cage. The prod in his hand hummed with charge.

"Now why'd you have to go and say a thing like that?" he asked as he swung the door of the cage wide open.

Predictably, the gray-haired man charged him in the feeble way that he could manage, but Henry was bigger, stronger, and quicker, and he jammed the prod into Wolfie's stomach. There was a sizzle from the electric charge and the man went limp briefly. Henry bent and dragged him out by his rags.

With Wolfie laid there at the big man's feet under the naked light of the shack's single bulb, Henry went to work on him. He rained down blows with his hard, meaty fists. One after another. Wolfie came to, cried out, and occasionally spat more words at Henry, even calling him a monster. Henry found that funny because, as he recalled, when he had come upon Wolfie in an abandoned warehouse somewhere in the dregs of Kansas City, the man had been in the throes of passion with his prick buried deep in the steaming wound of some streetwalker that he'd just slashed the red life out of.

"Who's the real monster here?" Henry growled as he pummeled the man at his feet, the shadows of his swinging arms long and terrible in the naked light as they played upon the spare frame of the shack.

Henry beat him for a while, though he took care to make sure all of his blows were to Wolfie's body and not his face. After all, it was the holiday season and he needed the man alive and looking well for Mummy's family picture on Christmas Eve.

❄ ❄ ❄

Later that night, as he sat in the darkness with the television flashing, his eyelids began to feel so very heavy. It was his routine, often sleeping in the chair and not in the bed that Mummy had once prepared for him.

It was a quiet evening and he could hear no noise from the shack. Apart from his new and captive siblings, there were many more cages in the shack, but only room for one more addition to the family. The most important of all. This one would round them out and make Mummy happy beyond words. To have her new family all together for the holidays!

The only problem was that he didn't know where to find

his next sibling. But she would tell him when he slept, just as she always had. Henry hoped that it would be another boy.

He grinned as he drifted off.

Yes, it would be a boy. For him, another brother. And how joyous that would be.

Corker's Tavern stood along the edge of State Route 13, several miles north of Lowry City, surrounded by nothing but farmland and endless sky. It was a bar and grill—though it was much more of the former than the latter—where farmhands and other locals gathered in the evening after a day's work. It was a rough place for hard-drinking men and women, and any passersby who wandered in from the road never found it very welcoming. In the winter, though, with the migrant workers gone, Corker's limped along, lucky to keep the lights on with the scant offering of regulars who came in from the cold every evening. During this time of the year, drifters and strangers would find the watering hole grudgingly accepting of them.

Silas had been basking in the warmth of their hospitality all evening as he sipped Cutty and Coke from highball glasses and picked at the lousy crockpot barbecue that had been piled on his plate. Christmas lights had been strung up all over the bar and the odd adornment of a Santa Claus or reindeer was hung haphazardly on the walls here and there along with a string of glittery letters that hung over the door that read, *Happy Holidays*! He had been making his way from one place to the next, in the way that he did, when he had got a hankering. Almost as if by divine provenance, Corker's had appeared, a bright star in an otherwise dark and cold Missouri night.

A sad parade of locals had come and gone during his time there, most of them jawing about the weather and the snow that was on the way, how much they'd get and so on. He had tried to engage in polite conversation with them, but most seemed unwilling to even acknowledge his presence. Eventually, the other patrons and cook wandered off into the chill, barren land, and it was ten o'clock at night when Brenda the bartender told him it was last call. He grumbled but agreed, though he managed to con one more drink out of her while she wiped down the bar.

The moment would come soon. Looking around at the dark, putrid walls of the bar, he had a sudden urge to go and lock the deadbolt on the front door of the place. He'd love to do her right here in the bar, but there was danger in that. There were probably weapons under the bar. A shotgun, maybe. There usually were in podunk shitholes like this.

After finishing his drink, he walked just ahead of her, determined to help her close up. When she protested, he summoned the affectation of a southern gentleman and made to tip a hat that he wasn't wearing.

"Couldn't abide leaving a woman all alone in a place like this," he said. "I'll see you to your car."

"Truck," she said, smirking.

"Whatever."

As luck would have it—and Sy was so often lucky that he had long ago taken the word itself as a nickname—he hadn't parked too far away from her beater of a truck in the now-empty parking lot. He followed her out, keeping a respectable distance between them. At the far edge of the lot, parked under a solitary street light, he noticed a van that must have been up on blocks, as dented and faded as it was.

"Well, goodnight, ma'am," he called, raising a hand.

She glanced at him, the keys in her fingers jingling as

she made her way to the old Ford.

"Night," she replied.

"Oh," he said, and stopped. "One more thing."

"Yeah?" she asked, turning toward him, an arm's length away from her truck.

Lucky gave her his very best and most disarming smile, but the wary bitch wasn't fooled. She turned away and stepped suddenly toward the truck. He followed, leaping at her like the bogeyman that he was. She scrambled to get away as her safe little world fell apart. One step, two, three steps... *boo!*

She might have been going home to a boyfriend, but he doubted it. She seemed more like the loner redneck kind of gal who devoted her life to a pack of dogs. Too bad. Those pups would be going hungry because Momma would not be coming home tonight.

He wrapped her throat in the crook of his arm and closed it while driving her forward. He aimed for the rear corner of the truck well above where the bed was attached to the chassis. A good, solid pillar of metal. When they were close, he placed his other hand at the back of her head and gave it a quick snap forward. Her forehead bounced against the truck, and when it did, the protestations and struggling stopped as she went floppy with unconsciousness.

A toothy, savage grin spread over Lucky's face as he dragged her across to his car. It was all in the wrist.

Opening the back door, he shoved her inside face first, then removed the belt from his trousers, bent the prong back, and slipped it back through the buckle. He slid the loop over Brenda the bartender's mop of bottle-blond hair and down to her neck, where he pulled it snug, but not tight. Not yet. She would need to be awake for that. In the meantime, he reached in and undid her jeans and pulled them down over her hips, leaving them crumpled around her ankles. While Lucky waited, he stimulated himself, though it wasn't much of an effort. The anticipation already had him well aroused.

Brenda began to stir, then to whimper as she became aware of her surroundings. Lucky dropped his trousers and grabbed the belt, pulled it tight around her neck. In her struggling and flailing, she inadvertently opened herself to him and he moved closer to make the connection with one, vicious thrust.

Then a hand was on his shoulder, and before he could even look to see what damned fool interloper had stumbled into the midst of Lucky's moment alone with Brenda, he was lifted off his feet, spun around, and tossed into the backseat, where he slid down to the floorboards and became wedged between the back and front seats. When he looked up, the street light at the other end of the parking lot was lighting the interloper from behind, rendering him in a silhouette. A fucking huge, hulking silhouette looming at the edge of the vehicle, with bright, thick flakes of snow coming down all around him.

Then the giant was reaching into the car to remove the belt from around Brenda's neck. She flipped over, struggling to get her jeans back up her legs.

"Thank you," she breathed through tears, her voice still aflutter with panic.

❄ ❄ ❄

Henry Collector placed a single finger against his lips and shushed the girl. And though she was relieved that he had come to her rescue and prevented the defiling that had been about to take place, she also saw something quietly menacing in his one dark eye. She was never to breathe a word about this to anyone, and Henry sensed that she knew this without having to be told and would abide by it.

In a single motion, Henry slid the belt loop over Lucky's head and pulled it tight around his neck. He jerked the man out of the backseat and onto the cold ground of the parking lot now covered with a dusting of snow. Clutching the worn leather belt, he dragged the man called Lucky across to the van. He did not even look back as the woman climbed into her truck, gunned it, and tore out of the tavern's gravel parking lot and into the black of a winter's night.

The drive back home to Mummy's was not such a long one, but it was lonely on account of the killer in the back being out cold. Henry had made sure of that courtesy of some animal tranquilizers he'd scored back when all of this started. It seemed like an age ago, though it must have been no more than six months or so. Back then, Henry hadn't been so unlike the man hogtied in the rear of the van; a common taker of lives, a drifter on the run from all the foul things he'd done. That was before he had met Mummy for the first time, though. One strange summer day that would change him forever. Of course, the coming change hadn't been so clear to him at first. Not at all, because just a few hours after coming across Mummy, he had murdered her right there in her own home.

But that had not been the end of their relationship.

Drifting through on a balmy July afternoon, he had come upon a tidy little ranch home in the middle of nowhere with a decrepit old van parked in the weedy dirt road that served as a driveway. It had been days since he'd had a meal, so he chanced knocking on the door to barter for one. What he found there was not a cattle-ranching family, but a frail old woman who answered the door and eyed him cautiously as he stated his circumstances and asked her for a bit of Christian charity. She had said that she no longer had any cattle and that she was too old for working the land, but she did have some fences in need of mending. She had asked him his name, so he had given it.

"Henry *Collector*, is that your real name? Or some kind of hobo moniker you picked up on the road?"

"It's my very own, ma'am," he had lied.

In truth, who he was before no longer mattered. He had seen the last of that person many years ago when he left his home in Kentucky with everyone in it except his sister sliced open from belly to brains with Daddy's hunting knife.

"Odd name," she had observed. "You an actual collector of anything?"

"Of a sort, I suppose," he had replied, unconsciously jiggling the strap of his knapsack that held his few worldly possessions; his Daddy's hunting knife and a pair of mason jars filled with a liquid that sloshed with his every movement.

She hadn't asked him to elaborate, and that was just as well because Henry was not fond of lying, even though he often had to.

"Well, Mister Collector, you do me the service of fixing my fences and I'll fix you a meal, even loan you a bed for the night, and give you a little something for the road when you clear out tomorrow."

He had agreed, of course, and as Henry now turned the van off the main road, the headlights washed across those same fences, the patchwork repairs he had made still holding as true as the day he'd nailed them into place.

Henry pulled the van past the house, through the stand of tall cedars that separated the house from the tracts of overgrown fields and the shack near the edge of the wood.

He remembered how Mummy had invited him in back then and showed him to the bedroom with two single beds that she said had once belonged to her son and daughter, who had long ago become estranged to her.

"My husband, God rest his evil soul, was a contrary sort, you see," she had explained. "He run them off years before they came of age. Boyd and Deena were too much like him that way. Contrary. Sometimes I think maybe they run themselves off."

Henry had dropped his bag in the room, taking a moment to slip the knife from it and belt it to his side. When tackling any job, a good knife was an indispensable tool. As she led him back through the house, he noticed another room that was unused and housed the dusty frame of an infant's crib.

"Your husband run the baby off, too?" he'd asked, thinking it a kind of joke.

In response, she had pulled the door closed and glanced down at her shoes. "'Fraid not. Little William didn't last much past his coming into this world."

Henry was notoriously ham-handed with jokes and he should have known better, so he had apologized profusely for the intrusion and was generously forgiven. Then the old woman had shown him to the outbuilding where she used to pen up breeding dogs, though that trade was also now well beyond her abilities. In the years since, she had filled it with the chaos of her husband's tools and bits of collected wood that Henry would be expected to use for the repairs.

And, true to his word, Henry had done it. He had worked all the long, hot afternoon mending the woman's fences even though there seemed to be no sense to it since she had no livestock to contain. But at the end of the day, he would have a meal and a soft place to lay his head. As the amber sun had begun to sink toward the horizon, he hung the claw of his hammer on the top board and watched the fields of tall grass sway in the summer breeze. Henry was enchanted with the old woman's ranch and he fancied that in a different life, he would have been happy to call such a place home.

But it was scant more than a dream and Henry understood that. He would take a meal with the old woman that night, and in the morning he would be on his way. That was the plan. Until he returned to the house that evening and found her rifling through his personal things.

❄ ❄ ❄

"What is this?" came the voice of the killer from the back, tearing Henry from his reminiscence.

"Oh, looky here, Lucky's awake," Henry remarked as he squeaked open the door of the van and stepped out.

He walked around to the back of the vehicle and opened the doors wide, peering at his quarry squirming there on the floor against the zip ties that bound him. After a moment, Silas stopped and craned his neck to see the one-eyed beast of a man that had taken him.

"How do you know my name?"

Even in the darkness of the van, he could see a pleasant grin on the big man's face.

Henry grabbed hold of the restraints at Lucky's feet and pulled him closer until his legs were hanging limp beyond the bumper of the van. He leaned over him and grinned. "Mummy told me all about you," he whispered. "But ain't no need to worry. You're part of the family now." Then he yanked him out of the van by the belt around his neck.

"Eat shit," the man managed to groan.

Henry smiled down at the man the way one might a child throwing a hissy fit and patted him on the shoulder. "You'll come around."

※ ※ ※

Lucky was about to spit something else at the man when the giant reached down, grabbed the belt loop around his neck, and hauled him off, dragging him through the snowy yard like a sack of feed.

He couldn't see where he was being taken, but after a moment the man dropped Lucky back down to the ground. He twisted around to see the big man busying himself with unlocking the doors on a shack that stood at the edge of a wall of towering trees that disappeared into the starless night above.

"Who are you? What're you doing with me?" Lucky asked.

The man pulled the shack door aside and flicked on a light inside before turning back to him. For a moment, Lucky could have sworn he heard the quiet murmur of voices coming from inside the structure.

"My name's Henry," he replied.

"All right," Lucky nodded, trying to keep cool. "Henry. What's this all about? I do something to piss you off?"

Henry snorted a laugh.

"'Fraid there ain't no time for that kind of thing right now," Henry said as he reached down and snatched up Lucky by the neck loop again. "Gotta get you penned up before Mummy wakes."

Lucky's feet dragged up the ramp and across the straw-covered wooden floor of the shack. It was warmer in there, at least. That was the last pleasant thought he would have about the place, though, as to his horror he saw two other people—a man and a woman—curled up like dogs in two of the half dozen cages that filled the shack.

The big man seemed to be heading toward an empty cage next to the blond woman, but then stopped and, seeming to have thought better of it, stepped across the aisle. He shoved Lucky into one of the empties next to the man with the gray hair and goatee, then slipped the belt loop from around his neck. He also slid a worn hunting knife from its sheath on his side and cut the zip ties binding him.

Then the one-eyed giant knelt down and slipped a padlock through the latch on the steel cage door. He cast a last look at Lucky, now penned up in his own cage.

"You be a good boy an' I won't have to put those back on," Henry said, nodding to the discarded plastic ties on the floor of the cage.

Lucky had nothing to say. This had to be a nightmare. A goddamned nightmare and that was all. Maybe the whole last day was: Corker's tavern, Brenda the bartender, even the drive from Illinois into Missouri itself. Perhaps he was still asleep in the feather bed of that cushy McMansion in Litchfield that he'd cleaned out, sleeping off a drunk he'd caught from the homeowner's cache of top-shelf scotch whisky. Any minute now, he would wake up. Any minute now.

Henry stood and turned on his heel. On his way out of the shack, he shut off the light.

"Wait!" Lucky cried out, but the giant paid him no mind. The shack's doors shut and he could hear Henry fidgeting with the outside lock, closing it up.

"Please!" Lucky continued, panicked.

❄ ❄ ❄

In the chill darkness of the shack, Lucky began to weep for his predicament, his teeth chattering together as his body erupted into violent spasms of trembling.

"Pick a corner and pull the straw in your cage up over you," came the gruff voice of the man in the cage next to him. "It ain't the Motel Six, but it'll keep you warmer than not."

This isn't happening.

"I'm gonna need to piss soon," Lucky spat.

"I wouldn't," offered the woman across the way, "or you'll be sleeping in it. He'll come back in the morning, and if you don't give him no trouble, he'll take you out to cop a squat or whatever."

This just cannot be happening, Lucky thought to himself again.

The gray-haired one chuckled in the black. "Welcome to the family," he said in his gravelly voice, then added, *"Brother."*

❄ ❄ ❄

Henry stood in the kitchen, a slab of meat sizzling in the frying pan, the air filling with that delectable aroma of searing flesh. Mummy was in the habit of waking obscenely early in the morning, well before the dawn broke over the horizon—and she always woke hungry.

There were a couple of minutes left on the steak—his, not hers—so he decided he should go ahead and take her supper to her. On the dining table in the kitchen there was a tray upon which sat a plate with a length of barely cooked meat and some chicken livers and giblets, raw and pooling in red. He had saved them from a roast he had done for himself a few nights before.

He heard her stirring, restless and hungry.

"Coming, Mummy!"

Henry picked up the tray and carried it into the den. His boot caught on one of the nails protruding from the torn-up floorboards and he noted that he would have to fix that before Christmas supper.

In the middle of the family den, the floor had been ripped up, right through the subfloor, leaving only a web of copper plumbing in place. The earth beneath the house was opened, a dark and yawning pit as wide across as two grown men laid head to toe. In the early days, getting food to Mummy had been an indelicate endeavor, but Henry had constructed a set of stairs that wound around the wall of the pit as they descended into it. He stepped carefully, always carefully, though the light filtering in from the den above was enough for him to see by.

He heard her moving below, Mummy, great and terrible. She hadn't always been that way, though. Certainly not on that day when he had come in from mending her fences and found her in the guest bedroom, staring down at the ghastliest and most prized of his few possessions.

"I reckon I know now," she had said, turning the jar over in her hands, "what it is that you collect, Henry."

Henry stretched out his hand, demanded she give it back, and she had handed it over without a word.

"I don't suppose that now that I've run across *that*," she nodded at the jar, "I'll be given the chance to wave goodbye to you when you leave come the morning?"

Henry closed his one good eye and shook his head.

When he looked up at her again, he felt the familiar sting

and tingle in his brain as his bad eye came to life behind that black-tinted swimming goggle and began to pulse terrible notions into his mind. His right hand drew Daddy's hunting knife from its sheath and brandished it at her.

"No, ma'am, but I believe I will take that meal before we get down to the nasty business."

Mummy had not made it necessary for Henry to see that she cooked his supper that night at the point of a knife. She had become quickly resigned to her fate, and after hearing the details of her hard life as she fried up steak and eggs for him, it was easy to understand why. The old gal was just plumb out of steam when it came to living.

But something had happened that night, a mercy that neither one of them had expected. In her final hours, as they took coffee and ate cookies in the den, she unburdened herself of all the darkness that had weighed her down for decades, shaking it free like slag. Confessing to Henry as if he were a kind of priest. Her husband had indeed run her eldest children off, and they had been lucky to escape him. She had not been so fortunate, though, and after withstanding his angry thrashings for many years, she repaid him by jamming the pointy end of a railroad spike into the soft flesh of his neck early one morning as he lay in the bed, stinking of the previous night's whiskey.

"He didn't even wake," she told Henry. "Just bled out, stopped breathing and continued on in a red, eternal sleep."

She left him there in the bed for days until he started stinking, and then she buried him in a shallow grave underneath the house.

Next to baby William.

When Henry had asked why the child was put to rest under the house rather than in a proper plot with a stone, the old woman had told him with a voice that was choked in sorrow that she had killed him, too. A mercy killing, but a killing all the same.

Mummy said that her youngest should never have made it into the world, and that after his birth, every breath had been a struggle for the child. Every cry an anguished one. She hadn't been able to bear it and had ended his suffering with the very pillow on which she still laid her head each night, for the smell of the infant—of baby powder and rose-water—still lingered upon it.

It had been heartbreaking to listen to, and even though his bad eye shed no tears—it never did anymore—the other half of Henry wept for the old woman. But what was done was done. He made it easy on her, though, taking Mummy outside so as not to make a mess. He let her watch the sun rise over the trees and fields, wreathed in the morning mist, as he slid his blade across her throat. In her death throes, they had pulled each other close, arms searching, fingers desperate to grasp that which was slipping away. They held each other tight until she crumpled in his arms like a rag doll and, even though it had lasted only moments, it was the most loved either one of them had felt in a very long time.

Henry buried Mummy under the house along with her husband and child. And to his credit, he had stayed his hand, willing himself not to take her eyes. Resisting the temptation to add them to the pair of quart-sized mason jars filled with formaldehyde and two dozen milky white orbs, including those of Henry's own mother and father, whose scornful eyes had been the very first.

❄ ❄ ❄

After a long night of getting to know each other, Henry had burst into the shack that morning more cheerful than any of his captives reckoned he had a right to be.

"It's Christmas Eve morning, y'all!" he had exclaimed, and then regaled them with a description of how much snow had fallen overnight and was continuing to come down, and how perfect it would all be for the evening's festivities. Disheartened at their lack of enthusiasm, he eventually got around to asking which one of them wanted bathroom break first.

Lucky, curled into a shivering ball in the corner of his cage with the pressure of his insides at the point of breaking, moaned about his pain, and the others had ceded the first turn to him.

Now, squatting in the trees along the edge of the yard and overcome with relief as he did his business, Lucky's eyes searched the dense forest for some safe haven, some sign of other life to which he might run if he could. There was nothing. There were remnants of a chicken-wire fence that had once spanned this side of the property, but it had long ago coiled into nothing more than a rusted obstruction, and the posts like the one he squatted near were rotting totems of wood with wayward nails and staples protruding from them. An idea began to form in his head and he grinned at this possible turn of fortune.

He had obviously lingered there for too long, however, because Henry tugged on the tie-out that connected to the leather collar around his neck. The big man urged him to finish up. And like a good dog, Lucky came shuffling back to his master when he was done, back into the yard and the unending blanket of quarter-sized snowflakes that drifted down from a cold winter sky.

When the bathroom breaks were done and the morning slop slid into their cages, Lucky devoured his as wantonly as did the others, but when he was done, he sat back with a smile that Wolfie and Squirrel found disconcerting. He would reveal nothing of its source to them, however, and they responded with taunting him about the day's inevitability. Tonight was Christmas Eve. The big night. The night the reason for their captivity would be answered.

The night when they would finally get to meet the oft-mentioned *Mummy*.

It was a joke that only the three of them were in on, for they had agreed during the long night before that there was no Mummy or that—at best—Henry the one-eyed giant was fixing to introduce them to the brittle remains of some old woman in a wheelchair that he had hacked to death with his knife.

But still Lucky grinned and assured them that whatever freak show their captor had planned, when that night came, he would not be a part of it. And if successful, he assured them, neither would they.

They laughed off his claim, for they had been there before. Each of them had masterminded an escape, had conceived of it to the point of exhaustion. Yet, for all the effort, here they were; caged pets of the one-eyed giant.

Lucky waited until their midday slop was delivered. He took it gratefully, earning a wink of approval from his captor and an endorsement that he was fitting in nicely. After Henry closed and locked the doors of the shack and Lucky heard the man's heavy footfalls diminish, crunching farther and farther away in the snow, he got to work.

His fingers slipped through the grates of his cage, and in the light filtering in from the day, he could see very well what he was up against. And it troubled him only a little.

"What're you doing?" Wolfie asked, deeply skeptical.

"I was shitting out near some decrepit fence post when I noticed a few nails and staples still stuck into the wood," he replied, fondling the tiny lengths of metal. "So I took them."

Wolfie waved it off. "I found some things like that once myself and tried the same as you. These locks are unpickable."

"Sure," Lucky nodded as he slipped the length of his narrow tools into the keyhole.

"I'm telling you it's a lost cause, brother."

Lucky stopped his machinations and took a breath. "I picked one just like this when I was fourteen," Lucky said. "On my old man's gun cabinet."

In truth, he had come across the same lock a couple of times since then, but they didn't need to know that. He figured it better to let them be in awe of his skills when he popped that sucker open.

"Oh yeah? How'd it go for you back then?" Squirrel asked.

"I shot the old man between the eyes with his Army sidearm," Lucky replied.

Wolfie scoffed in amusement and put two fingers to his brow in a mock salute. "Carry on, then."

"Thanks," Lucky replied.

He went back to work then, slipping the tiny nail and the bent length of a staple deeper into the lock. Silas was a killer, sure, but only when it suited or amused him. His stock and trade wasn't murder. It was theft. Breaking into the estates of the upper middle class and fencing their wares on the street was what bought him his drinks and filled his belly as he drifted from state to state.

Lucky had no idea how a rube like his captor had come across such fine locks to keep his quarry imprisoned, but on his way back from dropping his pants in the woods, he had taken care to survey them. As far as padlocks went, the Abloy Classic was one of the world's most unbreakable locks. A fastener comprised of a dozen sequential discs and half as many false gates, it demanded utter satisfaction even before the sweet spot was engaged.

It was a lock that was miles away from the ability of any common, snatch-and-grab hood, but thankfully it had been a long time since Lucky had counted himself among their dreadful number. He was a bona fide professional.

Lucky fiddled with the lock for the better part of the afternoon, biting back anger and frustration at his many failures. But just before the winter sun began to sink low behind a blanket of snowy clouds, he felt his tools slip into place, and from there on it was simply a matter of care and patience.

The others, nearly catatonic in their captivity, failed to notice this breakthrough event until several long minutes later when the droll silence of the shack was punctured by the metallic pop of the lock coming free.

"Holy hell!" Wolfie called out. "You did it!"

Lucky wiggled the lock until it was loose from the cage and fell with a *thud* onto the straw-covered floor. He pushed the cage door open wide and crawled out, standing free at last in the middle of the dog shack.

He crept over to the doors of the shack and pushed on them. There was a lock on the other side, true, but there was give in the movement, and he was willing to bet that with the proper amount of force the old wood of the shack doors would release the screws that held the latch without much complaint.

Lucky breathed a lungful of the cold air that stank of straw and mildew and gruel and excrement, bidding the shack a silent goodbye.

"How long will it take you to pick the locks on ours?" Squirrel asked.

Lucky glanced over his shoulder at them both and smiled.

"Not sure that's in the cards for you two," he replied and kicked against the door once, twice, three times before it broke free. The low light of the winter afternoon flooded into the space.

"Give my best to the one-eyed freak," he said over his shoulder as he ran out into the open air, hoping like hell that his exit would be unseen by his captor.

No sooner had his shoes started crunching through the snow when he heard the wailing of the others, cursing him for his betrayal and raising the alarm at his escape. But Lucky was in the wind, dashing through the snow into the woods behind the shack, his footfalls marvelously silenced by the blanketed ground.

As he put the shack behind him with growing distance, still the others cried, but he paid it no mind and felt no guilt. It was widely understood that there was no honor among thieves. Or murderers for that matter.

❄ ❄ ❄

Henry had been asleep, dozing on the couch, when he heard the screaming from outside. With haste, he stepped into his boots and went barreling out into the afternoon. Upon seeing the doors of the shack swinging free in the winter wind, he began to panic a little. When he saw his prize brother, Lucky, missing from his cage, he began to panic a great deal more. The others stammered their way through explanations of how the man had freed himself, but Henry could not have cared less. His mind was on Mummy and how this would positively ruin Christmas Eve for her.

He was about to get his coat from inside and pursue the man into the woods even though the light was failing when

Mummy's voice entered his mind and soothed him. *All will be well*, he was assured. Following Lucky would do no good, she told him. He should just get back into the house and continue preparations for their special supper.

Henry was not in the habit of second guessing Mummy. Ever since the dreaming times, when she had begun speaking to him from under the house, she had always guided him true. Early on, it had been hard for him to accept that the voice he heard in his head was not his own, but then he had torn up the floorboards in the den and had begun digging, heeding her commands.

Beneath the earth there, he had found not the bodies of the old woman, her husband, and child. Not exactly. What he had found instead was Mummy herself, who had become something more than all of those simple remains, a beautiful and harrowing thing that usurped the very notion of death and was fantastically alive in the midst of all that grave dirt and woe.

And in the time since, like any good son, he had attended to her, giving her food and companionship when she required it and leaving her be when her privacy was desired. In turn, she had cured him of his wanton bloodlust and given him focus. A focus that allowed Henry to collect not for his own needs, but for the needs of another. To renew a family and to find himself a part of it.

Standing there in the gentle but relentless snowfall, Henry once again had to look beyond his own need to track and kill the man he had hoped would be one of his new brothers. It was Mummy that he served now, after all. Mummy and the family.

And wasn't selflessness and family what Christmas was all about?

❄ ❄ ❄

Lucky's good fortune was holding out once again. For a city boy set loose in the wilds of wherever-the-hell, he was doing a damned impressive job of navigating them. After he had pushed into the thick woods around the shack and passed the fallen fence line, things had gotten confusing and it almost had him worried. But then clearer pathways of disturbed snow and bent vegetation had emerged in the dense forest labyrinth and he had begun following them. It made the going a lot easier, and just as the darkness overtook the land, he could now smell the burning of a distant fire.

A fire meant people. People that might deliver him from the backwoods, banjo-fucked nightmare in which he found himself trapped. He followed the path through the wilderness, keeping the scent of burning wood ahead of him, angling toward it. The sight of lights twinkling through the thick trees filled him with a renewed vigor and he doubled his pace toward them.

When he came out of the woods into a clearing, he saw a squat little home situated on flat land beyond the edge of the forest. Electric lights burned inside and a trickle of smoke rose from the chimney and disappeared into the starless night.

"Oh, thank God," he said, relieved and cold beyond belief. "Help! Help me, please!"

The house had a covered back porch on it, and against the backlighting he saw a man who had been sitting there spring into action.

"Hello?" the voice called out.

Lucky nearly wept at the sound of a friendly voice. He struggled to his feet, finding his legs numb with cold.

"Hey!" he called out as he watched the man come bounding off the porch toward him. The cold had gotten to him earlier and he had spent the evening pissed off at his chattering teeth. Lucky bit down and growled as his tongue was caught in the middle. He cursed and spat blood.

"You alright, brother?"

As opposed to what? Lucky thought. He quickly formulated a sarcastic and charming response, but stopped short of delivering it.

There was something awful in the man's familiarity, the casual way that he called him *brother*.

As the man approached, Lucky caught the glint from a floodlight on the black goggle of the giant and he nearly melted in defeat. But Lucky was a survivor. He scrambled back into the darkness of the wood.

There was little point to it, however; the giant was on his heels before he could gain any distance, and as he crawled desperately through the crisp, frosted leaves, he felt something grasp his legs from behind.

Lucky clawed maniacally at the earth, his fingers digging through snow and soil, hungry for purchase. And still he was dragged backward.

"No!" Lucky cried out. "Nononono!"

But the battle was over before it had begun. Lucky was cold and weak, and even on his best day, he couldn't have outmatched Henry Collector. The man was like an ox.

"Now, don't be that way," Henry sighed. "It's Christmas time, don't you know?"

Lucky was about to tell the giant that he could shove Christmas right up the darkest part of his ass, but the man picked him up and swung him around, banging the thief's head against the bottom-most step of the back porch. Then Henry was kneeling over him, a syringe in his mouth as, with one enormous hand, he pinned both of Lucky's to the ground behind his head.

Before he could offer any more protest, Henry snatched the syringe and plunged the needle into Lucky's throat.

"There's still time to clean you up before Christmas supper," Henry said. "Oh, my brother, we're gonna have such a time!"

Lucky watched as the world faded away along with the giant's smile, and in dreamy, echoed tones, he heard the tune of "Jingle Bell Rock" emanating from inside the house.

❄ ❄ ❄

The first thing that Silas noticed as he came to was the smell. The aroma of cooked meat and herbs and coffee brewing in a pot somewhere nearby. Fake aerosol pine and the sweetness of scented candles. It was all so very pleasant that he thought for a moment he had indeed dreamed all that had come before. Perhaps his entire life of dark deeds had been nothing more than the many small terrors of one night's sleep. Something was itching him, though, and as his vision cleared, he saw that he was dressed in a sweater. A horrible, horrible sweater. Looking down, he studied it and it took him a few moments to realize a pair of knitted eyes were looking back up at him.

Is that a red-nosed fucking reindeer?

He immediately began to twitch, but his hands and feet were tied well and a gag damn near split his head in two it was tied so tight. He sat on a couch with Wolfie at the far end and Squirrel in the middle, each of them bound, gagged, and likewise ridiculously dressed. Pinned onto the sweaters were name tags; Squirrel's read *Deena* and Wolfie's, *Boyd*. On the coffee table before them sat cups of steaming hot apple cider. In the center of the den, the floorboards had been torn away, exposing a great hole in the earth beneath. From it there arose a faint but foul odor that occasionally troubled his nose.

A buzzer went off and he looked toward the source of the sound. It was coming from the kitchen, and he could see Henry, the one-eyed giant, busy at the oven. He was clad in a button-down shirt over a mock turtleneck with an apron on that matched their sweaters, though it was spotty with the blood of someone or something that he had previously butchered.

Henry looked at Lucky and winked.

The roast he pulled from the oven smelled heavenly, though considering the cook, no one could be certain if the meat had once walked on four legs or only two. Vomit rose in his throat and he thought for sure that he would choke on it with the gag strapped across his face. He also considered that perhaps that was a better fate than what was to come. But he did not and could not. No matter how badly he wanted to.

The giant disappeared behind the kitchen wall to set the roast on the table, but after a moment he was back, grinning like the madman he was. He clapped his hands, rubbing them together.

"All right, family!" he exclaimed. "Picture time."

With a spring in his step, Henry skipped into the den and grabbed a tripod and camera from the wall next to the hi-fi that cheerily pumped holiday music from its speakers. Before he began setting it up, he peered into the hole in the floor and hollered, "Mummy! Picture time! Supper time!"

He was giddy with excitement as he set up the tripod at the edge of the broken floor, screwed the Polaroid camera onto it, and began to sight what would no doubt be the perfect picture in the viewfinder.

Mummy was going to be so very happy.

❄ ❄ ❄

Lucky heard the lunatic call down into the hole and he and his fellow captives shared skeptical but panicked looks with one another. This man was truly out of his mind. That much they knew.

Until they all heard something shuffle and scrape against the earth down there in the darkness of the pit.

Their eyes wide, watching as the giant maneuvered the camera and tripod to get the proper shot, they waited. They waited, for there was nothing else they could do. Waited as they listened to the sounds of something dragging its weight up the wooden steps that descended into the pit, not breathing, but hissing as it came, occasionally tearing into the soft dirt wall to steady itself.

When it cleared the topmost step and came into the room, Lucky and the others began to strain against their bonds, desperate to be free of them and to leave this place. To go screaming mad into the winter night even if their deaths out among the harsh elements were a certainty.

Mummy, or the thing called by such an affectionate name, was a moving heap of black earth and nightmare. The greater mass of it was nothing more than moist dirt and clay, clumps of which fell away as it shambled around the den toward them on a trio of corpse-like legs that seemed barely capable of supporting the whole of the thing. Standing about seven feet tall, the top of it was adorned with the decomposed head of what had once been a woman, the remains of white, stringy hair slack over the contours of her face, that lolled lifelessly from side to side. From there on, the thing tapered out, wider as it went.

Lucky shut his eyes tight against the sight of it, for as terrible as the woman's dead face was to behold, the rest of the thing was far worse, and even though he couldn't see them, he was sure Wolfie and Squirrel were doing likewise, turning their faces away.

"Open your eyes!" the one-eyed giant screamed at them. "Open your eyes or I'll gut every damned one of you right now and eat off you 'til spring!"

They all felt sure that they would not live past this Christmas Eve anyway, but the primordial demand to survive that was so embedded in the blood and bones and nature of humankind responded to the threat. The floorboards vibrated with the thumping chorus of *Frosty the Snowman* as they watched Mummy come closer and closer.

Below the woman's head, the mass of earth moved with all manner of terrible things. A host of serpents, entwined so thickly throughout it that they might have been mating in an enormous bolus, hissed and spat and slid among its contours. As Mummy moved and the lighting of the den passed over her, faces rose and fell within the shifting muck. A man's face old and withered with decay. The rounded, fleshy cheek of a child turned up in what almost seemed a smile. Bony arms and digits that writhed absently among the mud and the serpents, and the trio of once-dead legs that shuffled across the floor.

"Yes!" Henry shouted.

The thing moved around them, smelling of wet earth and rank flesh. It settled into position behind the couch, the floorboards creaking under its weight.

A hand of bone and putrid flesh settled on Lucky's shoulder.

Holy hell, Lucky thought, his stomach going cold. *It's posing for the goddamned picture.*

As the moment lingered, long, eyeless worms wriggled free of the dirt and dropped down, inching across the trio's holiday sweaters.

"Perfect," the giant smiled.

He clicked a button on the camera that caused a light on the front to start flashing rapidly. As he came around and stood behind them, it continued to flash more rapidly still.

"Say cheese," the giant commanded gleefully.

❄ ❄ ❄

Briefly, the room was filled with a bright, white light, and Henry, along with the members of his new family, squinted their eyes in its wake. How Henry would have loved to have those eyes for his own, but Mummy had taught him the new way. In the photograph, he would have their eyes captured. So white and so alive, forever and always. Each time he looked upon it, it would be like a fresh harvest.

Henry dropped the arm that had been hugging Mummy's form and scooted back around the pit to the tripod. The picture hung out the front of the Polaroid camera like a pale tongue, though its colors were changing. He watched as it developed. Waiting there, he was a captive to the moment of full realization. And when it finally formed, it was every bit as perfect as he had imagined it.

Framed by the white edges of the picture, his new brothers and sister there on the couch, dressed in the spirit of the season with cups of cheer set before them. The bay window behind them looked out on a night filled with fluffy snow-flakes dancing through the air, and despite the gags that obscured their smiles, the eyes of his family were wide with delight. He looked silly, of course, there in his apron, but his arm was draped around Mummy who stood next to him and… come to think of it… her dark shape, though it was rife with the limbs of her long dead *other* family, was not unlike the shape of a Christmas tree. A fortunate coincidence.

He smiled.

This picture had captured his boyhood hopes with the single white burst of a flash cube. This was the family he never had and had always yearned to have. Henry pulled the photograph from the camera and stroked it with affection. He was so lost in reverie that it was a moment before he even heard the screaming.

Turning to look, he saw Mummy there with her snakes and claws and dead, hungry jaws feasting upon his new sister, the last vestiges of her blond hair turning red with gore as she thrashed about.

Wolfie and Lucky were whimpering and wiggling toward the far ends of the couch, their faces aghast as if the murderers had never seen so much blood in their long, dark lives.

Henry clucked his tongue and put his hands on his hips.

"Oh, Mummy!" he remarked, shaking his head disdainfully. "Now I'll have to find another."

Still, it was Christmas after all; that special time of year when wishes were granted and loved ones were indulged. Mummy had her new family—even if they were now down by one—and it was all because of him.

Henry swelled with pride, feeling like goddamned Santa Claus.

He took up his cup of cheer and toasted his brothers with a smile as he sang along poorly with the familiar tune booming out of the stereo.

"There'll be scary ghost stories," he warbled like a

drunken caroler, "and tales of the glories of Christmases long, long ago."

Across the room, with the crunching of bone and tearing of flesh, the dark thing from the pit delighted in one of its gifts early. As he watched, Henry decided then and there that it would be a new tradition for many years to come.

The Ghosts of Christmas Past
Richard Farren Barber

"You've got two hours," the attendant in the smock coat said.

"You already told me. My mind isn't gone yet," Hazel snapped. Immediately she wanted to blame the outburst on her illness. The disease might not impact her memory, but she could see it bleeding through in other ways, and sometimes it seemed that the anger was not just in her—it was her. The attendant, though, had turned his back and was busy reading monitors and changing settings, and Hazel guessed he might be used to such outbursts from the patients he saw.

"My name's Jeremy, but everyone calls me Mark." He still had his back to her, and Hazel wondered if she'd just imagined him speaking.

"Mark Time," he explained. "The people I work with think they're funny. Mostly they're not."

Hazel's mouth was dry. She looked at the machine and realized that, until now, it had all been abstract for her, but standing in this room, with the tap of keys and the soft wheezing of the air conditioning, she had finally come to accept it was happening.

Mark turned to face her. He held a scrap of card in his hand that she recognized from her consultation. It was a different Hazel who had filled out that card, one who didn't believe what all the doctors were telling her. One who still believed she would live forever.

He looked down at the card. "You're sure about this?" But before Hazel could come back with a snide reply, he continued. "Don't worry. I'm the last one to ask you that. This is the point of no return."

"Has anyone ever changed their mind at this point?"

"Not so far."

"I thought not. Punch it in and let's get started."

He handed her a small earpiece. "Put this in now. Two hours," he reminded her. "It will go faster than you could possibly imagine."

"That's the joy of time travel," Hazel said, but before she heard Mark's reply, he was gone and she was standing in the front room of the house she had lived in forty years earlier.

It was darker than she remembered. The wallpaper was grubby and the flower pattern wasn't quite the same as the one in her memory. The floor was strewn with scraps of wrapping paper, and in amongst this debris, like a newly discovered toy, was Frances.

Hazel felt the breath sucked deep into her lungs. Frances. The little girl looked tiny, and for a moment Hazel thought that Mark had brought her to the wrong year. Then she saw the abandoned toys and they set the date as accurately as a calendar: Christmas Day 2005.

She ran forward, three quick steps, and tried to gather Frances into her arms. When the child remained seated where she was and Hazel was left holding nothing but air, she nearly sobbed.

"It's not fair," she whispered.

"I'm sorry." Mark's voice, so quiet. Hazel whirled around, but there was no sign of the man anywhere in the room.

She looked down at Frances.

"This was the last time we were happy. The three of us. After this..." Hazel let her voice trail away. She wondered how much Mark knew about her. Not about what was happening to her now—the ball of cells throbbing in her temples. He knew about that, why else would she be here? Hazel knew she didn't look like the type of woman who would be able to pay for the treatment from her own funds. No. She wondered how much Mark knew about before.

She wondered if he had any suspicions.

"Do you think that time travel proves the existence of fate?" Hazel asked.

"I don't know. I just press the buttons."

Hazel wondered why he felt the need to lie. Why he thought he had to hide himself from her. She wished that she could look into his eyes and read what he thought he was protecting her from, because she could tell him: Nothing. There was nothing she needed to be shielded from because she'd already experienced the worst that life had to throw at her back in 2005.

"Because if it is all fate, then what's the point?" Hazel said. She looked behind her, to where she imagined Mark would be standing if they were still together in his consulting room.

"It doesn't prove anything."

Hazel was about to argue with Mark. And then Jim opened the door and walked into the room.

Were you really ever that young? she thought. Her memory of him was corrupted. She knew she was to blame. She couldn't bear to remember him as he was in front of her now. Charming. Innocent.

Sober.

And then he started to speak and she heard the way he slurred his words. Someone else might assume he was using baby-speak for the young child, but Hazel was beyond such naiveté. He slurred his words because he was drunk. And he was drunk because... well, because he was Jim and that was what he did. Not yet two o' clock—he must have had his nose in the bottle since early in the morning. Hazel remembered those days.

"This can be difficult," she heard Mark say. "Troubling. Most people who take the trip..."

"Do so to try and find answers to questions that don't have answers," Hazel finished for him. "I know. I read the leaflets."

Again she sensed Mark's reaction—a pained embarrassment. She thought he wasn't used to being challenged, and maybe that was to be expected. Maybe if she'd come here for a final look at Jim and Frances, for the chance to live through a memory one last time, she would be equally pliable.

"I nearly didn't come," she said.

"That happens a lot."

"It's too passive, just standing here and watching."

Hazel looked around the room, almost expecting to see Mark's ghostly outline in a corner, watching over her. But of course the room was empty except for Jim and Frances and the presents scattered all over the floor. She tried to remember where she had been at this moment, but the memory was lost to her, and she wondered if that was deliberate—if she was repressing the knowledge, or if Mark had done something to block it. Some sort of space/time paradox protection so that she couldn't go and find herself and... and do what exactly? Wasn't that the whole point? She couldn't do anything. She couldn't change anything. Wasn't that why they called it ghosting?

Jim stumbled across the room toward Frances. Their beautiful daughter. Their only child because after today... well, after today there was no longer any of them. Bright wrapping paper clung to his ankles as he forced his way across the room. Frances looked up and Hazel almost expected her daughter to say something—to call for her Daddy or cry out in alarm, but of course Frances was too young for words and she didn't yet know that there was any reason to be afraid.

Hazel called out, "Jim!", but he didn't hear her. Hazel turned away for a moment, searching for Mark, but not finding him.

"Can you do something?" she begged.

"This has already happened. We're just witnesses."

"No," Hazel said. "You can do something. You can stop him."

"How?"

She heard the curiosity in his voice; that's what she'd been hoping for.

"We can do something," she told him.

"We're not really here. I thought you understood..."

"We're here," Hazel insisted. She began to walk forward. After a second she realized that although she had walked through the debris, her path had not disturbed any of the wrapping paper. It was true, she was back in 2005. But... not.

Jim swooped down, arms wide like airplane wings.

Frances giggled, and the sound was enough to rip Hazel's heart wide open. The sound of her daughter laughing.

She could feel the wetness of tears upon her cheeks, and for a moment she was overcome with the raw emotion. She turned towards where she imagined Mark was standing and almost asked him, *Get me out of here. Get me away.* This was so much harder than she had ever expected.

Jim wrapped his arms around their tiny daughter and threw her high into the air. Frances laughed again, the sound of glass trembling.

"I can't..." Hazel murmured. Her chest ached around the pain. She had wondered if it was possible that she could die here. Now she wondered whether that would be such a bad thing.

"Hold on, Hazel." The voice came from closer than she had expected, a point just off her shoulder. Mark was standing beside her, she could feel his spirit in the room with her.

Jim put their daughter down and reached over to the stone mantelpiece above the fire place to pick up the car keys.

"Please stop," Hazel begged. "You don't know what you're doing."

Her words were as thin as broken promises.

Jim held the keys in his hand. "Do you want to go for a drive?" he asked Frances.

"You can't," Hazel shouted. But he didn't hear. *Maybe if he was sober he might notice,* Hazel thought. But he was drunk. Two o'clock on Christmas Day and he was already drunk. She recognized the poison she had been carrying around inside her for the last forty years.

Hazel remembered the showroom where they had bought the car. She remembered Jim's hand casually anchored in the back pocket of her jeans, tracing the curve of her bum.

And it was like she was travelling within time because she was in that showroom and she was in the front room with Jim and Frances and she was strapped into the machine in Mark's operating theatre all at once. Other memories folded in on her. Walking across Market Square on a wet Saturday, plastic bag handles cutting her palms as she hurried out of the rain. Crying herself to sleep in the too-wide bed. That first moment when she had noticed Jim watching her, his face dappled with silver and blue light. Walking down the aisle. The hotel in Santorini. Staring at the roof of the maternity suite and then hearing Frances' first cry. And sitting in the plastic bucket chair in A&E, her hands covered in blood. And standing beside the grave on a cold January morning. And... And... And...

"Stop it," Hazel shouted. "I can't do it."

She saw her husband's head turn toward her.

But that was impossible.

Wasn't it?

Hazel had read the police report. Her lawyer had given her a copy—a young man with razor burn on his cheeks. "I don't know if this will help you," he'd told her. Even now she still didn't know if learning what had happened made it easier to live with. The report had been factual, dispassionate. It spoke about reaction times and braking distances and blood-alcohol levels. She knew what had happened. She didn't accept it. It was impossible ever to accept what had happened that Christmas morning, but she knew the facts.

Hazel shouted again. And this time there was no doubt that Jim heard her. He turned toward her and she could see the confusion in his face. He heard her, but he couldn't see her. Hazel watched the doubt creeping into his features. She knew what he was thinking now—it was the booze that was doing this to him. The booze stole hours and days from his memory, and now it was causing him to hear voices.

"Lemme alone," he slurred.

"No, Jim. It's me."

"Hazel?"

She took a step toward him even though she understood he couldn't see her. She wanted to reach out and hold him. All the hate she had built up in her heart was still there, she felt it like a weight she could never release, but there was also love. The love she had once felt for him. A love that existed before the hate, before the loneliness and the rage and every other emotion she had lived with for the last forty years. She felt love.

"Hazel, you can't..." Mark said from behind her. She heard his voice in her ear, close as a lover's whisper.

"Can't?" she said. "Can't? Surely it's the opposite. I have to."

"You can't change the past," he said.

"I can try."

Jim looked pained, as if he could hear the conversation, but understood none of it. As if listening to the exchange between herself and Mark just reinforced the belief that it was alcohol that was driving the voices he heard.

"Jim, listen to me," she said softly. "You need to leave Frances. You need to..." She could feel wetness on her cheeks and realized she was crying, and for a moment she was no longer in the living room with Jim and Frances, but instead she was back in the theatre strapped into Mark's chair. She felt her body forming around her mind, layers upon her soul. Dragging her back to the present, to reality.

"No," she shouted.

For a second her vision flickered and she saw the two scenes overlaid upon each other: Jim and Frances and the living room and Mark and the white walls of the theatre. She heard the slow beeping of the monitors on her right and she smelled the sharp scent of pine from the Christmas tree in the corner of the room, and they were both the truth and both lies.

"No." She pushed. She forced her mind back to Jim and Frances because she had only one chance—she had never needed Mark to tell her so.

"You have to listen to me, Jim," she said. Her vision wavered, and although the two scenes remained in her sight, the white walls of the operating theatre faded until they were out of focus. The fireplace was real. The settee and the rug in the middle of the floor was real. Jim was real. Frances was real.

"You can't..." Mark said.

Hazel lifted her hands up to her head to plug her ears from his voice. For a moment she felt a tug of resistance from the leather restraints tied around her wrists, but then the sensation faded.

"Please, Jim."

He was crying. Thick, booze-sodden tears rolled down his cheeks.

"If you love Frances, leave now, before you hurt her."

He seemed to look at her, to really notice her, and then Hazel watched him dismiss her from his mind as just another sign that he needed a drink. What did she look like to him? A sixty-five-year old woman that he didn't recognize?

He snatched hold of Frances' hand and pulled their daughter across the room after him, her feet trailing through the curls of discarded wrapping paper.

"No, Jim. I won't let you do it."

Hazel reached out toward Frances, to pull the pair of them apart. Her hand smacked against her husband's shoulder.

The contact was solid. Real.

Jim began to fall. Backwards. Towards the fireplace.

Hazel heard the sound—like a bomb exploding in the next room—and then her head filled with Mark screaming at someone that it wasn't his fault.

Blackness slammed down upon her. The last fragment of a second was filled with Jim's face and the blood pooling beneath his head. And her final thought before the blackness took her—*I've done enough.*

She awoke into chaos.

The small room of Mark's theatre was crammed with bodies, and at first she thought something terrible had happened—an explosion or an earthquake. A disaster that had ripped the place apart and summoned the emergency services.

A mob of black-suited men huddled around the machine. From somewhere in the middle of the swarm she could hear Mark's voice protesting his innocence. "It's not my fault. I didn't know. How the hell could I know she…?" and then one of the soldiers barked at him to shut up.

Soldiers. As soon as her vision had settled enough for her to take in the scene, Hazel realized what she was looking at: A unit of soldiers in their black fatigues with heavy rifles slung around their waists.

"What are they…?" she tried to ask Mark, but Christmas 2005 was still working through her system. Instead of words, her lips issued a pathetic squeal like a frightened piglet.

The soldiers had their backs to her as they grilled Mark and poured over the readouts from the machines that clustered around the bed.

"What do they want?" she tried to ask. The thin sounds

she made bore no resemblance to the voice in her head.

And then some unseen signal passed between them and they flooded back through the door.

Mark stood opposite her. The cockiness she had seen in him was gone.

"I'm sorry," he said.

"What for?"

He looked at her and she realized he couldn't understand the noise she had made.

"The sedative will wear off soon."

"What did they want?"

"I'm sorry," he said again.

Hazel realized she wanted to scream with frustration. *Who were they? What are they doing?*

Mark turned away from her, and Hazel thought it was because he couldn't bear to look at her any longer. There was a terrible knowledge in his face, an understanding that slowly dawned on her—like a jigsaw puzzle built in front of her eyes, one piece at a time.

"No."

The word came out strangled, but whole enough for Mark to understand.

"It's the rules," Mark said. "I tried to tell you."

He turned away and Hazel realized he was crying.

"What are they going to do?" she slurred.

Mark looked beyond her as he spoke, as if he couldn't meet her eye. "They're going to put it right," he told her.

Deck the Halls

Chantal Boudreau

"Ward! Ward, did you get the ornaments out of the attic?"

The shrill voice of his aged mother, her words followed by a round of phlegm-filled coughing, was harsh enough to make his ears bleed. It caused Ward to grit his teeth, cringe, and shudder. *Why was she still alive?* he asked himself. Once her health had begun to fail and she had become a burden to him, he had expected her to die rather quickly. Instead, once he had started anticipating her death, she had clung to life for two years, her condition only declining bit by bit.

"No, Ma," he yelled back. "It's not even December yet! We've got weeks to go!" Then under his breath he grumbled: "… And I'm hoping you'll be dead by then."

"You can't leave it until December, dummy. You need to check to see if anything needs replacing. Go through the light strings for dead bulbs and switch them for new ones, look for broken ornaments that have to go, and figure out if any garland is too tangled to use. You have to put things up the way I always did. You have to—you promised!"

Ward shuddered and cursed himself, remembering that promise. She had been considered palliative at the time, supposedly on her death bed in the middle of July. She wouldn't make it to Labor Day, the doctors had said. Ward certainly hadn't expected to have to make good on that promise. Then his mother had made an incredible and inexplicable comeback. Something of a miracle, the doctors had claimed, thanks to an iron will to live. She had stared death in the face and had lived.

That would be enough to scare off even the Grim Reaper, Ward thought snidely.

Still an invalid, but no longer considered critical or palliative, she had demanded to go home instead of into a long-term care facility. At first, she had hired caretakers to clean her house, keep her fed, administer her medication, and run any errands she needed done. While this set-up had remained in place, Ward had been forced to watch his potential inheritance dwindle—and that just wasn't acceptable. He had decided after a couple of months that since those arrangements weren't working for him, he would have to find a way to rectify the situation. Ward had insisted on taking over her caretaking duties, moving in with his mother so her money would stay with him.

Becoming his mother's keeper hadn't been as easy as Ward had anticipated. Her demands were constant and harrying. She rarely let him rest for any amount of time before she would ask for something new, and he ended up both irritated and exhausted most days. He was tired of waiting for her to die, and he had already decided he couldn't tolerate one more Christmas season with her persistent nagging. He wanted her out of his hair—and that meant accelerating her annoyingly slow demise.

Ward had concocted what he felt was a rather clever plan, one that involved substituting over-the-counter pain-killers for her regular heart and hypertension medication. He had been switching the contents of her capsules and his mother had thought she was taking her proper pills, unknowingly. He had been foisting off the fakes on her for two weeks and was already witnessing noticeable changes in her overall well-being as a result: shortness of breath, complaints of heart palpitations, pale, clammy skin, and joint and muscle tenderness. Ward had repeatedly dismissed his mother's concerns, pointing out that the doctor had warned her symptoms would worsen with time, medication or not. He had convinced her that it was nothing she should worry about for the moment, but Ward figured he might need to cause her some sort of extreme stress to finally end things for her before she suspected any funny business on his part.

"Jesus, Mom! I don't have the time to mess with that crap now!" Ward was in the middle of watching a closely matched hockey game involving his favorite team and a comparable rival, beer cracked open, chips and dip at the ready.

"Anita always had the time. I think Anita cared about me more than you do—my own pathetic son. Maybe I should get her back. She certainly earned her pay."

Anita had been his mother's last caretaker. Ward wasn't about to let the intrusive and caustic woman return—more of what should soon be his money lining someone else's pocket. Not only that, but if Anita came back in, it would destroy all the progress he had made so far, possibly reversing the damage he had already done. She would question the changes in his mother's health and demand answers.

"No, Ma. You don't have to do that. If it's that important to you, I'll go to the attic right now."

Ward swore that this would be the last game he would miss for her sake—the last sacrifice he would make of any kind. He would find a way to give her a shock that would drive her to the grave sooner rather than later. Getting an eyeful of the ridiculous amount of Christmas junk she kept in storage gave him a wicked idea. While his mother loved her Christmas decor, there were a few items in particular that were extra special to her, things she would actually mourn if they were lost. Ward made sure to dig for the box with those treasured trinkets first. With a devious cackle, he reached into the box and pulled out two particular angel baubles. His mother had bought both of those ornaments, delicate china pieces, when first his father and then his sister had died. His mother liked to claim that a little piece of their spirits was preserved in those angels. She had made Ward promise to buy an angel like that for her spirit once she had passed on. If he didn't, she insisted, she would have to haunt him for it.

"That's crazy," Ward had told her, before agreeing to do her bidding. "Why the hell would they stick around in stupid Christmas ornaments? Dad and Shelly weren't Christmas nuts like you."

"I'm not crazy," his mother had insisted. "A part of them stayed behind with me because we're family, and since I love Christmas, it only makes sense that that's where they would go. You're just a big, ole' cynic—you don't believe in anything. You'll regret that someday."

Ward believed in plenty, actually. He believed in making sure he had power of attorney for his mother to keep the prying hands of nieces, nephews, and cousins away from her money. Once that was done, Ward had signed the house over to his name. He also believed in keeping up the premiums on her life insurance, paying them out of her personal pension fund every month. He believed in using her Social Security checks to keep the fridge stocked with beer, as well as his favorite foods, and to use it to pay the oil costs to keep the house warm. He needed to keep it in good shape so he could sell it as soon as she died. He would sock away the proceeds, and then he'd be set for life.

"Check things," his mother had said — like it made a difference if a few dumb ornaments had been dinged or nicked while packing them up or one of her multitude of light strands didn't work. Most of that junk didn't really mean all that much to her individually. But Ward did know the state of those angel ornaments was especially important to her.

Why... if they were broken, it might be enough to kill her...

Unfortunately, the angels were in pristine condition.

"Not for long," Ward snickered. He snatched up the glittery pair and crushed them with his brawny hands, an act that required only a single gesture. He didn't even wince when a sharp shard of the porcelain dug deeply enough into his palm to draw blood. Instead of expressing pain, he smiled.

"Hey, Ma." Ward made a beeline for his mother's bedroom, grinning from ear to ear. "I'm afraid I have some bad news for you."

When he stepped into the elderly woman's bedroom, broken angels in hand, his mother was already sitting up in bed, pale, shaky, and looking anxious.

"You were right to have me check. Looks like we have a couple of casualties that didn't survive the year."

Ward held out the smashed angels so she could take in

the full extent of the damage and he waited. His mother's anguished response was immediate. She cried and wrung her hands, screeching at him for not being careful enough when he had put them away the prior year. He pushed back, trying to get as much of a rise out of her as possible, telling her that they were only stupid ornaments anyway and he didn't get why she would make such a fuss over them. The final reaction he was waiting for came much more quickly than he had been expecting, probably because of his interference with her drugs.

His mother suddenly clutched at her chest. She gasped for breath, reaching for Ward with her other hand.

"My heart... I need a doctor, Ward. I need paramedics. Call 9-1-1."

She certainly did need medical attention, but Ward wasn't about to supply it, or even acknowledge that there was a real problem.

"We'll just wait it out, Ma. You can get fined if you call 9-1-1 when you don't really need it. You're having a panic attack because you got yourself so upset over the dumb broken angels." He held the damaged ornaments up again just to rub salt in the wounds and maybe speed things up a little, watching the small dribbles of blood rolling away from the cut in his palm.

A look of distress flashed across the elderly woman's face. She tried to get out of bed, perhaps hoping to make the call herself, but her efforts failed and she slipped to the floor. She was already starting to look quite gray.

"Ward, please... help me. Ward?"

He stood there watching, wearing a blank expression on his face, as she moaned, wheezed, and strained, struggling futilely to rise. Ward ignored her pleas as they weakened and she went from gray to blue in color; he waited for the inevitable, knowing it would come soon. When she lost consciousness, lying still on the floor, he smiled.

"As far as I was concerned, you were asleep for the night. I was downstairs, watching the game." Ward tossed her broken angels into the wastepaper basket without a second thought. "I never heard a peep from you. I'll find you like this when I check in on you before I head for bed, long past the point of resuscitation."

He walked out of the room, closing the door behind him, pausing only to wipe away the smear of blood his palm left on the knob.

"Goodbye, Ma, and merry Christmas to me, only this time it's coming early."

❄ ❄ ❄

The house was lonelier than Ward thought it would be without his mother there, even though he didn't really miss her. Now that it was the week before Christmas and Ward had had one too many celebratory rum and eggnogs—heavy on the rum—he had decided it was time to decorate... only this time he would do it his way.

"I don't need anyone to bring me any lame-ass ol' presents this year," he slurred as he pulled out the storage bins, talking to nobody in particular. "I can buy plenty of my own damn presents, thanks to that insurance money. All I need to do now is sell this crappy house—probably in the spring. Then I can go anywhere I feel like going and do anything I want to do."

He stumbled along with the bulky boxes in hand, headed for the hallway where he had already set up the artificial tree. He had bought that tree himself during a celebratory shopping spree a few days after his mother had died. She had always insisted on a real tree, so he had gotten it just to snub her memory—proof that she could no longer order him around or decide things for him.

Ward staggered around carelessly as he decorated, dropping more than one ornament when he attempted to hang them on the tree. He cut his finger on one of the sharper shards, but just laughed at the pain, shoveling all of the broken bits into a garbage bag along with a few of the undamaged but tacky baubles his mother had adored, but he had always hated. They were mostly ones with a religious motif. Ward was hoping to eventually replace them with monster snowmen and mooning Santas.

"I don't have to look at that shit anymore, and I don't have to listen to your nagging ever again either. I get to 'deck the halls' any way I choose." Ward sang those three words like the Christmas carol. "I get to hang my hockey team ornaments wherever I want, not just in my room, and I get to put up my naked girly garland that I got at the novelty store. This is my home now—and my decorations. So fa-la-la-la-la-la-la-la."

Ward belched and threw a couple of her favorite gaudy antique ornaments against the wall, where they shattered with a loud crash. He laughed uproariously as they smashed to smithereens.

"That one's for you, Ma. No more 'Jesus is the reason for the season.'"

Once the lights were strung and the ornaments hung, he decided it was time for his special garland. He set off to fetch it.

Skipping the eggnog this time, Ward returned to the fake tree with the bottle of rum in one hand and his garland composed of foil nudie silhouettes in the other. He had also shed most of his clothing and was now clad only in his ho-

ho-ho underwear, red and green wool socks, and a Santa hat.

After catching himself in a wobble and almost taking the less-than-secure tree down by falling into it, Ward started winding the garland around the phony branches. He paused, goose-bumps rising on his flesh. He noticed a chill to the air but figured it was one of the old drafts that ran through the old, poorly insulated house, one he could feel more so than normal because of his skimpy attire. Weaving and swaying, he shrugged and returned his attention to the task at hand, while humming *Jingle Bells* slightly off key.

He had the garland partially strung when he reached the halfway point on his bottle of rum. In a drunken haze, Ward tripped as he reached for it, grabbing for the tree to halt his fall and toppling into it. He tumbled down in a man/tree tangle. He tried to free himself, but before he knew it, he was thoroughly entwined in the garland. He swore loudly, thrashing against the artificial branches. Each flailing motion merely tightened the garland's hold, especially the part looped around his throat.

"Aw crap!" Ward exclaimed, sputtering and gagging. "Ma's revenge—I'm going to have to wreck my own special decoration to get out of this. That would have made her happy. I can just picture her ghost smiling over this, wherever she happens to be." He had never bought that angel ornament for her spirit.

Ward tried to curl his fingers around the garland to rip it free, but the loop continued to constrict and he couldn't get a proper grip around the slippery strands. Even through his drink-induced fog, he felt a flash of panic, his breathing now restricted.

"This is bullshit!" he wheezed, feeling very dizzy.

Ward pulled at the garland even harder, but it wouldn't

break away. That didn't make sense—it was a flashy piece of cheap trash that normally came apart with little prompting. It should have snapped like nothing. Instead it was proving to be impossibly strong, as if he were being strangled by piano wire instead of decorative tinsel.

He cursed again, but Ward's foul protests were growing less audible due to a lack of air. As fear overcame him, a sense of utter doom, his booze- and eggnog-laden belly rebelled. He vomited, and much of it became trapped in his mouth, nose, and throat. The little air he could suck in was now just an aspiration of the mess that choked him. His suffocation came on quickly, his lungs partially clogged by the sticky acidic swill. Ward convulsed his way into death, garroted by the garland and drowned by his own alcoholic filth.

❄ ❄ ❄

Nobody found Ward like that until sometime after Christmas, because nobody in particular was interested in what had become of him. The emergency workers who broke through his door had to leave the house to get some air, overwhelmed by the gruesome sight and stench of his decaying body.

"A case of a little too much Christmas cheer," one man said to the other. "Some people just don't know when enough is enough."

"You can say that again," his co-worker agreed. "Kind of sad. These things always happen around the holidays—people get self-destructive or even suicidal. I heard the poor bugger's mother died recently on his watch. It might have been the guilt that got him. You know, all alone at Christmas, dwelling on her death and blaming himself for it. That, or it might have been loneliness. He wasn't married. No kids, and his parents and only sister dead and gone."

"Yup... pathetic. And what's worse is how long it took before anyone noticed he was dead. The postman saw that the mail piling up and the strange smell coming from the house. I wouldn't want to be the one to have to clean that mess up. I'd be tempted to just burn all those Christmas decorations in there, if not the whole decrepit house."

Both men noticed a new chill in the air following that comment. When they carted out Ward's corpse, they were forced to do so tree, garland, and all, his flesh having rotted to the point where it was now one with the tacky decorations.

"I don't think this was what they meant by 'deck the halls'. Looks like he took that a little too personally," the first man said. His co-worker chuckled, and then grimaced at the smell.

Trying to ignore the gruesomeness of Ward's end as the pair toted him off, they sang off-key, "Fa-la-la-la-la-la-la-la-la!"

ALL I WANT FOR CHRISTMAS
Raymond Gates

Ryan stared at the computer screen. The screen stared back. They'd been testing their wills against one another for a long time. The computer was still winning.

He reached for a cigarette, found the last one in the pack, and placed it between his lips. A Zippo appeared in his hand as if by magic. With a well-practiced snap of his fingers, a flame flared into life. As he touched it to the end of the cigarette, he wondered if he'd asked Karly to get more smokes while she was out. Or if she'd listened to him. She'd been pretty pissed that he wasn't going with her and Emily to the carols, and given that she didn't approve of his smoking, there was a good chance she wouldn't. Though she'd never refused before, this time was different. This time, it wasn't just about her and him. It was about Emily, too.

Emily. He pictured her; her beautiful, doll-like face glowing with the wide-eyed wonder only a six year old has at Christmas time. Those big blue eyes, filled with disappointment as he told her he couldn't go to Carols by Candle-light with her and Mummy because of his work. His novel. He had to finish his novel.

She hadn't argued; she hadn't whined or pouted or pleaded with him. She'd whispered, "Okay, Daddy," and turned to go. Somehow, that was worse than any tantrum she might have thrown. Worse than the look Karly had given him. Worse than hearing the woman he'd cherished and loved for nearly ten years mutter, "You fucking asshole," as she stormed out with their daughter in tow.

I'll make it up to her, he thought, leaning back in the chair and drawing deeply on the cigarette. The burning tang of smoke filled his throat and lungs. He held it in, allowing the buzz to seek out the gnawing guilt and beat it into silence. Or at least quieten it down. *The moment I finish it, the moment the file finishes saving, I'll make it up to both of them.* He closed his eyes and exhaled, imagining the guilt leaving his body along with the smoke. He didn't believe it would, but it enabled him to sit up and look at the screen again.

The cursor rested exactly where he had left it; a faithful dog waiting for its master. Above it, *Chapter 22* sat in solitude. He'd typed that almost three months ago. Until then, words had flown freely, almost too easily, as he'd ripped through chapter after chapter of his greatest work to date. The New Year's Eve deadline became irrelevant as page after page rolled off the printer. Even Don, his panic attack-prone publisher, had been relaxed, even happy, with the progress he'd made. He and Karly had laughed with delight about this being his Big Break, and deep down he truly believed it would be.

That ended in September, when he sat down, opened the file, typed *Chapter 22* and... nothing. No thoughts, no ideas, no inkling of what should happen next. Nothing.

He'd tried all his old tricks: writing random words on a page; reading some of his favorite authors; distracting himself by going for walks. Numerous times he'd belted out the beginning of a paragraph, trying to break through the block that had cemented itself in his mind. They'd been clumsy, ineffective, the words of a novice, and summarily deleted.

Now he had less than a week to deadline, and still nothing. *Well that's not entirely true*, the guilt piped up. *You've managed to break your daughter's heart and make your wife loathe you.*

Fuck off, he thought, sucking down smoke until the filter started burning.

He stood and shuffled out of his study, not knowing, or even caring, where he was going. He had to get away from the computer's cursed blinking eye. He followed the noise coming from the lounge room. The TV was still on, tuned to the coverage of some celebrity Christmas concert. The latest *Australian Idol* winner crooned their way through *All I Want For Christmas*, while a green, buck-toothed dinosaur he recognized from one of Emily's favorite shows danced and encouraged the audience to sing along. Ryan snorted. Two front teeth? All *he* wanted was a finished first draft.

The shrill ring of the phone jolted him as it cut through the air. It rang again, the backlit display coming to life, confirming he hadn't imagined it. He glanced at his watch—twenty past nine—and wondered where his wife and daughter were.

As the third ring ended, he thumbed the answer button. "Yeah?" he said.

"Merry Christmas, Ryan," a smooth, masculine voice said.

"Who's this?" It didn't sound like Don, nor Karly's father.

A low, rumbling chuckle answered him. "Oh, really,

what's in a name?"

Great, Ryan thought. *Some moron with nothing better to do on Christmas Eve.*

"Yeah, I think you've got the wrong number."

"You're Ryan Harper, the author."

Ryan sighed. Worse than a prank call; a crazed fan. So much for unlisted numbers. Telstra was going to get blasted over this.

"Yeah, listen. I appreciate your support, but you can find out all about me on the webs—"

"Ryan..." The voice was firm. "...I'm not one of your crazed fans. I'm calling to help you."

Ryan frowned.

"With your novel."

A tingle crept down Ryan's spine. Three people knew about the novel. Two were at Carols by Candlelight; the third was probably giving a secretary her Christmas bonus on top of a desk. Don wouldn't have told anyone. Would Karly? Why would she?

Then again, if the guy knew he was an author, it wouldn't be much of a stretch to guess he was probably working on another novel.

"Oh, okay," he sneered as he spoke. "What do you think you can help me with?"

"The ending."

The room shifted, started to spin.

"The ending that's eluded you for the last three months," the voice said.

Ryan swooned, and grabbed the wall to steady himself. *Karly had talked to someone about this? Some guy? What the hell was going on?*

"Who the fuck *is* this?" he asked through clenched teeth.

The silence felt longer than the few seconds it lasted.

"You're on a deadline, correct? December thirty-one, if I'm not mistaken."

Ryan's eyes bulged. He stared at the phone, holding it at arm's length as if it had turned into a venomous creature. His name buzzed through the speaker, as if a swarm of bees were calling him. "Ryan. Ryan."

With trepidation, he raised the receiver back towards his ear, keeping it a finger's width away from him.

"I understand your concern, Ryan, but you've nothing to worry about. I'm here to help you." He could almost hear the smile behind the voice. "It is Christmas after all."

Ryan swallowed. This was ridiculous. Fear told him to hang up on this freak, but he couldn't bring himself to push the button.

"Tell you what," the caller interrupted his thoughts. "Let me offer you something as a show of good faith. A taste of what I've got for you."

The stranger whispered down the line, the sound of silk dragged over broken glass. Ryan gaped, eyes wide, as the stranger carried his story on from where he'd left it. His grip on the phone turned white. He strained to hear every word, every syllable being spoken to him. A veil lifted away from his mind's eye, revealing what he'd been searching for.

The voice stopped. The veil cast itself back and shrouded the ideas that had been coming forth. "No!" he cried out, though whether aloud or in his mind he wasn't sure.

"What do you think of that?" The voice was a lover's purr.

Ryan licked his lips. He felt as if he hadn't drunk in days. *It's perfect*, he thought. He could imagine the stranger smiling on the other end of the phone.

"Shall I continue?"

Ryan was already moving towards the study. Something

hard and plastic uttered a squeak as it was crushed under-foot; he ignored the pain as he scrambled onto his chair. A voice in his mind demanded to know why this stranger would help him. Grinning through clenched teeth at the white space he'd been trying to fill, he silenced the voice with a mental slap. He cradled the phone between his shoulder and neck and flexed his fingers above the keys.

"Okay, I'm ready," he said.

The rapid clacking of keys chased the whispers coming from the phone. Words, sentences, paragraphs hurtled across the screen. Ryan felt an odd sense of detachment; his fingers seemed to be under the direct command of his strange benefactor.

He processed the content as it was laid out, and it was *good*. The threads of his tale wove together in a pattern he doubted he could have conceived of himself. Loose ends were tied up, and sub-plots were given closure. The main story reached its glorious crescendo, and then settled into a comfortable finale.

Ryan blinked. His eyes stung as if they'd been rubbed with sandpaper. He straightened, the phone dropping to the floor as he winced from the dagger of pain in his neck. He stretched, wiped away fresh tears, and stared at the screen.

The cursor rested to the right of the word, *END*, panting from its exertions.

Ryan sat, staring, unmoving, in front of the screen. He closed his eyes, scrunched them shut, and kneaded his temples. When he opened them again, the screen told the same story.

"Ha!" His trembling hand guided the on-screen pointer to the icon that would save his previous work. A simple click and the hard drive hummed in response. "Ha HA!" The chair crashed back into the wall as he leapt to his feet.

He double-pumped his fists in the air as his face screwed up in exquisite joy.

A buzzing came from the floor and he froze. He looked down at the handset, lying on its side where it had fallen. He snatched it up and pressed it to his ear.

"Merry Christmas, Ryan." The voice was like a warm breeze.

"Oh, mate," he said. "You're an absolute fucking life-saver!" He retrieved the chair and sat in front of the screen again. "This shit is gold!" He scrolled through the section, scanning as he went, shaking his head with an ever-growing smile as the realization of what he'd accomplished set in. "How'd you know?"

"Ah," the voice took a humorous tone. "I make it my business to know these things. It's what I do."

Ryan shook his head. "Well, mate, I can't thank you enough. You've really made my Christmas."

"My pleasure." The man on the other end of the line cleared his throat. "Now... What are you going to give me in return?"

His smile faltered. "Pardon?"

"Your gift. To me. In return for mine." Ryan heard a low, ominous chuckle. "Tis the season, after all."

His mouth opened without a sound. His brow creased and he leaned back in the chair. A mental alarm bell clanged away in his subconscious. "What do you want?"

A sharp intake of breath, the sound of a nest of angry vipers, preceded the response. "How about your two front teeth?"

Ryan blinked, then barked a short laugh. "What?"

"Your two front teeth. You know. Like the song."

An image of the dinosaur cavorting around the stage to the tune of *All I Want for Christmas* played in Ryan's mind. He took a breath to say, *You're joking*, but let it out without uttering a word. He felt his elation fading away, a sense of dread rising up to take its place.

"One gift deserves another, wouldn't you agree?" The voice was losing its smoothness, becoming sinister. "Isn't that the spirit of Christmas? The joy of giving?"

Ryan placed his thumb against the button that would end the call. "I appreciate your help," he said. "But if this isn't a joke, you're out of your fucking mind."

A laugh that would curdle milk echoed through the phone. "Oh, Ryan. I'm not *asking* you for them."

Strong, cold hands grasped Ryan's head on either side. He dropped the phone, reflexes firing as he clawed at the vice-like grip. His head was jerked backwards and he stared into a nightmare.

"You're giving them to me," the voice's hideous owner proclaimed.

The thing's bulbous, pustulant face split apart in a mockery of a smile. Puffy, purple gums displayed a chaotic assortment of teeth that looked like they'd been implanted by a blind, insane dentist. The maw descended towards him. Ryan gagged from its fetid breath. He struggled, tried to break the grip on his head, tried to pull away from the horrid, rank pit that was now bare inches above his face.

"Stop," it commanded.

Ryan stopped struggling. He couldn't move. He couldn't breathe. As panic took hold, it even seemed his heart had stopped beating. He wailed inside his mind, now a prisoner of his inanimate body.

The thing sighed, a sickly, sulfurous stench. "Oh, Ryan. Where's your Christmas spirit?" It gurgled in apparent humor. The grip on Ryan's head released. Bone-white hands came into his frozen view. Each long finger was tipped with a black nail shaped like the flat head of a screwdriver, only paper thin, and tapered almost to a point. The nails slipped between his lips and teeth and pried open his mouth with minimal effort.

"So typical of this world," the thing leered above him. "This could have been so much easier if you'd thought more about giving than getting."

Ryan felt like crying, though no tears came to his eyes. He felt pressure against one of his upper front teeth, felt something pushing against his gum. He summoned every ounce of mental energy to will his lifeless muscles to move, to pull away from the inevitable.

The thing's flat fingernails worked under his gum line, in front and behind the tooth, following its root. The pain was dull at first, and then escalated, like a spike being driven through his mouth, past his nose, to seed itself behind his eye. As the nails traced the root to its socket, and then into the socket, pain rolled in a wave across his face. A cold hand held his forehead. The fingers in his mouth tugged, pulled, and jerked at the tooth. Each effort sent a pulse of agony throbbing through Ryan's head, drowning out his mental screams. With a final tug, the tooth popped free of its home. A metallic taste assailed him as warm liquid trickled over his tongue and down his throat.

Unable to do anything but watch, Ryan saw the demon — as he now thought of it — open its mouth wide. Holding its ivory trophy close, it used its free hand to search for a free space amidst the haphazard rows of teeth. Ryan noticed for the first time that, although the teeth were of innumerable shapes and sizes, they were all grouped in pairs. All central incisors.

Having found a suitable spot, it pressed the bloody root of Ryan's tooth against its gum, and then twisted it back and forth. Yellowish-green ichor dripped from the wound as the tooth was worked into its jaw, unaware, or not caring, that the tooth protruded sideways from its mouth. It smacked its lips together, ran its lumpy, purple tongue over its new, secured denticle, and bent to retrieve the other one.

"I must say," its words rang through Ryan's torment as it worked on releasing the other incisor, "I've never been so well rewarded for performing a single service.' With a crunch, the tooth was released from Ryan's jaw. It soon found a place beside its partner in the demon's mouth.

The monstrous face filled Ryan's vision. Violet eyes regarded him without warmth. "Now, that was a fair exchange, don't you think?" It smiled, revealing its latest acquisitions. Ryan could only stare and pray for his overwhelmed mind to lose consciousness.

"Well," it said, straightening, "I'd love to stay and discuss your new book, but I've more gifts to collect before the night is over. And my gift to you just keeps on giving." It grinned. "Thank you, Ryan, and Merry Christmas to you."

There was a shimmer, as if the demon was surrounded by heat haze, and then it was gone.

Ryan fell back and thumped to the floor, coughing and gagging. He spat gobs of clotted blood onto the carpet. A gnawing ache was taking residence in the front of his mouth. His tongue gingerly explored the new gap in his smile. He winced as it found the open sockets, and fresh blood spilled into his mouth.

He knew he should find something to press against the wound. He knew he should call for help. All he wanted to do was curl into a ball and weep.

The trill of the phone cut through his awareness. The handset was only inches away from his head. Karly's name lit up the display.

He grabbed it and connected the line. He tried to speak through closed lips. "Karly?"

"Hi, Daddy!"

"Baby?" Blood spattered the phone as he spoke.

"Mommy said I could call." Emily sounded excited. "Will you come to the carols now?"

Ryan's head swam. "What?"

"Your book's finished, so now you can come to the carols."

Ryan sat bolt upright. His breath caught in his throat. "How did you know I was finished?"

Emily giggled. "You sound funny."

He spat out a fresh clot of blood. "Baby, how'd you know?"

"The man told me."

His heart skipped a beat. "What man?"

"The man who gave you your wish. He does that at Christmas time. He said Santa doesn't mind."

He stood, ignoring the blood spilling down his chin and staining his clothes. "Where's Mommy, darling?"

"She's talking to the man. He gave us our wishes, too! I wished for you to finish you book so you can have fun again." Emily's voice lowered to a whisper. "I think Mommy wished for that, too."

"Baby, listen to me. Put Mommy on the phone. Right now, okay?"

There was a pause before Emily's faint words sounded through the receiver. "Okay, Mommy."

"Emily, give the phone to Mommy." Ryan's hands were shaking.

"Mommy said I gotta go. The man wants his presents."

The phone's casing cracked from the force of Ryan's grasp. "No, baby! Stay away from the man!"

"Come soon, okay? I love you, Daddy."

"EMILY!"

A low-pitched buzz sounded through the receiver. Ryan heard a faint, growling chuckle.

The line dropped out.

You Better Watch Out

Randy Lindsay

"You better not," Jimmy said with his hands on his hips. "If you keep being mean to me, Santa won't bring you anything tonight."

"There is no Santa," Mike said with a smirk.

Jimmy's lip trembled for a moment, and then he squared up his shoulders and faced his brother. "I'm gonna tell Mom and Dad!"

"Go ahead, you brat." Mike picked up one of building blocks scattered on the floor and flung it at his younger brother as the boy fled the bedroom.

Once the nudge was gone, Mike sat on his bed. He sat through a scolding from his mother. He sat through his brother's bedtime ritual. He sat as the lights were turned off and the house was at last dark and quiet. He sat there until he heard noises coming from the living room.

With slow, quiet steps, Mike moved through the house.

From the hall, he peered at the figure next to the Christmas tree. Dressed in a red suit with white trim, it looked like the pictures of Santa Claus that everyone knew. But something was not quite right.

"Santa?" said Mike.

"Krrisssssss," came the serpentine reply.

"What?"

"I am Kris Kringle." The figure turned and faced Mike. Made for someone with a wide girth, the suit hung on Kris' gaunt frame. A few strands of wiry gray hair stuck out from under a cap that threatened to fall and cover his eyes. Pale orbs stood out in dark contrast to the darkened sockets that held them. Dry, wrinkled skin covered his face and hands, making him look more like the Grim Reaper than a jolly old elf.

Mike stood there, mouth open.

Kringle made a rasping sound like a blade being sharpened, and its body shook in a parody of laughter. Then it bent over and grabbed a cookie from the plate that had been set on the fireplace mantel.

"You're not Santa," Mike mumbled, horror clearly present in his voice.

"Krrisssssss." The cookie disappeared into Kringle's mouth. "The sweet sacrifices help to restore the energy I use on this night. Still, they are not enough. What sustains me most is the faith of the innocent. They believe I exist and in turn—I do." Kringle's eyes swept over Mike and its cracked lips pulled back into a grimace of sadistic joy. "I understand that you do not believe in me."

"I... it's not real," Mike stammered. "Santa, the reindeer, presents under the tree, they're all part of a fairy tale. None of it's real."

"There lies the problem," Kringle shook its head. "Belief

in the old gods has faded away. I barely survive. You can understand why I cannot have the faith of my believers diminished with lies of my nonexistence."

"Wh-What do you mean?" Mike tried to lift his feet, but they remained where they were, as if glued to the floor.

"You should not have told Jimmy that there was no such thing as Santa."

Kringle's hands rose up until they bracketed Mike's head. Mike shook violently as a glowing stream flowed out of him into Kringle. As Mike shriveled, Kringle expanded. Energy passed from boy to pagan god until Kringle filled out his bright red suit and there was nothing left of Mike except a couple of pieces of coal. Bending over, Kringle picked up the coal and deposited them into Mike's stocking.

"Of course, unbelievers have their uses as well." When Kringle laughed, its belly shook like a bowl full of jelly.

Saint Nick Sticks
Peter White

The black BMW 5 Series uttered a low, guttural growl as it crawled along through the slush on Sycamore. Ethan was in the driver's seat and he was dressed as Santa Claus. Riding shotgun was Ethan's older brother, Frank. He palmed a magazine into his Desert Eagle pistol, chambered a round, and then tucked it into the waistband of his own Santa Claus suit. Behind them both, the morbidly obese frame of Country Bob was sprawled across the rear seats. Country Bob was chewing strawberry Hubba Bubba and trying to remember that he, too, was wearing a Santa suit. If he tried to blow a bubble through his fake chin whiskers, it was going to end up in one almighty gloopy mess.

"What's this guy's name again?"

Ethan knew the guy's name, but when he was nervous, he couldn't stop himself from yakking. It was just the way he was.

"Sticks. The man's called Sticks," replied Frank.

There was a loud snort of derision from the back seat. Frank flicked his eyes to the rear-view mirror and then back to the road as Ethan gently guided the car to a stop on the corner of Willow, killing the engine.

"Something to say there, big fella?" Frank's eyes were back on the mirror as he addressed the fat man in the back seat.

"What kind of dumbass name is Sticks?"

Frank thought the beard improved Bob's looks. It meant you didn't have to watch his chins wobble when he laughed. Or spoke. Or breathed.

"Well, gee whiz, *Country* Bob, I guess that would be a nickname. He used to be a drummer. A good one by all accounts."

Bob snorted again, but didn't say anymore; instead, he turned to look through the window at the last-minute shoppers waddling around under the combined weight of layers of winter clothing and bags full of gifts.

"What's his real name, Frank?" Ethan pressed, still jittery and not ready to let it go just yet. That was okay because there was family, and then there was family. And while fat Bob could go fuck himself (assuming he could even find his itty-bitty pecker under that gargantuan gut of his), Frank had infinite patience with his little brother.

"Sticks is all I know," Frank said. "That's was his handle inside and we don't need to know any more than that."

"Don't seem right to me, doing a job with a stranger." There was a trace of petulance in Ethan's voice now. Sometimes Frank forgot how young he was.

"He ain't a stranger to me, little bro. We did three years in the same cell block, remember? Besides—we didn't have a lot of choice after Trey got his stupid ass busted, did we?"

Country Bob grunted, but carried on staring out the window. Trey was Bob's step brother and the crew's enforcer of choice. He had been busted the week before by a couple of State Troopers, pulled over for a broken taillight while hauling a trunk full of grass. Cousin Trey's third strike. Season of goodwill or not, he wouldn't be seeing daylight anytime soon.

"We could do it ourselves, Frank. I could come in with you, it would be fine." Even though they were pulled over, Ethan still gripped the wheel in both hands.

"Ethan, look at me." Frank introduced a subtle edge to his voice; a stranger wouldn't have noticed, but Ethan immediately recognized the difference. This was Frank's taking-care-of-business voice, his you-listen-up-and-don't-answer-back voice.

"The gig is four people, you know that. The Driver never comes inside. Never, do you hear? Doesn't make a difference if it takes thirty seconds or thirty minutes, the driver stays with the car. Inside we need three men. One to watch the door, one to grab the cash, and one to put the fear of God into everyone. Trey was our badass motherfucker, but he's gone now. That's why we need Sticks. Now, we okay to do this?"

"Yeah, we're okay, Frank. Sorry, I know you know best."

"Oh, fuck me sideways!" howled Bob from the rear. "Don't tell me this is him coming now, Frank. Don't tell me this is your *Badass Mutha-fucka!*"

He used the sleeve of his suit to wipe the condensation from the window and pressed his fat face up against the glass to get a better look. Frank and Ethan both turned to look out of the front passenger window. Shambling up Willow Street towards them was a scarecrow in scarlet. He was maybe five feet six in his boots and as thin as a rake; the arms and legs of his suit flapped in the breeze around his wasted limbs. Extra holes had been punched in the wide black belt, cinching his jacket tight to his waist, but it fell open above to reveal a scrawny pigeon chest clad in a grimy vest, what Frank would have called a wife beater. A thick mass of chest hair sprang forth over the neckline and seemed to be entangled with the fake white beard he wore.

"Yep, that's my boy," confirmed Frank.

"Well, shit on me," said Bob, laughing. "Drummer my ass. He's made of twigs. That's why they call him Sticks."

"Frank..."' began Ethan, but Frank cut him off.

"Shhhh, it's okay, Ethan, trust me. This guy will not let us down."

As he drew close to the car, Frank lowered the window. "Hey, Sticks, you found us okay?"

Sticks leaned down and stuck his head through the window. His pale blue eyes were heavily bloodshot and he looked and smelled like he was on the tail end of a bad drunk. Up close the man could have been any age between thirty and sixty. "Hey, Frank. Yeah, found it no problem. You give good directions." To Ethan, it sounded like Sticks kept his singing voice in shape by gargling with rusty nails. He seemed to be wheezing as well.

"Okay, well hop in the back next to Bob there. Bob, move your fat ass over and make room for Sticks."

Bob begrudgingly did as he was told, but even squashed right up against the driver's side door, he still took up most of the space. Luckily, Sticks didn't need much room.

"Okay, then," said Frank. "Let's head out."

Ethan started the engine and slowly got them moving again.

"What you got in that sack for me, Frank?" asked Sticks.

Frank reached down to the big burlap sack stuffed into

the passenger-side footwell and pulled out a long, narrow box with a big gold bow stuck on it and a gift tag proclaiming *Merry Xmas* in red lettering. He lifted it over the back of his seat with some effort and handed it to Sticks, who laid it across his knees and lifted the lid. Inside, wrapped in tissue paper, was a Remington pump-action shotgun. Sticks nodded approvingly and then replaced the lid.

"Thank you kindly, Frank. It's just what I wanted."

Frank then pulled out a shorter, squarer box and handed it to Country Bob. Bob didn't need to look inside to know that it contained a Steyr machine pistol. It was Bob's favorite and what he always asked for when they did a job. Frank didn't know why—guessed he'd probably seen it in some movie—but it didn't matter. The guns were for show; if it got to the point you actually needed to use them on a job, then you were probably already fucked. And the Steyr looked nice and lethal, even if he suspected Bob might struggle to hit the side of a truck from ten paces.

"What time you got, Ethan?" asked Frank, turning back to face front.

Ethan looked at the Casio on his wrist without taking his hand off the wheel. "I got eleven thirty-seven, Frank."

"Okay, little brother, I want us walking in the door at eleven forty exactly. Sticks, Bob. The Sheriff's office is within spitting distance of the bank. If anyone triggers the alarms, they'll be on us in two minutes tops. Even if they're out on patrol, they always leave at least one deputy dawg behind for just such an occasion as this. Course, they very rarely get it, and they tend to wet their panties when the call comes through, but we should be prepared for them nonetheless. Sheriff's men we can handle. But when they get the call, they will notify the State Troopers as well, and we don't want anything to do with those guys. To avoid that, we walk out of there in under five minutes. Sticks, you're our man. You got to persuade them that it's in their best interests to help us get out of there as quickly as possible. But you can't kill anyone. None of us want to be looking at a murder rap if this gets fucked. Is that gonna be a problem?"

Sticks did not answer immediately and actually seemed to be carefully considering the question, as if *not* killing someone might call into question his professionalism. But in the end he agreed to the terms. "Okay, Frank, I won't kill anyone."

And in the end, as Country Bob took great delight in pointing out, they didn't actually walk through the door until eleven forty two. Ethan, after timing his drive immaculately, parked the car nose first in one of the half dozen slanted parking bays in front of the bank. His face turned as red as his suit when Frank had to remind him they were there to rob the place and it might be handy if the getaway car was pointing away rather than toward the scene of the crime. After he had swiftly pulled out and reversed it back into the space, Frank and the others got out.

Frank went in first. The Desert Eagle was still tucked in his waistband; in his right hand he held a collecting tin for the Children's Defense Fund. Sticks and Country Bob followed behind carrying their gift boxes. All three wore surgical gloves and had empty burlap sacks tucked through their belts.

As Frank had anticipated, the place was doing frantic pre-Christmas business. Every window was manned by a teller, every teller was dealing with a customer, and the queue waiting to be served was at least twenty people long. There were assorted hangers on as well: a couple of young kids in one corner waiting on a parent, a fat woman with a half dozen shopping bags sitting at the loan officer's desk fanning herself with a mortgage brochure, the loan officer himself drafted in to help behind the counter. And then there was the security guard, of course; he was posted just inside the door, and as they entered, he tipped his hand to his hat in greeting. As soon as Frank had finished his quick assessment of the main floor, he turned his attention to the guard. The guy was big, middle aged, a bit paunchy, but strong looking. He raised his eyebrows as he saw Sticks and Bob follow in close behind and Frank understood he wasn't dumb either. He wouldn't be packing—the most these rent-a-cops got was a Taser and some pepper spray if they were lucky—but he still looked like trouble. Frank knew the type. Too much to prove to not at least try and intervene, he'd put his life on the line rather than risk coming out of this without a war wound and a story. So be it. Without taking his eyes off the guard, Frank spoke. "You're up, Sticks."

Sticks was at Frank's side now, and without hesitation he flipped over his gift box so that the lid fell off. He caught the barrel of the shotgun in one hand at the same time as letting go of the bottom of the box with the other, using it to grab the stock as both parts of the box tumbled to the floor.

The guard was lunging forward as soon he saw Sticks' hands flip the box. Add fast reflexes to his size and his wits, but he had been thrown off by the movement. He should have gone for Frank, who was closest to him; fast as he was, he would have had time to grab him and either put him down or use him as a shield. As it was, Sticks had the shotgun in both hands and was swinging it hard, up and towards the guard as he was still closing on him, head tipping low as his momentum carried him forward. The stock caught him full in the face and there was a sickening crunch as his nose exploded. His legs went out from under him, and as he went down hard, Frank saw the blood running between the fingers of the hands clasped to his face. The guard ended up on his knees, bent forward, head touching the carpet as if in prayer, and there was a thick, wet sound as he tried to breathe through his mouth and choke down the blood at the same time. It made Frank think of someone vacuuming up the dregs of a thick shake with a straw.

The rest of the bank was completely silent. Every pair of eyes was turned towards the three men in the Santa Claus costumes. Deer frozen in the headlights, they couldn't have forced themselves to act even if they wanted to, and Frank was pretty sure that they didn't want to do anything but live through this ordeal. This was going to be easier than he thought. He dropped the collection box and reached inside his jacket to draw out the Desert Eagle, intending to make his way to the tellers and to start issuing orders.

And then Sticks started to speak. He didn't raise his voice, but his sandpaper whisper commanded attention nonetheless.

Using the shotgun that he still held in both hands, he gestured toward the crumpled figure of the guard. "This man did what he had to do. That's okay, that's his job, and I respect a man who does the job he's paid to do. That's why I took it easy on him." As he said this, he made a show of slapping his palm against the stock of the shotgun. "But none of the rest of you are paid to be heroes, and if any of you try, we will have words. Just to be clear, the next time I have to talk to somebody, it will be with the business end of this thing. And you don't want that, not if you were planning on having an open casket at your funeral."

Frank stood next to Sticks with gun in hand, but he might as well have not been there. These people were terrified, but they only had eyes for Sticks.

"'Course the problem with this gun is that it only holds eight rounds, and I don't need to be no genius at math to see we got a lot more than eight people here. So after I've spoken to the first eight of you, I will have to make the rest of you try and see my point of view by talking to you with this."

He took one hand off the shotgun and reached down into his boot. He pulled out something small and black that from a distance looked a little like the plastic combs that they had in boxes next to the register at the drug store. Then he gave a quick flick of the wrist and there was a flash as the silver blade of the straight razor reflected the light from above. Sticks wielded it deftly, his little finger and his ring finger curled around the handle just below the hinge, the blade lightly gripped between thumb and forefinger. He moved it back and forth in front of his eyes, flicking his wrist with each change of direction; it shimmered like a trout in a mountain stream.

"And that's a conversation none of you want to have."

Then, with another flourish, the razor vanished as quickly as it had appeared, stowed somewhere safely on Sticks' skinny little body, and he had two hands on the shotgun again.

"Okay, everyone hit the floor, hands behind your heads, eyes closed."

They all obeyed, dropping like stones.

Sticks gave a little nod of his head towards Frank as if to say, *Okay boss, I got them warmed up for you, they're all yours now.*

Frank looked at Bob, who was already in position covering the door.

"You," he said to Sticks. "Put a hole in anything that moves."

He said it on every job to instill fear and promote compliance. Of course, Sticks little performance had already taken care of that, but he said it anyway and he made sure he said it loud. It wouldn't do any harm to remind everybody exactly who was in charge here.

He grabbed the sacks from the others' belts and made towards the tellers, picking his way between the bodies on the floor. When he got to the desks, he stood on tip toe to look behind the glass at the tellers lying on the floor. There were six in total, two old maids, an old geezer, the loan officer, a young male teller, and a little slip of a thing with red hair.

"Hey, Red!"

The girl whimpered, but did not look up.

"Hey, Red," Frank repeated. "I'm talking to you."

"You l-leave her alone."

It was the loan officer. Frank ignored him. He hadn't seen her face yet, but if the front matched the back, she was undoubtedly one tasty dish. No doubt the young buck in the expensive looking suit thought so, too. Why else would he be risking so much to impress her?

"Red, look at me or I'm going to tell my friend over there to start explaining the situation, and I'll tell him to start with the kids."

From somewhere behind him a woman screamed, the mother no doubt, and someone else, a man, found enough balls to call him a bastard, but he ignored it. He had gotten the redhead's attention; when he looked back, she was looking up at him, tears streaming down her cheeks. She looked like she was just out of high school.

"Red, I need you to get up and open the security door for me." He jabbed a finger to indicate the door to the left of the desks. It was big and had a wooden veneer, though Frank knew it would be steel underneath. There was a security key pad on the wall next to it. That was how the tellers got to and from their desks. Behind it was the money. There was the cash at the tellers' desks, of course, but more importantly, on a busy day like today just before closing time, there would be two or three trolleys stacked high with currency in a holding room waiting to be transported to the vault.

The terrified girl looked imploringly towards her colleagues for some sort of guidance, but her head snapped back at the sound of Frank's voice again.

"Don't look at those dumb bastards! Look at me!"

She looked up again to see Santa Claus using two fingers on his left hand to indicate his two eyes.

"Now you've got ten seconds to get that door open, or people are gonna start dying."

This elicited more whimpering from behind him, but it had the desired effect; the girl got to her feet and disappeared from his view. Seconds later the door swung open and Frank walked through, gun in one hand, empty sacks grasped by their necks in the other.

The trolleys were there just as he thought, and he emerged three minutes later pushing one loaded with the three full brown sacks. The redheaded girl walked in front of him, head down, shaking as she wept.

"Walk me to the door, sugar." He trained his gun on her as their little convoy made the short trip to where Bob was standing.

Frank handed Bob one of the sacks, which he took and hefted it over one of his massive shoulders, but he seemed more interested in the girl than the money.

"Hey," Bob said, looking her up and down. "Why don't we take her with us?"

Frank saw a momentary flash of pink between the nylon whiskers as the fat man licked his lips.

"She can help Santa guide his sleigh." There was an evil gleam in his little piggy eyes.

Frank turned to the girl. "We're done here. Get back behind that desk."

She didn't need to be told twice. Sticks was walking

among the customers lying on the floor, looking for an excuse to do something. Frank wondered if the man had even noticed that he was back.

"Hey, Saint Nick!" he yelled. "Time to hit the bricks."

Ethan had been studying the door of the bank in the rear-view mirror, and when he saw it swing open and the three Santas emerge, each one carrying a full sack over his shoulder, he slapped both hands down on the steering wheel and gave a triumphant yelp.

"Drive," was all Frank said as he slid into the passenger seat beside Ethan, and Ethan didn't need telling twice. He accelerated and the Beemer fishtailed in the slush, but he brought it under control easily enough. Despite the conditions, the needle was touching fifty by the time they left Cooper's Mill. No sign of the cops.

They stayed on the back roads. Sticks' little performance had ensured that the bank staff were too scared to try and trigger the silent alarms during the robbery, but there was little doubt they would have been reaching for the button as soon as they'd left the building. Ethan had made the most of the head start they'd been given, but there would be no avoiding the law on the highway.

They drove mostly in silence. Ethan asked how things had gone inside the bank and Frank said, "Fine, just fine."

After about half an hour, Ethan left the stretch of tree-lined, two-lane blacktop and turned onto an old dirt road. The tarmac had provided a relatively good driving surface—it was at least ploughed in between heavy falls of snow—but whoever owned this old access road was either unwilling or unable to keep it clear. Ethan had to bring the speed right down as he struggled to keep control of the car over frozen snow that dipped into deep troughs on the uneven surface. The heads of the four men inside rocked from side to side and the suspension complained loudly that it hadn't been meant for this. After about a quarter of a mile, the road began to slope gradually upwards and the car began to struggle for grip, but Ethan was able to nurse it delicately up the incline. When they crested the top, they could see the blackened timber skeleton of a burnt-out farmhouse. Next to it, close enough for the wood to have been scorched, but not close enough for it to have gone up itself, was a barn. Ethan brought the car to a stop in front of the double doors. They were secured by a chain run through the handles and held in place by a large, solid-looking padlock. Ethan killed the engine and got out; everyone else followed.

"We changing up, Frank?" asked Sticks.

"That's the plan."

Frank produced a small key from a pocket in his Santa pants, opened the padlock, unwrapped the chain, and flung open one of the doors so hard that it banged against the side of the barn. A crow, which had been perched on the roof, cawed once angrily and took to the air. Sticks turned to watch the bird fly low across the fields, wings flapping lazily, a perfect black silhouette against the snow.

Inside the barn was a large vehicle under a tarpaulin. Frank dragged off the cover to reveal a battered-looking Land Cruiser. He opened up the tail gate to reveal the carcass of a deer. He reached behind it to pull out a couple of canvas sports bags that he hauled out and dropped on the floor of the barn.

"From now on we're hunters," said Frank. The bags gaped open to reveal orange high-visibility vests, checked shirts, and thermal underwear. Everything a good old boy needed to look his best on a little pre-Christmas hunting trip with his buddies. Ethan and Bob started stripping off their Santa clothes to get changed.

Sticks thought about the crow. *Bad luck for someone. Maybe for me.*

"Frank, I got to take a piss," he said, heading back out of the barn door. "Don't run off without me, now, boys."

"Wouldn't dream of it, Sticks,"' answered Frank.

Sticks checked the driver's side window of the BMW on the off-chance, but it confirmed what he thought—Ethan hadn't been dumb enough to leave the keys in the ignition.

He carried on round to the side of the barn, didn't look back. He could hear footsteps in the snow behind him. He got to the back of the barn and faced it, legs apart, hands at his crotch as he would if he really was taking a piss.

Frank rounded the corner, gun in hand.

"Frank, it doesn't have to go like thi—" Sticks began, but then a .50-caliber shell punched a hole in his forehead and blew out the back of his skull. Blood and brain matter the color and consistency of oatmeal splashed over the snow and began to steam immediately.

"Sorry, Sticks, take came up short. Can't afford four cuts. Nothing personal. It's just business."

Frank, Ethan, and Bob finished changing in the barn. Frank briefly thought about torching the BMW and the Santa costumes, but didn't want a fire to bring anyone running while their tracks were still fresh. He settled for getting Ethan to bury the clothes under the snow and for getting Bob to wipe down the car even though they had all been wearing gloves. The guns went in a compartment underneath the deer carcass, which was starting to smell, but which would look pretty good to the cops if they were stopped. Hooked over the rear seats of the Land Cruiser was a gun rack with three high-powered rifles, all with permits. The guns on display would mean that no one would think to look for the ones that were not, or so Frank figured. They rolled out in the new wheels, Ethan driving again, a case of beer on the back seat next to Bob. They drove for an hour and a half, slowly following the road into the mountains. As they ascended, the air grew colder and the road grew more icy and treacherous. Even with four-wheel drive, Ethan had to nurse the Land Cruiser in low gear to stop it from spinning its wheels and slipping back on the incline. They reached the hunting lodge just as the light was beginning to fade and the first flakes of a fresh snow fall were beginning to appear in the air. Ethan, who had been tensed up over the wheel, allowed himself to relax as he turned off the ignition and put on the emergency brake.

"We made it, boys" Frank laughed as he clapped one hand onto his brother's shoulder and turned to offer Country Bob a huge grin.

❄ ❄ ❄

"Kid, I ain't messing around. Open the fucking door or there will be no presents for anyone this year."

Charlie was six years old, which was young enough to still believe in Santa Claus, but old enough to know that the guy in the red suit who sat you on his knee at the department store wasn't the real deal. How could he be? He was there from the end of November and the real Santa was too busy to leave the North Pole before Christmas Eve. But today was Christmas Eve, so it was at least possible that the skinny old guy with the scratchy voice standing in the hospital parking lot and banging on the window of his mother's Prius was the real Santa. He just didn't look like Santa. Even though he had the suit and the beard, he looked like someone Charlie's mother might call a "lousy bum."

"If you're Santa, you should be in Australia already. They get Christmas first. Miss Hitchin told us that in school.'

Sticks cleared his sinuses noisily and spat something blackish-red and about the size of an oyster onto the tarmac. It was dark now, and the sodium lights that lit the front of the parking lot caught the wetness and made it twinkle. Sticks regarded it with something like awe. He had been dead, there was no doubt about that. He remembered Frank following him out of the barn, he remembered the gun being raised, and he remembered the deafening roar as the muzzle flashed and his world turned dark.

When he had opened his eyes again, the light was already fading, but he had no trouble seeing that the rotten old timbers of the barn were painted with his blood. He was slumped on his side, in the same position he had fallen after the bullet ripped through his skull. He rolled onto his back, then shakily got to his feet. He probed gently around his forehead with one finger, feeling for a hole that wasn't there. He took off his Santa hat and found that to be intact as well. Pulling it back on, he noticed the wall of the barn and the blood-stained snow were peppered with bits of brain and skull. He didn't even have a headache.

Good deal, he thought. *Fucked up beyond all reason, but good deal.*

He had headed out across the fields; there was business to attend to and he meant to get to it sooner rather than later. His path was straight and true and he didn't think about the direction he had picked; for Sticks, it was enough that his instincts told him he should go that way. Had he thought about it, he would have realized that he was travelling on the same bearing as the crow that had taken flight from the barn just before he died. Eventually that bearing led him out of the fields and across a road to the Stone County Hospital patients' parking lot. And here Sticks started systematically trying the handles of cars with no luck. Then he came across Charlie. The Santa costume had been enough to get the kid to crack the window so he could talk to him, but it was going to take more to get him to open the door.

"The reason I'm not in Australia is because my sleigh was stolen. By terrorists."

Charlie gave a sharp intake of breath and his eyes grew wide.

"Terrorists?" he repeated in an awed and fearful voice.

"That's right, son. Terrorists. Those filthy bastards hate Christmas and they want to ruin it for everyone. They tried to kill me. Left me for dead in the snow and stole my sleigh, they did. If I don't catch up to them soon, they'll kill my reindeer and then they'll eat them."

"No!" Charlie cried.

Sticks nodded. "No fooling, son. Now open the fucking door. I need these wheels to go catch those heathen bastards and save Christmas."

Charlie looked at the keys stuck in the ignition. Charlie's mom was delivering a change of clothes and some "women's things" to Mrs. Eversham, the lady who lived across the road. Mrs. Eversham had had a fall and broken her hip, and while Charlie's mom didn't mind helping out, she didn't want to get stuck talking to the old girl on Christmas Eve when she still had so much to do. With that in mind, she had left Charlie in the car to give her an excuse to rush back. She had left the keys in the car so Charlie could listen to the radio and she had watched from outside as he had leaned forward between the seats to push the button on the key fob that engaged the central locking. When she was sure it was locked, she held up one gloved hand with the fingers spread to indicate that she would be back in five minutes before hurrying inside. That had been ten minutes ago.

"I should probably wait until my mom gets back," offered Charlie. "I don't think she'll be long."

Sticks shook his head slowly from side to side. "That won't do, son. Every minute we waste, Rudolph is getting closer to being turned into hamburger. Now are you going to man up and help me, or not?"

Charlie considered his options, then sighed to himself in imitation of the way that grown-ups did when they found themselves forced into doing something they didn't really want to do. Mom would just have to understand; this was Christmas they were taking about, after all. Once again he pushed himself between the gap in the front seats and reached out to the key. The central locking disengaged.

Sticks immediately threw open the door and climbed into the driving seat, then turned to face Charlie. "Thanks, son, now get the fuck out. Santa's got some dirty work to do."

"You shouldn't curse so much, Santa. My mom says it's not nice."

"Is that so? Well, you might want to remind your mom of that when you tell her what happened to her car. I have a feeling she's liable to forget. Now get the fuck out."

The boy did as he was told and Sticks tore out of the parking lot as fast as the Toyota would take him, which wasn't nearly fast enough.

❄ ❄ ❄

"Pair of eights and a pair of tens. Hand it over, boys." Bob roared with laughter as he threw his cards down on the rickety little table and began gathering up the cash. The hunting lodge really wasn't much more than a shack with a tin roof, but Frank and Ethan's father had called it the 'Hunting Lodge' when he had brought them here as kids and the name had stuck with them. Frank had no idea who it belonged to—back then it had been a friend of a friend of their pop's, or some such. Frank had come up a week earlier to check it out and had seen straight off that it hadn't been used in a long time, maybe years. It wasn't the Ritz; hell, it wasn't even a cheap motel, but it was perfect for laying low for a day or two. He'd come back with Ethan and stocked it with food, booze, and wood for the stove.

When they arrived, Bob and Frank got to drinking pretty quickly—Ethan never touched a drop—and as there wasn't anything for entertainment but a deck of cards, it wasn't long before they got a poker game going. The snow started coming in thick and heavy after they arrived, and the wind howled, shaking the windows in their frames and threatening to lift the thin, corrugated roof clean off. No one cared, though; the stove was loaded up to bursting and was putting out enough heat to keep them from hypothermia. And of course, the take had been a dream. Frank hadn't counted it yet, but he reckoned over a hundred grand at least, maybe a hundred and fifty.

"You're a cheating bastard, Bob!' screamed Frank, picking up his Desert Eagle off the table and pressing it against Bob's jowls. "And we don't take kindly to cheaters here." Then he erupted into howls of laughter himself.

Bob slapped the pistol away, and this only made Frank laugh harder. Ethan looked at Bob and shrugged, as if to say, "What ya gonna do?"

"Screw this," said Bob, staggering to his feet. "I need a piss."

He walked into the small kitchenette that adjoined the main living area and began unbuckling his belt. He pushed his belly up against the sink and raised up on tip toe. He was reaching in with one hand to pull his pecker out when Frank shouted at him.

"What the hell do you think you're doing? Go outside."

There was no toilet inside the lodge; the outhouse was about twenty yards beyond the back door. It was just a plank over a deep hole in the ground, and their father had told them that was why it was put so far from the cabin, because the smell in the summer would choke you.

"It's blowing a Goddam blizzard outside," Bob protested.

Frank picked up the gun again and pointed it in Bob's direction. "Outside, or I will put a hole in you. No fooling this time."

Bob cursed incoherently, but he tucked himself back in and stomped to the back door. When he opened it, the wind screamed in victory and a flurry of snowflakes blew in before he pulled it shut behind him again.

Frank snorted with laughter and then grabbed the bottle of Johnny Walker he'd been working on, raising it aloft. "Merry Christmas, little brother."

"Not quite," Ethan replied, tapping his watch. "It's only just past eleven. Still Christmas Eve."

Frank reached under the table into one of the sacks and pulled out a huge wad of bills and slapped it down on the scarred wooden surface. "Well, I'm buying an extra hour. Now Merry Christmas, you smart-ass bastard."

"And a very Merry Christmas to you, too, Frank," said Ethan, grinning broadly.

After five minutes, Frank was restless and itching to get another hand going. Ordinarily he wasn't much of a card player, but there wasn't anything else to do up here. There weren't even any books.

"What's keeping that moron? How long does a man

need to take a piss, for Chrissakes?" Frank slurred the last word badly.

"Maybe he's taking a dump," offered Ethan.

"That could take all night. That boy's full of it." Frank laughed at his own witticism and actually slapped his thigh.

Ethan got up from the table. "I'd better go check on him. He's been hitting the sauce pretty hard. He could fall asleep on the john and freeze to death out there."

Frank snorted his derision as he watched his brother head out into the snow. He took another pull from the bottle, then started peeling cards off the deck one by one and building a house. His buzz was turning into a pretty good drunk and his perception of time escaped him. It was only when he ran out of cards that he realized Ethan hadn't come back, either. They were probably playing some sort of joke at his expense, but if not, something was very wrong. Frank picked up his gun; it didn't hurt to be prepared.

He could hear the muffled howl of the wind through the lodge walls, but when he opened the back door, it shrieked in his face and he tried to force it shut again. He had to get his shoulder behind it and push hard to swing it back on its hinges, but then he gave up and let the wind take it, allowing it to slam back against the outside of the cabin. He couldn't see much more than a couple of yards in front of him as snow whipped into his face, making his cheeks burn and forcing him to squint his eyes against the onslaught.

"Ethan!" he yelled at the top of his lungs, but the words were carried away on the wind as soon as they left his mouth. He looked down at his feet and saw two sets of footprints trailing off in the direction of the outhouse. He squeezed the gun in his hand and the weight of it felt reassuring. He thought there might be a torch in the Land Cruiser and briefly considered going back through the cabin to the front where the car was parked to get it. *Pussy!* he thought, and instead dug in and got moving towards the outhouse. It was up a slight incline, and the wind and snow made it hard going. The drifts were piling up against the cabin and were already above his knees. Despite the obstacles nature was throwing at him, it still took less than a minute to reach it.

It was a relic from a bygone era, similar in size and shape to a phone booth, but made from wood and with a swing door with a half-moon cut out of it. Frank hammered on the door with the pistol, the weight of it making the flimsy wooden door shake.

"Bob! Ethan! Get out here and stop messing around." He was screaming to be heard over the wind; it was driving harder now, chilling him to the bone even through his heavy clothes and his thermal underwear. There was no answer, of course. He tried pulling the door open, but even though it shook and bent in the frame, it didn't give, which he couldn't understand. He knew there was a simple hook-and-eye catch on the inside to secure the door, hardly enough to withstand his assault.

"Last chance. I'll give you to the count of three, then I'm kicking the door in."

The snow blasted against his body; his left side was coated, making him look like a giant, half-iced gingerbread man. There was still no answer, and he hadn't expected one. Grabbing the sides of the outhouse to brace himself, he kicked out with his right foot. The lock broke first time. The door swung in hard, then rebounded almost immediately as it hit something solid.

Someone solid.

Frank slowly pulled the door open and held it so the wind couldn't slam it shut again. At first he didn't understand what he was seeing, but then, as his brain slowly began to accept the evidence before him, his stomach rebelled and threw up a gutful of whisky into the snow.

What Frank saw was Bob's massive torso, upside down, feet leaning against the rear of the outhouse, head invisible because it had been shoved through the hole in the plank. The shit chute. The stench was unbearable, but it wasn't coming from the pit beneath the outhouse; it was coming from what decorated the walls. Bob had been gutted. Cut open from crotch to sternum and his bowels were a steaming, stinking pile on the floor. Blood coated the walls and the ceiling, rained down in fat, dark drops. Frank's legs turned to rubber and it took all his strength not to collapse.

He tried to call for his brother, but words failed him. He tried again, unsuccessfully. And finally, "Ethan!" He screamed again into the wind and was answered by the piercing squeal of the Land Cruiser's alarm.

In the heat of the moment, he assumed it was Bob's murderer trying to make a getaway and he ran back to the cabin, then circled around it to the front. He came at the vehicle from the rear and saw the turn signals flashing in time with the alarm. All four doors were wide open, and even with the drifting snow he could tell from the way the vehicle canted to one side that the tires had been slashed.

He raised the gun and held it out in front of him at eye level in a two-handed grip. He began to sidestep his way carefully around the side of the car, seeing the outline of some-thing on the hood through the rear window.

It was Ethan.

"Oh Jesus, no!" It was barely a whisper.

His little brother had been stripped to the waist and laid out on the hood, arms stretched out to his sides as if he'd been crucified. His head was tilted up at a slight angle where it lay against the slope of the windshield. His legs were together and ran down the length of the hood, feet dangling off the edge. His throat had been slashed and it gaped open, revealing the ruined gristle of his windpipe in the bloody canyon. Both cheeks had been laid open from the corners of his mouth right up to his ears, face frozen forever in an insane grin of death. A string of fairy lights wound around his head and he wore it like a crown of thorns. They flashed, multicolored, the flex trailing around through the open door and jammed into the cigarette lighter. "Merry Christmas" was carved into the flesh of Ethan's pigeon chest.

This time his legs did give out, and he collapsed into a wailing, shaking heap of snot in the snow. He heard a bottle smash inside the cabin and managed to haul himself to his feet and stagger towards the door, determined to have his revenge. As he shoved the door open and barged inside, something big and heavy came down on the back of his head. He sprawled forward awkwardly, propelled by his own momentum. He was unconscious before he hit the floor.

When he woke up again, he couldn't move. He was in a sitting position, arms and legs lashed to one of the crappy little wooden chairs with duct tape. There was another strip of tape across his mouth. He tried to scream anyway, and even though it was muffled, it was loud enough to attract the attention of his captor. The back door opened and in walked Sticks.

Frank's eyes grew wide and a damp patch bloomed on the front of his pants.

Sticks walked over to his former prison mate and ripped the tape from his mouth, taking some skin with it. Frank immediately started screaming.

"You're dead! You're dead, motherfucker! I blew your brains out."

He strained and writhed in the chair, almost toppling it over. His face was purple and cords stood out on his neck with the effort.

Sticks was perfectly calm. "Yeah, funny thing about that Frank—and I just figured this out myself a couple of hours ago, so don't feel bad for not knowing—but apparently you can't kill Santa Claus on Christmas Eve." His voice was a testament to years of hard living.

Frank shook even more violently in the chair and began howling incoherently with rage.

"I know," Sticks continued. "Ain't that just one almighty kick in the ass. I mean, I should be dead. You *did* blow my brains out, but I woke up. Look, not even a goddam hole!" Stick pulled the red floppy hat off his head and pointed towards his forehead. He then turned around to demonstrate that the back of his skull was also intact.

Frank gave a final heave and succeeded in toppling himself and the chair to the floor. Sticks continued regardless.

"See, I figured it out when I was talking to this kid. I think it's because they all believe in Santa, all the little ones at least. Even if they pretend they know there isn't a Santa Claus, they secretly still believe because they want it to be true. And not just for the presents, either. It's because they want there to be something magic."

"Arrrrrgggggghhhhhhh! You're... not... Santa... fucking... Claus!" Frank was on his side, still stuck in the chair and trying to propel himself along with his feet. Splinters dug into his cheek as he slid across the unsanded floor boards.

Sticks sighed, then bent down and dragged the chair and Frank back into an upright position. "Obviously I'm not *the* Santa Claus, but I'm *a* Santa Claus. At least today I am. And there's a lot of kids out there with a lot of Christmas spirit. More than enough to go round, it would seem. Fuck me,

Frank! You and your boys made a hell of a mistake when you changed your clothes." Sticks gave a throaty chuckle. His eyes, which had been old and tired before, were now a vibrant blue, and they twinkled with mischief.

Frank felt his gorge rise, but he had voided it all outside and his stomach didn't have anything left to give.

Sticks grabbed another chair and set it down directly in front of Frank. Then he sat down cross-legged in front of his betrayer and reached inside his jacket to remove his straight razor. Without warning, his wrist flicked; there was a flash of steel and he lunged forward, arm outstretched, then just as suddenly he resumed his position in the seat as if he had never moved. For a fraction of a second, Frank didn't realize what had happened, just that a shadow had suddenly appeared on the left of his field of vision. Then he felt the wet thickness oozing down his cheek and he screamed.

"Don't worry, I won't take your other eye before the end. I'd hate for you not to be able to see all the fun things I have in store for you." He paused a moment, watching the blood run down the other man's face. "Did I ever tell you how I came by the name Sticks, Frank?"

Frank only moaned.

"It's not my real name, in case you haven't guessed. My parent's christened me Nicholas. Can you dig it? Little Nicky." As he spoke, he absent-mindedly opened the blade of his razor again and carefully wiped off the gore on the leg of his Santa pants.

"I was a serious little boy, Frank. Took everything seriously. Schoolwork. Chores. Didn't matter. To me, it was all business, and even though I was too young to know what business really was, I knew it needed to be taken care of. If there was a job to be done, I'd keep at it and keep at it and I wouldn't stop until it was done. And my pop, he would watch me and he would say, 'Little Nicky sticks at things. Oh yes, our Nick sticks.' And my little brother eventually picked up on it, and then his friends, and soon they were all calling me Nick Sticks, and eventually that became plain old Sticks."

Frank moaned again and started to cry.

"And now the business I need to take care of is putting a hurt on you, Frank, and believe me when I tell you that that serious little boy grew up to be a very serious man. When the pain finally becomes unbearable and you heart gives out under the strain, I will crawl down into Hell after you and keep right on going because Nick still sticks."

Then he opened the blade of his razor and he didn't close it again for a long time.

❄ ❄ ❄

Dear Charlie,

Thank you for helping me to save Christmas. I eventually managed to catch up those terrorist bastards and I made them sorry they was ever born and Rudorf and the other raindeer did not get ate.

I have brung back your moms car. If you look out your window you will see it parked across the street. But frankly you can tell her from me it's a reel peace of shit and it's a wonder I was ever able to catch up to them. Sorry it is late but I wanted to get you a special present for helping me out but I forgot to ask you what you like so I hope money is okay. There is fifty grand under the spare tyre. By yourself something nice. If you are feeling generous by your mom a decent car. That thing really is a peace of shit.

Your Pal
   Santa

With Their Eyes All Aglow
Jeff C. Carter

Thick snow drifted silently in the dark front yard, turning the mailbox and bushes into faceless snowmen. Cindy gazed out past her own corn-yellow hair in the reflection of the bay window to watch the lights twinkle on the roof of the neighbor's house. She was eager to decorate her own home, but her mother said they had to wait until daddy got back from his trip.

Christmas music wafted through the house, the church kind that her mother liked. Cindy turned to look at the carved African mask on the wall. It had long, spiraling horns and a pointy snout. She pretended it was a reindeer. She pretended the strange bugs pinned inside the picture frames were toys. There were only a few chocolate-filled windows left on the Advent Calendar, but Christmas still seemed like a million years away. Just like daddy.

Cindy looked up and found her mother watching her.

129

"Hi, sweetie. Want some cocoa?"

Cindy shook her head. "When is Daddy home?"

Her mother frowned and sat by the fire place.

"We talked about this, remember? He may not make it for Christmas this year."

Cindy tugged at her pink princess pajamas and pouted. Her mother pulled out a sketch pad and the crayon bin.

"I have an idea. Why don't you write a letter to Santa?"

"Can I ask Santa to bring Daddy home faster?"

Her mother rubbed her on the back. "You can ask for anything you want. When you're done, we'll send it off to the North Pole. Sound good?"

Cindy nodded and dug into the colorful bin of mismatched crayons.

❄ ❄ ❄

Thick fog drifted silently down the Himalayas, turning the jungle valley of Northern Myanmar into a winter wonderland. Ray thought about Cindy and Beth back home. As he swung his machete through the underbrush, he started to hum, *I'll Be Home for Christmas.*

Ray's native guide, Muang, stopped and pointed at his ear. "What song?"

Ray laughed. "Christmas song."

A big smile crept across Muang's face, revealing red-stained teeth. He spat a wad of betel nut, lime, and tobacco from his cheek and gestured for Ray to sing. Muang was a devout Christian with an impressive knowledge of hymns and carols, but he was always on the hunt for more. When Ray came to Myanmar, he never thought he'd spend it singing about Frosty and the Grinch.

He was about to break into his best impersonation of

Bing Crosby when the silhouette of a bat broke through the fog. Thick silk threads stretched the dead bat taut in a macabre imitation of flight.

Ray used the tip of his machete to cut it free. The dried-leather corpse hit the wet, leafy forest floor with a thud. Alive, it must have been enormous. Muang picked over the body for meat, but it was deflated, like beef jerky. Ray wasn't interested in the bat. He was looking for whatever had spun those webs.

Ray's love of insects had propelled him to his master's degree in entomology. His obsession with spiders had brought him to Myanmar. The Northern Forest Complex was one of the greatest hotspots of bio-diversity in the world, and Ray had convinced his PhD advisors that it was also the home of a mysterious specimen, glimpsed only once, a hundred years before.

In 1925, famed fossil-hunter Barnum Brown got lost in this same jungle. He described an encounter with a glowing creature the size of his thumb, a spider unlike anything known to science. He failed to capture his 'luminous spider', however, and his discovery became a mere footnote in the annals of entomology.

Ray had spent the bulk of his expedition heading out into the jungle every night, stumbling after fireflies and glowing mushrooms. It wasn't until his visa was about to expire that he discovered the perfect habitat for a predator that hunted with light; the cloud forests, eerie twilight jungles between the frigid mountains and the sweltering low lands.

A scream split through the fog, shrill and hysterical. Ray's heart jumped into his throat, and for some reason he thought of Cindy. Muang peered into the forest canopy.

"Woi." The Jingpho word for 'monkey'.

As they moved closer, they saw more bats strung up in

the trees, tangled together with dead rats, snakes, and tropical birds. The branches thrashed in time with the panicked screams, jostling the bloodless corpses into restless life.

The screaming stopped and a sinister silence closed in. Ray held out his machete, afraid a leopard or tiger would leap out of the trees.

Muang pointed to a pale shape in the branches of the teak tree overhead. Ray thought the heavy fog had poured into a hole left by the fleeing primate, but he soon realized that the cloudy tuft and human outline told a different story. The body of the monkey quivered inside a snowdrift of spider silk. A constellation of lights twinkled in the dripping gloom and hovered around the corpse.

Ray pulled the binoculars off his chest. The terror-stricken face of the monkey filled his eyes. Its gaping mouth was lit from inside by crawling lights. Ray pushed down a surge of horror and focused on the shining orbs. Beautiful eight-fold symmetry projected from luminous, oval bodies. He'd found them. Barnum's luminous spiders were real!

Muang cut a length of vine free and looped it around the bark of the teak tree. He leaned back, put his feet against the trunk, and scurried half way up the tree before Ray could react.

"Stop!"

Muang looked down, confused. "These are them you wanted?"

Ray hopped from foot to foot and flailed his arms. "Come down! Now!"

When Muang let go of the vine and landed softly, Ray gestured at the dead monkey. "Bad poison!"

Muang held his fingers a few inches apart and spat a red stream of betel nut juice from a corner of his mouth. "Little poison."

Ray shook his head and pointed at the sprawling web that spanned the surrounding trees. Glowing spiders continued to emerge from the leaves, setting the tree alight like a sunset over water. "Many. Clan. Hunt together."

Muang nodded and chewed on his wad of betel nut.

Ray observed the spiders converging on the cocooned monkey. He had seen something like it in Brazil—social spiders. They were not as organized or specialized as bees or ants, but they were capable of working together to construct vast communal webs. The larger webs caught bigger prey, thus everyone ate well. But capturing a monkey? Ray didn't know of any spider venom potent enough to take down something so strong and agile in such a short time. It would require a dozen bites, perhaps a hundred, flooding the victim's body and liquefying its veins. Killer bees on eight legs. He pulled his thin coat around himself and shivered.

He backed away from the killing tree and looked for other pinpricks of light. Now that he knew what to look for, he saw the sparkling trail through the jungle canopy. He wondered if they were all part of one colony, or if each tree was a world unto itself. There would be time to fill his field notebook with questions and observations later. The first order of business was to succeed where Barnum failed and capture one of the spiders.

He checked his shoulder bag and made sure his forceps and killing jars were ready. He had everything he needed but a ladder. Should he risk his only insect net in the high branches and sticky webs? Muang could reach the tree tops easily, but Ray didn't want him to get a spider bite. He looked around for a log to climb. Seeing nothing, he decided to push deeper into the jungle.

Ray whacked a broad fern with his machete and it fell, revealing a long, flat field. He and Muang both stared in disbelief at what they saw—a small forest of Christmas trees.

Muang pushed past Ray and then spun around. "Oh Christmas Tree!"

Muang laughed and sang as he skipped into a clearing the size of a football field, packed with conical, furry, green trees in neat, ordered rows. Mangled stumps and burned timber lined the edges of the field—the tell-tale signs of slash and burn. Deforestation was a major problem in Myanmar, and wholesale logging was illegal. So why was there a Christmas tree farm in the middle of the jungle? It was surreal.

Muang rushed to one of the alien trees and stroked its thin bristled branches. There were conifers in the northern jungles, but nothing like this. Ray looked up at the perpetual cloak of rain and fog that swirled around the snow-capped Himalayans and thought of Washington State or the Swiss Alps. He understood how the trees could be grown in this climate, but who would bother?

He recognized the distinctive outline and needles. They were Nordmann Firs. They had been ultra-trendy a few years back. Beth had begged for one every year, but Ray refused to spend that kind of money on something they would toss out by New Year's Day. That variety had been in high demand, even before the beetle infestation.

The Asian Bark Beetle had completely devastated the Nordmann fir population of the United States and Europe. As an undergrad, Ray had helped his professor deliver a keynote speech about the beetles and other invasive species at a Forest Ecology and Management conference.

Now it made sense. The beetles had driven supply so low that it was economically feasible to export them. Ray laughed. Asian Bark Beetles were native to this region, so there were plenty of natural predators to keep them in check. It was the perfect place to farm Nordmann firs.

A chill wind blew through the rows of conical trees. The fresh scent stirred up memories of stuffed stockings and long family dinners. He thought of Cindy's joy on Christmas morning as she sprawled in piles of shredded wrapping paper. He smiled. He had what he had come for, and he could rejoin his family soon.

He ran his hand across the branch and found a clump of dark nodules. He stuck his head into the tree and looked closely. Thousands of spider egg sacs studded the spine of the tree. He had never seen an egg sac like them. They were mottled grey, with thin spikes that spread in a swath around the branch.

He pulled out his forceps and gently plucked at one of the sacs. The membrane tore open and a cascade of tiny spiderlings poured out. They glimmered weakly in the shade of the tree.

Ray lurched back and ran to another tree. Spiky egg sacs festooned its spine. He checked another at random, and then one a dozen feet beyond that. Without exception, every tree contained luminous spiders.

Ray knew the average live Christmas tree carried thousands of mites, lice, and spiders into the home. People rarely noticed, because the stowaways were small and harmless. The luminous spiders were organized, aggressive, and deadly, and the Nordmann firs were going to bring them into people's homes. Ray had to stop them before they were exported.

"We have to go!"

Muang sagged against the tree, a thick, red stream of betel nut juice drooling down his chin. Ray jogged over and tapped him on the shoulder.

"Muang? We have to go. Important."

Ray inched around and looked into the man's eyes. They bulged wide and juddered in their sockets. The smell of blood mixed with the pine-fresh aroma of the tree. The red liquid on his lips and chin was not betel nut juice.

Ray pulled Muang out and eased him to the ground. Wisps of silk clung to Muang's arm, and the flesh was already dark and swollen from dozens of oozing bites. A juvenile spider crawled out of Muang's trembling fist. Ray seized it with the forceps, squeezing until a comet of incandescent ichor shot into the air.

"Muang! Can you hear me?"

A bloody bubble of saliva boiled up on Muang's scarlet-stained lips. His body jumped and shuddered as his muscles slammed tight like bear traps. The necrotizing venom darkened his skin, a shadow creeping towards his heart.

Ray lifted Muang under the shoulders and groaned. He looked around for the path back to town. It was a nine-hour hike with Muang's expert guidance, and there was no doctor. He would have to take an ox-drawn cart to the capitol.

Ray looked around the Christmas tree farm. If there were loggers, there must be a road. It was a safer bet than dragging Muang through the jungle at night.

Leaving Muang near the tree, he sprinted along the perimeter until he came to the far corner lined with freshly planted saplings. A rusted blue-and-white pick-up truck painted with the logging company logo sat next to a wall of felled trees. Beyond the truck, a rough road of mud wound off into the dim, green horizon.

Ray ran towards the truck, shouting and waving his arms. No one answered. He yanked open the door and leaned on the horn. The sound blared out across the alien, symmetrical forest like the wail of a wounded animal. The noise hit the fog and vanished, ensnared in its dense, white mass.

He searched the truck for keys and found nothing but a

slim screwdriver tucked between the seats. He climbed behind the wheel and stabbed the tool into the ignition and twisted. The truck sputtered and grunted awake. Ray swerved and sped across the field.

Muang was mumbling something through his clenched jaws. Ray couldn't make out the words, but he recognized the rhythms of prayers. He wiped a layer of hot sweat off of Muang's forehead.

"I'm taking you to a hospital. Hang on."

Muang grabbed Ray with his good arm and squeezed. His bleary eyes opened and searched Ray's face. Ray dredged his mind for a proper prayer, but was unable to come up with anything except for the lyrics to *I'll Be Home for Christmas*. He cleared his throat and began to sing. The corner of Muang's paralyzed mouth twitched upward for a fleeting second, and then his body fell still.

Ray sat with the body until the sun dissolved into the mist. The spiders twinkled in the trees like emerging stars. Cursing, Ray stomped around to the back of the truck. He grabbed a plastic jug of petrol.

He splashed the fuel onto the Christmas tree where he'd found Muang. The bitter tang filled the air and assaulted his nostrils. Ray stalked through the grove, spraying trees at random. He circled the entire field, making sure that every drop of petrol was spent.

Ray rooted through his backpack until he found his lighter. A thin drizzle fell across the field as the mist settled to the earth. Ray dropped to his knees and scooped dry, brown needles into a pile. He shielded the lighter from the wet wind and sparked it to life.

The needles began to exhale puffs of aromatic smoke. The wind kicked up and threatened to extinguish the pile. A sudden whoosh of flame shot up from the tree and Ray fell backwards. He rubbed his eyes to clear them of the neon-green blur.

Ray watched with satisfaction as the heat drove a cluster of spiderlings to burst from their fragile egg sac. They scurried outward along the branches, but they could not escape their doom. They melted and boiled away without a trace.

The fire prowled through the grove, giving each tree a delicate lick. It grew bolder with each taste of petrol, finally sinking its teeth into the wood, gutting trees and consuming their insides with frenzied abandon.

Ray collapsed into the truck and watched the green boughs curl and scatter their glowing needles. He wept, and his sobs joined the angry hiss and pop of boiling sap.

He put the truck in gear and a hot ache throbbed in his right hand. He flicked on the dome light. A small bite puckered his flesh on the edge of his hand. Ray swallowed a surge of bile and drove onward.

❊ ❊ ❊

The Kachin State Police Station was a small concrete box with a sheet metal roof. A warped, wooden railing separated Ray and the tiny lobby from two desks and two policemen. A relentless rain hammered against the roof, thickening the cramped room with oppressive noise and humidity.

Painful cramps marched up Ray's right arm as he paced the lobby. A sullen officer stared at him and sucked on a cigarette. An AK-47 hung from one drooping shoulder.

The Police Lieutenant stood at his desk and spoke into his phone in rapid Myanmar. Ray strained his ears, grasping for what few words he understood. He heard *naing-ngan gya-tha*, the word for 'foreigner'. That was all.

The Lieutenant set down the phone with a sharp click

and barked an order to the slouching officer. Together, they stepped out from behind the chipped, wooden counter. Ray perked up.

"Were any of the trees exported?"

The Lieutenant stepped directly up to Ray. The other officer hemmed him in from behind.

Ray looked down at the stone-faced Lieutenant, expectant.

"You are under arrest."

Ray scrunched up his bleary eyes in confusion. "What?"

The young officer grabbed Ray's arm. Ray gasped when his swollen arm was twisted and pinned behind his back.

The Lieutenant grunted, "Murder and theft."

Ray struggled with the officer while trying to face the Lieutenant at the same time. "What? What are you talking about?"

The slouching officer shoved Ray off balance towards the back of the station. Ray tripped and fell into the corner. The officer slammed Ray's swollen wrist against a thick metal pipe in the wall. Ray cried out as his bones clanged off the metal.

"Let me go! I didn't do anything!"

The officer ratcheted one end of a hand cuff around Ray's swollen wrist and snapped the other onto the pipe. The young man looked down at Ray and took a last, satisfied drag of his smoldering cigarette. He dropped it onto the floor and crushed it out.

The Lieutenant took a cursory glance, nodded, and then stepped outside. The slouching officer joined him beneath the metal overhang. They lit new cigarettes and stared out into the rain.

Ray looked over to the small, wooden desk. It was only a few feet away. He leaned away from the wall and the hand cuff bit into the purple flesh of his wrist. His outstretched hand tickled the edge of the desk drawer. If he could get his hands on a key, or even something to pry off the cuffs, he might have a chance.

He grabbed the bottom of the desk and dragged the entire desk closer. The wooden legs creaked and scraped against the dirty cement floor, but the relentless rain masked the noise.

Twin arcs of fluorescent rain drops slashed through the night air. Ray shook his head and they resolved into a pair of headlights. A pick-up truck swung around the station. Ray spotted the logging company logo on its door. Of course. The Lieutenant was in the logging company's pocket.

Ray eased the desk to the floor and his head began to spin. The activity must have pumped more venom through his bloodstream. His legs began to cramp and seize up. There would be no daring jail break or escape into the jungle. His only hope was the phone. If he reached Beth, she could contact the embassy; maybe they could stop the export of the trees. Maybe he could just hear Cindy's voice one last time.

He fumbled for the receiver. Cradling the handset against his neck, he used his free hand to peck out the country code for the United States, followed by his home number.

There was a long pause filled with static. In Ray's fevered imagination, the rain was leaking into the phone line. A dial tone warbled like a jungle bird. He clamped the receiver to his sweaty ear to trap the sound. Beth's voice tripped down the line, faint and stuttering. There were more clicks than words. Ray pictured a mass of glowing spiders feasting on the other end of the line.

✳ ✳ ✳

Cindy heard the phone ring and rubbed a fist into her sleepy eye. She gazed up at the naked Christmas tree. The heat from the fireplace had made everything cozy and warm, and the excited sound of her mother's voice rang through the house like music.

"We miss you! Are you almost done?"

Cindy tiptoed to the edge of the living room and leaned against the wall. She liked to listen to her mother talk to Daddy on the phone.

"What? You're breaking up. The tree? Yeah, I finally got a Nordmann fir, how did you know?"

Her mother's voice suddenly dropped. "Hello? Hello?"

A twinkle of light pulled Cindy back to the tree. She rubbed her eyes again. Small lights continued to emerge and wink from the thick, green branches. It was a Christmas miracle!

The twinkling lights swarmed over the tree and beckoned her closer. She smiled and reached out with her soft, pink fingers.

S*HOP T*ILL Y*OU D*ROP
Michael McCarty & Mark McLaughlin

It was a dark, snowy Christmas Eve in Tuttlesburg, and Neil Gluckman was mad at his job, his wife, and himself. Mostly himself. He was a busy man, and in the wild hurly-burly of managing Gluckman Gifts & Goodies during the holiday season, he'd completely forgotten about buying a present for his own daughter.

He couldn't give her any of the toys or novelties from his own shop, for he knew exactly how his wife Cynthia would respond to that: "Oh, look what Mister Gotbucks got his daughter for Christmas. A piece of crap from the warehouse. Something he bought wholesale for—what, two bucks, maybe three? They say you can't buy love, but Christ, that's not even a down payment!"

There was once a time when he'd been enthralled by Cynthia's crisp wit and clever turns of phrase. That time had passed long years ago.

Neil steered his Toyota Prius Hybrid down Pepper Street, looking for a lit-up store window. He glanced at the time, spelled out in green, glowing digits on his dashboard clock. 7:17. The streets rolled up early in this small Wisconsin town, but surely some store owner was greedy enough to stay open on Christmas Eve and make a few extra bucks.

Then he saw it: at the end of the block, a two-story brick building with a front window blazing with welcome light. He drove closer.

A weatherworn wooden sign above the door read, in quaintly curlicued forest-green letters, PROFESSOR LaGUNGO'S EXOTIC ARTIFACTS & ASSORTED MYSTIC COLLECTIBLES.

Even though he'd lived in Tuttlesburg his whole life, he couldn't remember ever seeing this shop before. It had to be very new, even though the sign looked very old.

He pulled the Prius into the empty parking lot. He wondered why the owner's car wasn't in the lot. Maybe this Professor LaGungo guy had forgotten to turn the lights off because he was in a hurry to get home. Or, maybe he didn't have a car and he lived up on the second floor.

As Neil stepped out of the car, a bitterly cold wind blew snow in his face. He felt like he had just been hit between the eyes with a snowball.

He opened the front door and a bell chimed *ting-a-ling!* From wall to wall, shelves and cabinets were packed with a bewildering array of trinkets and artifacts, pictures and puzzles, and gizmos and whatchamacallits—most of which were extremely dusty. He sneezed twice.

"Bless you and bless you again," said the proprietor, a thin, elderly man in a light-gray suit that matched his wispy hair and thick mustache. He wore dust-flecked glasses with lenses as thick as the bottoms of soda bottles. He waved a gaunt, liver-spotted hand. "Welcome to Hell!" he cried. "A Hell of a mess, that is. The place really needs dusting."

"I've noticed," Neil said.

"I am Professor LaGungo—but please, just call me Teddy."

"I'm Neil Gluckman. I was hoping to do a little last-minute Christmas shopping. I've been so busy lately, I've barely had time to eat. I sure was glad to see your lights on!"

"And I'm glad to see you, Mister Busy Businessman!" Teddy said. He gestured toward a stuffed green iguana on the counter. "I was so lonely, I found myself talking to Bertram here. You came at the perfect time. I'm having a special holiday sale—everything is half off. Look around! There's so much to see! Shop till you drop!"

"Half off? Wow! Usually stores jack up the prices before the big day," Neil said. "You're a great guy, Teddy. I need to get something for my daughter, Missy. Have anything a ten-year-old girl would like?"

Teddy cocked his head to one side. "Nothing for the wife...?"

"Cynthia and I don't exchange gifts," Neil said.

"Really? What a pity." Teddy walked slowly from behind the counter. "Are you absolutely sure you wouldn't like to treat the wife to something special? For the couple that has everything, over to your left you will see a his-and-hers bed of nails. Only used once."

Neil grimaced at the horrid heart-shaped bed. "Are the nails rusty, or is that blood on them?"

"Both."

Neil sneezed a third time.

"Once again, bless you."

"So Professor, just what are you a professor *of*? Dust collecting?"

"Dead languages," Teddy said. "I used to teach at a private college in Asia for about thirty-five years. Of course these days, students have enough trouble with live languages, let alone dead ones."

"I suppose so."

"I bought this shop with my savings. Something to keep me busy in my retirement. The shop was originally located in Tibet, but besides yetis and spiritual gurus and the occasional mountain hikers, there weren't a lot of costumers. So I came to Wisconsin—the cheese here is so much better. That Tibetan yak cheese... Blech! Have you ever tried it?"

"Can't say that I have."

"Over there," Teddy said, pointing toward the rear of the shop, which was not as well lit as the front, "you will see a brass maiden."

Neil squinted into the far shadows. "What's a brass maiden?"

"Same as an iron maiden, except made of brass. This one has the prettiest opal eyes."

"Remember, I'm looking for something a ten-year-old girl would enjoy."

Teddy pouted. "The *right* ten-year-old girl might enjoy a brass maiden... But not to worry! I have plenty of other gift options. Like this!" From a nearby shelf he picked up a large, dusty bone covered with cobwebs. "This petrified bone was once part of the ugliest, most vicious and evil dinosaur of all—the dreaded Two-Headed Hellosaurus."

"Hellosaurus!" Neil cried. "Never heard of it."

"The Hellosaurs didn't have feet—just a muscular, slime-exuding belly, like a giant snail, useful for sliding around and biting other dinosaurs. It was low to the ground, so it could bite the privates off the taller dinosaurs. In fact, that may be why the dinosaurs went extinct." The professor set the bone back on its shelf. "Some scientists think the Two-Headed Hellosaurus came from outer space, but I believe that demons have been evolving, too, just like us regular-type critters, and that the Two-Headed Hellosaurs was, in fact, a dinosaur demon. I also believe that pterodactyls were dinosaur angels. In their honor, I always put a little toy pterodactyl on top of my Christmas tree."

"Missy does love dinosaurs," Neil said, "but a dirty old bone isn't much of a gift." He looked around. "I don't see your Christmas tree…"

"It's upstairs, along with some especially rare collectibles. I also live up there."

"Ah! I wondered why I didn't see a car outside."

Teddy waved a hand dismissively. "Cars! I manage to get around without using those awful, smoky things. How do you think I moved this building from Tibet all the way to Wisconsin?"

Neil looked around, confused. "An entire brick building? Well, I don't know… You'll have to tell me some other time. Right now, I need to find something for Missy. They're expecting me at home."

"Not to worry! I have a nice little dolly right over here." The professor walked over to a side-table and picked up a busty doll without a head. "This is the Jayne Mansfield doll. I also have a Marie Antoinette doll in the back that—"

"No, no, no!" Neil said. "Please, Missy is your typical cute, sweet, ten-year-old girl. Do you have anything in stock that won't give her nightmares?"

The professor snapped his fingers. "Follow me!" he said as he walked to the front of the store. He stood grinning by a wooden rocking horse. "Isn't this the loveliest thing you ever saw?"

"It certainly is," Neil said, kneeling by the toy, admiring its craftsmanship.

"It's made out of cedar... it has that lovely forest smell to it. Hand carved and hand painted! Just look at the right eye! That little painted twinkle is so whimsical, so mischievous, as though the horse is saying, 'I've got a secret!' As a matter of fact, this particular rocking horse *does* have a secret..."

"I'll take it! It's perfect." Neil stood up and pulled his wallet from his back pocket. "How much?"

"You don't want to know the secret?" Professor LaGungo asked, his eyes round with surprise.

"The only secret I want to know is the price."

"Like I said, it is made by hand, not manufactured. It comes from a faraway land, too. Normally it goes for three-hundred dollars, but since I'm having a half-off sale, it goes for one hundred and fifty. And since you've been so extremely patient with all my stories—I do tend to ramble on!—I will let you have it for only one-hundred dollars."

"You've got a deal, Teddy!" Neil opened the wallet, took out two crisp fifty-dollar bills and handed them to the professor.

A few minutes later they were in the parking lot, loading the rocking horse into the backseat of the Prius. It was a tight fit, but they managed it.

"Merry Christmas, Teddy," Neil said. "And thank you." He then drove off into the night.

The professor shuffled back into the shop. He brushed snow off his sleeves as he walked up to the stuffed green iguana. "You know, Bertram, I really wish he'd allowed me to tell him the secret of the rocking horse. Would *you* like to hear the secret?"

Yes, Professor! Of course I would, Bertram did not say.

"The secret, my dear Bertram, is this: that delightful rocking horse came from Zombie Island. It was specially designed by grown-up zombies to help zombie brats hunt down their prey. Little zombie arms have hugged its smooth, graceful neck. Wee zombie butts have ridden on its finely crafted saddle. Good thing it's made of cedar, or else it would have probably reeked from all that constant exposure to zombies, zombies, zombies!" Teddy smiled. "Ah, well! He'll learn the secret soon enough."

It was 8:00 pm when the next customer entered Professor LaGungo's shop. *Ting-a-ling!*

Helga Pennywhistle, age sixty-two. Mother of four, grandmother of eight. She was just a little over five feet tall, if you counted the thick salt-and pepper bun of hair on top of her head. Like Teddy, she wore glasses with bottle-thick lenses.

"Welcome to my humble shop," the proprietor said, closing the large, dusty volume he was reading—*Countess Bathory's Big Book of Beauty Secrets.* "I'm Professor LaGungo, but you can call me Teddy. How can I help you? I'm having a half-off sale tonight. Please, look around! Shop till you drop!"

"A fifty-percent discount? You don't say!" the petite grandmother said. "I'm looking to buy a present for my grandson, Andy. I thought I'd done all my Christmas shopping and then at the last minute I realized I'd forgotten all about Andy. Probably because I've been so busy! Work, work, work! I run a day-care center and my little angels run me ragged!"

"I understand," the professor said. "My parents were always very busy, just like you. Sadly, they never remembered to buy me any gifts. No birthday gifts, nothing for Christmas... But I digress. Exactly how old is Andy?"

"Eight—and as cute as a button."

"You know, little boys love to pretend they're spacemen!" He picked up a shiny metal and plastic gizmo. "This item is a real doozy. Einstein's death-ray gun. Albert, you see, used to go out with a cocktail waitress named Lisa LaGungo. My aunt."

"You don't say!" Helga exclaimed.

"Lisa LaGungo was a very beautiful woman," Teddy continued, "but she was married with three kids, so she could never tell the world about her love affair with Albert Einstein. Eventually, she broke it off—the relationship, that is. Albert became so enraged, he started work on a death-ray gun to destroy humanity."

"Goodness!" Helga said.

"But then Albert met and started... let's saying 'pitching woo,' that's a good euphemism... with Marilyn Monroe. So he never finished his vile, terrible weapon of utter destruction. He gave this harmless prototype to my aunt as a memento. His way of saying, 'Hey, no hard feelings.' In a way, Marilyn Monroe saved the world. What a gal."

"That certainly is interesting," Helga said, "but I'm looking for something less violent and more educational."

"Educational! I have just the thing..." The professor reached under his counter and brought out a doll. It looked like a stone head from Easter Island, except it had long, flexible limbs and was clutching a spear, which also had a stone head. Unlike the doll's blunt head, this one came to a sharp point.

"Mercy! What in the world is that?" Helga asked.

"A doll from the island of Pokaluhu in the South Pacific. This will teach your grandson about a little-known foreign culture. Very exotic—and educational!"

"True! You've even taught me something. Before this evening, I'd never even heard of the island of Pokaluhu. How much is it?"

"Normally it goes for one-hundred dollars. But tonight, everything is half off. Only fifty dollars... and since you have such a nice smile, let's make it forty."

They chatted for a few more minutes and then Helga wished Teddy a very merry Christmas and sailed out the door.

"Oh, don't look at me that way, Bertram!" said the professor to his stuffed green iguana. "Yes, I should have told her about the doll's fully functional jaws. Dollies can't eat, of course, but they do love to chew! I'm sure she will soon become aware of that particular feature—for which there was no additional charge, I might add!"

How generous, Bertram did not say.

❄ ❄ ❄

Ting-a-ling!

The next customer who came in, fifteen minutes after Helga Pennywhistle's departure, was blanketed in snow. Roger Sinclair resembled a walking snowman until he brushed himself off, revealing himself to be a police officer.

"Good evening!" Professor LaGungo said. "'Twas was the night before Christmas and all through the shop, not a public servant was stirring, not even a cop—except you! No offense."

The policeman smiled.

"I've always wondered why they said, 'the night before Christmas.'" Teddy continued. "They should have said, 'Christmas Eve.' It's a lot shorter and rolls off the tongue more easily. I'm Professor LaGungo, but you can call me Teddy."

"Thanks, Teddy—I'm Roger. I had to work twelve hours today and still needed to do some last-minute shopping. I'm finally off my shift and all the other stores are closed. I'm surprised you're still open."

"There are plenty of surprises in here," the professor said. "Plus, everything is half off. My big Christmas Eve sale! Look around! There's so much to see, my busy, busy friend! Shop till you drop!"

"Great!" the police officer said. "All I need is a gift for my seven-year-old daughter, Emily. Let's see what you've got."

"Perhaps you should get something for yourself, too. I have some rare items that you might enjoy displaying in your home. Real conversation starters for cocktail parties!" The professor walked to a cherrywood table and pointed to a glass box with a curiously stained stone inside. "Here we have a moon rock with some alien blood on it. I keep this item sealed up tight. Old things can have such frightening germs on them—especially this thing." He pointed to another glass box, which held another oddly stained item. "Do you remember Typhoid Mary from the pages of history?"

"I've heard of her, yes," the officer said.

"Nice lady," the professor continued. "Loved to cook. Worked for different families. Left a trail of sickness and death. This is a coloring book from her childhood. I don't think all those colors came from crayons. Especially the earth tones. Perhaps if she were alive today, she'd be one of those avant-garde artists who make statues and paintings out of poop and whatnot. I hear museums pay big money for that sort of thing."

"Sounds like you have some potentially dangerous items in this shop. We'll have to talk about that some other time. Right now, let's concentrate on a gift for Emily. Something fun. Something safe. Something…" The police officer paused. "…traditional."

The professor picked up a pink, fluffy toy bunny. "Something like this?" he asked.

"Yes, that's more like it! How much?"

"Normally it goes for twenty dollars, but with a half-off discount, it's only ten," the shop owner said. "For a fine protector of the streets, let's make it seven bucks! Seven bucks for a bucktoothed hare!"

The police officer handed Teddy the money, picked up the bunny, and left the shop.

Bertram stared at Professor LaGungo with dead, shiny eyes.

"I know what you're thinking," Teddy said, "and yes, I probably should have told the nice officer that the bunny came to our world through a trans-dimensional gateway. But really, do you think he would have believed me? Would he have believed that such a cute, adorable, fluffy toy originated from the Galaxy of Death?"

Hmmm. Probably not, Bertram did not say.

❉ ❉ ❉

In his garage, Neil Gluckman maneuvered the rocking horse out of the car and placed it on the concrete floor. How, he wondered, was he going to wrap it? Would there be enough wrapping paper in the house to cover it? Even if there was, Missy would still be able to tell what was under all that paper.

As he stood thinking, he absent-mindedly pushed on the horse's nose, rocking it back and forth a few times. He then looked around the garage at his motley collection of tools and odds and ends, hoping that inspiration would strike him.

He looked back at the horse.

It was still rocking.

Faster and faster. All by itself.

He backed away from the horse.

The toy responded by rocking toward him. Twin steel blades slid forth out of the horse's curved rockers.

Neil rushed to open the garage door. He only had time to open the door halfway—but that was enough.

Enough to allow the rocking horse to leave when it was finished.

❄ ❄ ❄

Helga Pennywhistle lived alone, but you couldn't tell by her Christmas tree. Under its branches rested presents for her four children, the spouses of her four children, and her eight grandchildren. In the morning, all her loved ones would arrive to open their presents. The house was completely silent: one could not even hear the wee scratchings and scramblings of any meandering mice. Helga had placed the doll from Pokaluhu in a shoebox, which she'd then wrapped with shiny green paper.

The spear pierced the box and wrapping paper easily. The doll then climbed out of the box and headed up the stairs toward Helga's bedroom, snapping his little jaws all the way. His teeth, previously hidden behind rigid lips, resembled thin, jagged shards of broken bones.

In fact, that's just what they were.

❄ ❄ ❄

When he came home, Roger Sinclair hurried to his home office—he refused to call it a den, since that sounded so pretentious—and pulled the fluffy bunny out from under his coat.

"Hello!" the bunny squealed in a high-pitched, yet raspy voice.

"Hey, you talk!" the policeman said. "Cool! Emily will love   you."

"Thank you, Roger!" the bunny said.

The policeman laughed. Toys these days really were amazing. He wondered what kind of technology the manufacturer had used to get the toy to say the buyer's name. "Are you voice activated?" he said.

"Of course! All living things with ears are voice activated," stated the bunny from the Galaxy of Death. "We listen to what others have to say to us and we react accordingly. I must say, that was actually a rather stupid question! Would you like to know how I respond to stupid questions?"

Frightened and confused, Roger dropped the bunny. "With a stupid answer?" he said.

"No!" the bunny roared, looking up. His eyes began to glow bright red. "With a cutting reply!"

At that moment, sizzling laser beams shot out of the

bunny's eyes.

* * *

In the back room of the shop known as Professor LaGungo's Exotic Artifacts & Assorted Mystic Collectibles, Teddy sat at his desk, smiling as he counted his money. Another successful Christmas Eve. Tuttlesburg was certainly a great deal more profitable than Tibet. He'd brought Bertram into the back room to keep him company, and he couldn't help but notice that the iguana's hide was the same shade of green as the fifty-dollar bill he was holding.

Suddenly, a tiny rapping sounded at the back door. The professor shuffled to the door and flung it open. The wind blew in a flurry of snow as three small figures made their way into the room.

"Welcome home!" he said, closing the door behind them. "I hope you had no trouble making your way back."

Tenderly, lovingly, the professor brushed the snow off the rocking horse, the doll from Pokaluhu, and the adorable pink bunny from the Galaxy of Death. Then he used a soft, red towel to wipe off the bloodstains. They would all require a more thorough cleaning in the morning.

"It's important to spend the holidays with loved ones," Teddy said, gazing fondly at his little companions. "I do hate people who put work before family. I absolutely hate them! They're just like Mommy and Daddy, always busy, busy, busy!"

He turned to look at a picture frame on the wall to his left. The frame did not hold a painting or a photograph. It featured a yellowed newspaper clipping—an article with the headline, COUPLE DIES IN XMAS FIRE: CHILD MISSING. He wiped a single tear from his cheek. "Well, you know what they say. 'Busy people become the Devil's playthings' — or something like that. Bertram, do you think I should have told the customers that the term 'half off' would apply to them as well as the prices?"

At that moment, the psychotic cuckoo clock on the wall, which had little straight-edge razors for hands, struck midnight. A wee bird in a straitjacket popped out of its hiding place inside the clock and screamed twelve shrill notes of rage.

Merry Christmas, Professor LaGungo, Bertram did not say.

THE ANTIPHON
John Boden

The letter beneath the phone bill was curious. No return address. The handwritten rendering of their address was written in a large, flowing script, oddly historical looking. The edges of the envelope were brown and would convey a perception of extreme aging were it not for the recent postmark and the accompanying smell of smoke. The letter had been near a fire. Darren carefully opened the letter that was addressed to his eight-year-old son. He slid his glasses further down his nose and began to read.

My dear boy, Arthur...
    It would be an untruth, were I to tell you I was not pleased to have received your letter. I get so little correspondence. Well, very little that is not "I want! I want!" or "I would sell my..." or similar pleas. I would like to take a moment of your time and explain a little about who I am and what I do. You have no doubt heard of me... be it from Church or Sunday school... or your

parents... or maybe some ridiculous rendering on a television show or a cartoon. Truth be told, I am not as any of those paint me. I was never a man, so I cannot be held in comparison to them. Though my name is a traditional benchmark of evil and sin and all around debauchery, I rather look at myself as the weight on the other end of the balance than the cornerstone of bad behavior... without me, you can have no good... no God. Without one of us, you would sit on one side of the teeter-totter, going nowhere. Where is the fun in that?

I was with him once—God... He was great in his kindness and boundless in his compassion. Things were perfect until I got a bit uppity; I grew envious of the Lord and wanted to be as he was. I caused a bit of trouble and soon found myself on the receiving end of the foot of God. I was thrown from heaven.

After that fall, I was bitter... very bitter. I ruined Eden... and changed the scope of mankind forever. It is not something I am always proud of... I mean, on one hand, had I not done such a thing, then man would not have the chance to choose their own path... they would simply be as cattle... loping here and there with no care or thought, just an ingrained "this is what we do" mentality. I changed that... of course, who wouldn't be so awestruck as to not listen to a talking snake!?

Since that day, I have had to do very little. Mankind has proven, time and time again, they are more than capable of acting as their own damnation... dreaming up horrors and travesties that have literally kept ME awake nights. The holocaust, genocide, war, the list can literally go for miles. I spend my days wandering these sour halls... bored by the screams of the damned... these souls who cockily did as they wished upon the earth... knowing the afterlife consequences, but never worrying... my how they carry on like infants when confronted with their eternity. It is stated that I want nothing more than all the souls, that I have not a nice bone in this body. That could be true.

It is often assumed I am the great enemy of God, chief hater of the Heavenly Father. That is untrue. I loved him and still do. He is my creator as he is yours. I was thrown into a role—an important one. Were I without my position... Well, I will not go into it again. I know this is all over your little head, as it should be. You have years to ponder this. For now, busy yourself with playing and laughing and all that glorious youth, for in a blink, it shall be gone. Choose your path, and choose wisely. I am never at loss of company, but sadly I am lonely in a sea of millions. I am sure you have been a good boy, as I am sure in a few weeks you will be more than pleased with what you find under that tree.

I bid you well, wish you happiness... and a long fruitful life, for now.

Thanks for the letter... even it was not meant for me.

—S.

The man folded the letter and put it back in the envelope. He looked at the fingerprint smudges on the paper, scorched into the pulp. He smelled the letter again, and the sulfuric tang made his eyes water. He looked at the young boy sleeping on the sofa, the flicker of the tree lights dancing on his still face. The man walked towards the kitchen, where he could hear his wife making dinner. "Honey, I think the boy might be dyslexic."

A Christmas to Remember

JP Behrens

"Honey, you're overreacting. Nathan is just going through a phase."

"No, Charles, I'm not. I found drawings of dead animals in Nathan's notebook. On every page. Some of them were just..."

"Wanda, he's ten years old. How bad could these pictures possibly be?"

Black-and-white images flashed through her mind, twisted, broken, and mangled diagrams of cats, dogs, and birds illustrated in great detail.

"I'm sure he'll grow out of it. Stop worrying."

Charles smiled as he navigated the Christmas traffic swelling around the mall.

Wanda hugged herself to combat the chill writhing in her stomach. The car heater blasted, but did nothing to melt away the twisted images. Her husband always said the same thing, yet this phase had persisted for almost two years now. Nathan snuck away into the forest more and more often. His attitude toward the family had gone from hostile to ominous. She caught Nathan threatening his little brother, Simon, only last week for trying to tag along.

Part of her was glad Simon wasn't allowed to follow. The venomous look in Nathan's eyes frightened her. After she'd pulled Simon away and admonished the both of them for arguing, Nathan walked into the woods without a word.

The car shuddered to a stop. The subtle jerk brought Wanda out of her dismal reverie. Shaking the twisted images from her mind once more, she exited the car to begin their final Christmas shopping. Maneuvering through the crush of people snatching at items helped to get Wanda's mind off her troubles. Unfortunately, the hectic reprieve did not last as they entered the sporting goods store.

A brand new, high-gloss cherry wood-stock air rifle was displayed in a glass case. It was exactly what Nathan had asked for.

"They actually still have it in stock, Honey. Nathan will go bonkers."

"Absolutely not, Charles. Until he's through with this morbid fascination of his, I will not allow him to own that… thing."

Charles sighed. "Fine, maybe I'll give it to Simon. He's been asking for it as well. I'll teach him how to use it. It'll be fun. You've wanted me to spend more time with the boys."

"No. What'll stop Nathan from getting a hold of it?"

"I'll keep it locked up in the den. If one wants it, they'll have to ask, and I'll be there to supervise. Fair?"

Wanda nodded reluctantly.

Charles walked through the mall with his purchase tucked under his arm, beaming as if it were his own Christmas gift. In many ways, it probably was. She wouldn't be surprised to find him firing off a few rounds some morning while the boys were still asleep. The child-like grin on Charles' face coaxed one out of Wanda as well. Wander-ing from store to store, they hunted for one last item for Nathan. She wanted something to divert his strange interests, but found nothing.

After a couple of hours, they finally decided to make their way home, feeling defeated, until they passed a hardware display in one of the department stores.

"One sec, Wanda. I want to see if they have that Miter Saw on sale yet. Maybe I'll get lucky."

As Charles trotted off to check on the machine he'd been eyeing for the last three months, Wanda browsed the aisles. She drifted through the various wrench sets, ratchet sets, and toolboxes until she same across a children's carpentry set. The wooden box was small and contained a saw, hammer, nails, screwdriver, ruler, level, and several other tools for which she didn't know the names.

"Not on sale yet. Maybe after the holidays." Charles sidled up to Wanda.

"What do you think of this?"

"I have all those tools."

"No, I mean for Nathan. You could teach him how to do repairs and build things. Maybe it would get him away from all the other craziness he's involved in."

Charles nodded, scrutinizing the set. He examined each one, and finally said, "Looks like an okay first set. Not good, but it'll definitely do to help teach him the proper ways to use the tools. I think it's a great idea."

"I hope the boys like their gifts." There was a lightness to Wanda's voice she didn't remember having the last few years. Not since she found Nathan dismembering a dead mouse on the kitchen floor. In the car, she watched the scenery flash by without fearing what lurked hidden within.

He'd sliced away at the rodent with surgical precision using a simple paring knife. The look of fascination etched across his face haunted Wanda still. Over time, his actions grew more gruesome until finally they seemed to disappear. After a brief mental respite, Wanda suspected Nathan moved his activities to a location away from her watchful gaze.

"I'm sure they'll go crazy over them. Don't worry about it."

The drive home was quick. Gravel crunched under the car as they pulled up to the house. The babysitter, Shelly, must have heard their arrival. She came bursting from the front door before they came to a full stop. Wanda opened her car door to meet her. Shelly stood, beads of sweat sparkled across her brow.

"Thank God you're back. Don't worry about paying me. Just don't call me again. I can't watch your son anymore. Simon is great, but Nathan... Just no."

"What happened?" Wanda placed her hand on the young girl's shoulder. She could feel Shelly shaking.

"He wanted to leave the house, go play in the woods, but I told them not until you got back. When he demanded to be allowed out, I told him to go to his room." Tears began trickling from her eyes. "The things he said as he walked up the stairs... It was horrible, disgusting. I can't repeat them. I will not watch him again. I'm sorry."

Shelly rushed off before anyone could say another word. Charles came up behind Wanda. "I'll go talk to him. Maybe this *has* all gotten out of hand."

Relief washed over Wanda as her husband marched into the house, ready to take control of the situation. She gathered the gifts, preparing to sneak them inside later when she heard Charles yelling in the back yard.

"You come back here right now!"

Wanda ran over in time to catch a glimpse of Nathan diving into the brush bordering the woods. Charles was hanging out of Nathan's window staring after their son.

"I'll go follow him. You watch Simon."

Nathan knew his way through the woods. Wanda almost never set foot in the wilderness. Crashing through the unknown, she tried to keep up. Soon she lost sight of Nathan or any trail he might have left. Still she kept going. After running through the woods for almost fifteen minutes, Wanda stopped. The only noise was her hard, ragged breathing. She realized Nathan had eluded her and she was hopelessly lost.

Wanda began walking in a direction she hoped would take her home. She kept an eye out for anything that might serve as a landmark. She stumbled through brush and over collapsed trees. By sunset, Wanda still had no idea which way to go. The chill wind cut through her clothes. For the first time, Wanda feared she might never find Nathan or a way out.

A deep thud echoed to her left. Hoping for salvation, she followed the sound. It repeated at a steady rhythm, growing louder as she neared. Wanda pressed through thick bramble. The growth opened into a small clearing filled with tables constructed of refuse gathered from the forest. On the opposite end of the clearing, standing over a wobbling table, Nathan hammered at something with a branch.

It took a moment for Wanda to register the thin wires stretched across the clearing like crude clotheslines and the lifeless beasts hanging from them, always in pairs, strung up by their tails like shoes tossed over power lines. Chipmunks, small dogs, cats. The animals were covered in gaping lacerations, mottled fur, and dried blood. A loud screech to her right brought attention to two cats flailing at one another, slashing, futilely trying to escape their fate. It wasn't long before the frantic creatures succumbed to their wounds and hung limp from the clotheslines like the rest.

On the makeshift tables spread out across the clearing she saw dark stains that made her throat burn with bile. Animal bones were strewn about, some hanging from wire, others just tossed to the side in small piles.

The horror of Nathan's time in the woods settled in. Wanda's shock held her in place as Nathan continued working at the table, unaware of his horrified audience. She didn't make a sound until she felt a small vibration under her feet. She looked down to find the fresh-turned soil jittering. Her fingers brushed the dirt, probing for answers. The kitten mewling for release from the shallow grave was more than she could handle.

Her terrified scream roused the attention of Nathan. As she scratched at the earth to release the tortured kitten, Nathan just stared at her. He watched as if he were studying something beyond comprehension. He was not angry or surprised, merely curious. Blood dripped from the stick in his hand. Nathan stepped aside, revealing a bound and gagged dog on the table behind him. Its rear legs were crushed.

Vomit covered the ground and Wanda's hands. The cries from the earth had ended. She rose from her knees, grabbed Nathan by the collar and said, "We're going home. Walk."

He shrugged and led the way. Neither of them spoke during the long trek home.

When they emerged from the forest, they found Charles dressed in a heavy jacket, wielding a flashlight and ready to come looking for them as shadows swallowed the forest. Nathan brushed past him and disappeared into the house.

"It was awful, Charles." She crumpled onto the lawn,

tears cutting lines down her dirt-covered face.

While Nathan busied himself with dinner, Charles took the opportunity to screw Nathan's bedroom window closed. They had no idea if he was sneaking out at night, but they weren't taking any chances. After Nathan and Simon were asleep, Charles moved the presents from the car to the living room. He was trying to wrap the air gun, but made a mess of it. Wanda managed to wrap Nathan's tool set before her shaking hands made it impossible to do more. Charles took over without a word.

"I'll go out there tomorrow and tear it all down. Hopefully, with his new tool set, he'll move on."

"Seriously, Charles? A new tool set isn't going to fix this. He needs help."

"I won't have some doctor poking at his brain. We just need to be more attentive. He's a boy who just got bored and wanted our attention. Now he has it, he'll be okay."

"You didn't see him, Charles, beating that dog. All those animals. You didn't see it."

"I will tomorrow. Now, why don't you take a warm bath, relax, and get some sleep. This'll all be over in a couple days."

Her dreams were red-washed images of squealing animals, hissing undead cats, and an innocent little boy waving his hands like a conductor, controlling the bloody carnival of horror. Wanda woke drenched in sweat. The sun bled through the curtains. She took a deep breath and got out of bed. There was a lot to do.

On a normal morning, she would sip a cup of coffee, let her mind wander, and appreciate the natural beauty surrounding her backyard. Now the forest was nothing more than a labyrinth of shadows and death. Wanda tossed the dregs of her coffee into the sink, unable to taste it. Everything was ash in her mouth. Her children roamed the house, waiting for their grandparents to pick them up and take them out for the day.

She heard the unmistakable crunching of gravel in the driveway. It took all of her will power not to run out of the house, just as Shelly had, and beg her parents to take Nathan away. Instead, she called to the boys, "Your grandparents are here. Go outside and be good!"

Simon exploded into the hall, all excitement and joy. Nathan walked to the door, reserved and steady.

When they were gone, Wanda released a huge sigh. She didn't even know she'd been holding it in until the wind rushed out of her lungs. With Nathan out of the house, the world seemed lighter. Charles came down the steps.

"Did they already leave?"

"Yes." Wanda couldn't keep the relief out of her voice.

Charles smiled. "I'm sure it isn't as bad as you made it out to be. I'll go out and clean the mess. In a few days, this will all be a bad memory. Relax."

Wanda nodded, but said nothing. He would understand soon enough.

Charles put on his coat and pants. He gulped down a cup of coffee and set out into the woods. Wanda watched from the kitchen window. Dread colored the forest bordering her existence. The withered branches of the leafless trees looked like claws ready to rend her into bloody pieces that Nathan might later examine on one of his wicked tables. She closed her eyes, but still the images assailed her. The house needed cleaning, the gifts placing, but none of her chores were able to dispel the scenes flashing through her head.

Whenever she saw Nathan's name on a present, she feared touching it, as if something could be trapped inside, suffocating. Whenever she wiped dust from furniture, it reminded her of the filth caking the make-shift tables of the miserable clearing in the woods. The vacuum sounded like an orchestra of screams being torn from innocent, mutilated animals.

Preparing dinner was the worst. Every slice of the knife made her wonder how often her son had done the same thing to some living creature. She cleaned the knives over and over again, constantly wondering if any of them had been used for his sick hobby. Finally, she couldn't take it anymore and went to watch television. Everything on was either too happy or too violent, so in the end, the house and Wanda fell into silence.

The warm glow of the Christmas tree covered her in soft light, but it did nothing to improve her mood. Charles had left over six hours ago to find and destroy their son's grotto of death, but still no word, and soon the boys would be returning. Per their Christmas Eve tradition, after dinner the boys would be allowed to open one gift each. Wanda and Charles had already decided which gifts to offer, hoping they might soften the blow when Nathan discovered his Frankenstein's laboratory destroyed.

The back door slammed. Wanda jumped. A muffled shuffling echoed through the stillness.

"Charles?"

"Yes."

"Is it done?"

"Yes."

"Did you see the dog?"

"It's done."

Charles drifted into the living room. He wavered between the shadows and the multi-hued aura of the Christmas tree. Wanda knew a new burden weighed on her husband's shoulders. They heard a car door slam shut. Both parents watched the front entrance with trepidation.

"God, how can I even look at him?" Charles whispered.

Wanda felt as though anger or shame was the proper response to Charles' disgust, but she just couldn't muster the emotion.

The front door opened with joyous tidings of grandparents spoiling grandchildren. Simon giggled uncontrollably, a sharp contrast to Nathan, who glided into the house silent as death. A trembling smile stretched across Wanda's face as her eldest son entered the room. Simon was gabbing about all the things they had done during the day, but neither parent truly heard. Both tried to look Nathan in the eye, willing themselves to show love for their son. Wanda's smile was on the verge of collapse. Charles just gave up. Confusion tilted Nathan's head, then for the first time in a long time, true horror flashed across his face.

His understanding made Wanda want to cackle in triumph, but the urge made her sick. She felt wicked for reveling in his pain, but the poor, tortured animals in the middle of the woods plagued her thoughts.

"No!" Nathan cried, flying out the back door before anyone could intervene.

"What was that about?" Wanda's mother started to follow Nathan.

Wanda's insides curdled at the sight of someone showing Nathan genuine concern. She wanted to reveal his atrocities to everyone. Instead, she remained silent. Only his parents knew of his sickness. For Nathan's sake, it would stay that way.

"Nothing, Mom. It'll work itself out. Let's just get dinner on the table."

After a great deal of bustle, the food was ready. Simon was his usual bubbly self, making the occasional silly comment that normally put an irrepressible smile on his parents' faces. Not today.

Wanda's mother kept looking toward the woods. "It's getting dark, Wanda. Maybe he's lost."

Charles, his face drawn and haggard, mumbled, "Doubtful."

Wanda waved off her mother. "He's always running around back there. Knows the place better than we do."

The comment sparked one of her father's long-winded recollections of the trouble he got into as a child. Charles maneuvered across the room and started in on the bourbon early. Wanda slapped on a smile, trying to ignore her father's morbid tales of practical jokes on wild life.

The soft whisper of the back door signaled Nathan's return. Charles poured his fifth shot and swallowed it down before taking his place at the head of the table. Wanda's father sat across from him, thrilling Simon with further tales of mischief. Her mother welcomed the missing member of the family back into the house. Neither Wanda nor Charles looked at their eldest child during dinner. Wanda could feel his hard, accusing gaze on them all throughout the meal. Simon prattled on over the awkward clicking of utensils, his voice the only bright spot in a house darkened by gruesome memories and silent recriminations.

After dinner, everyone gathered in the living room, ready to watch the children open their first gift of the holiday. Two packages were placed at the base of the tree. Nathan grabbed the long, poorly wrapped air rifle. He saw the name on the label and paused. His face darkened. Without a word he shifted it over to his little brother. Nathan dragged the neatly wrapped box onto his lap, looking at it to consider its contents.

"Wow! My own gun! BANG! BANG!"

"Wanda! What kind of gift is that?"

"Mom, it's okay."

"Look, Grandpa! I'm a soldier! BANG! BANG!"

"Go get 'em, boy!"

"Harold!"

"Mom, please. We have it under control."

"Now, Simon, there are rules you need to follow if you are going to use the rifle." Charles broke in, using his best fatherly voice. "Rule number one is you never use it in the house. Rule number two is you never use it without me. To make sure, I'm going to hold onto it. You'll have to come and ask to use it. Okay?"

Simon cradled the rifle in his arms, agreeing to each stipulation.

"Can we use it now? Can we?"

A deep laugh rumbled from Charles. "Not tonight. First thing tomorrow, I promise. Glad you like it."

"I love it. Thank you!" Simon turned to Nathan, "What did you get?"

Nathan stared at the rifle in his brother's hands. "That's a very nice gift, Simon. Just like the one I wanted."

"It's great, isn't it?"

"Yeah. Great."

Wanda shot a worried glance to Charles, but her husband didn't seem to notice. Instead, he said, "Go on, Nathan. Open yours. I think you'll really like it."

Tearing his eyes way from the rifle, Nathan began to unwrap the box. He undid the latch and swung the lid open.

"Now that is a proper gift for a young man," said Wanda's mother.

"Hey, Charles, whatever the boy makes first, would you mind if I got it?" asked her father.

"No problem."

Nathan pulled each item out of the box, examining the

tools in great detail.

"Don't worry, buddy. I'll show you tomorrow how each of those is used. It's about time I taught you how to be more handy. This way you can help me out more around the house."

Nathan placed each tool back into the box and closed the lid. Nothing registered on his face. His attention returned to the rifle that his little brother held in his arms.

"Cool! I want a tool set!"

"No, sorry, you're still too young for one of those."

"But he's not too young for a gun?"

"Mom! Stop!"

Charles interjected again. "So, Nathan, do you like it?"

The room went silent. Nathan looked from the rifle to the toolbox to his father. "What? Yeah, it's fine. Quite fine. Thank you."

Charles took the rifle and locked it away while the children were ushered to bed. Nathan carried his toolbox to his room without a word. Meanwhile, Simon speculated with great excitement on the rest of the gifts gathered under the tree. After both children were tucked in, the adults chatted for another hour, shared a few drinks, and eventually said their farewells.

"Well, that went better than I expected," said Wanda.

"What did?" Charles mumbled through his drunken haze.

"Nathan. Though I suspect tomorrow will be much harder."

"Hmm… yeah. Probably."

Shaking her head, Wanda guided her husband to bed. The tight feeling in her gut had loosened as the evening progressed. She still felt queasy remembering the things Nathan had done. At least the worst was behind her. Tomorrow was a new day.

In the middle of the night, she awoke to a sharp scream. Lying in bed, listening, the house was silent, but she could have sworn she heard a scream. She turned to look at Charles, who was sleeping like the dead, snoring and drunk. The darkness in the room was solid. Even as her eyes adjusted, she could barely see. The scream rang in her head. The way it cut off with a wet gurgle sent a shiver through her whole body. Wanda knew sleep would escape her. She decided to go and check on the children.

Watching them sleep, innocent and pure, always reassured her of not only the world, but her ability as a mother. She used to think there was nothing more wonderful than a sleeping child. As they grew up, that wonderful innocence disappeared, bit by bit. They developed into their own people, found their own way, brought about their own joys and sorrows. In sleep, the innocence life burned away returned. It was only then a parent could relish those lost moments.

As Wanda crept through the house, she caught a whiff of a strange odor—meat and humidity. It reminded her of a butcher's shop, but with a strange acrid undertone.

Wanda followed the stench until she came to Simon's door. Her heart froze. The blood in her body stopped flowing to her brain. She couldn't stop herself from opening the door. Simon's star light machine whirled, creating a shower of revolving cosmos. Nathan stood over his little brother, a chisel in one hand and a hammer held high in the other. A bloody saw hung off the edge of the bed, dripping onto the carpet.

Simon's eyes were locked open, heart and lungs exposed and still.

"You were right, Mom. This tool set will definitely help

my studies."

Nathan set aside the bloody tools and grasped a pair of sharp-edged pliers. Paralyzed into inaction, Wanda heard herself scream as Nathan continued the dissection, one careful snip at a time.

It's the Most Wonderful Crime of the Year

Nicky Peacock

"So, let me get this straight. Your idea is to have links through all the company logos online?" My manager, David, narrowed his eyes at me.

"Umm… yes, I think that we would increase activity on our, umm… website by adding the links," I replied, trying to avoid his stare.

"That's an awful idea, Sally. Look, let's keep your little idea between us. I wouldn't want it to affect your position here at Storm Marketing."

I nodded, wishing the ground would just crack open and I could tumble off my swivel chair into a black chasm of shame. He smiled at me, though; it was the kind of smile that mental patients get when they're telling doctors that they're 'better now'. I'd not been at Storm long enough to float ideas and watch them sail. David was being kind.

The door to the boardroom burst open and five more employees flooded in, all clutching clipboards and chatting like birds lined up on a telephone wire. I tried to avoid eye contact with any of them lest they note my stupidity.

Five minutes later the MD arrived, clapped his hands together, and energetically started the last meeting before the Christmas holidays.

"Well, guys, I'd just like to thank you all for your hard work this year. The recession still may be biting Britain's arse, but Storm is light years ahead of its competitors, and that's all due to your efforts." He smiled and mimicked a 'pat on the back' motion.

Todd from finance then chimed in about the year-end figures, and I tuned out, my mind wandering to the next activity of Secret Santa.

"...then we put links on all the online logos," said David.

What? Had David just thrust forward my rubbish idea? And was he getting a round of applause for it? Yes! The MD's smile became even broader and he pointed at David.

"Great thinking! That's why you're the manager, David. Take note guys, that's how you get ahead in this industry."

David grinned like Alice's Cheshire Cat. I still couldn't meet his eyes.

❉ ❉ ❉

The company Christmas tree was black. Apparently it was in fashion. It looked like an evil doppelganger of a real pine tree, one that was more likely to consume your presents rather than protectively nestle with them. The flashing lights strangling the tree caught my eyes and held me transfixed for a moment, just like they use to do when I was little. For the briefest second my mind was quiet, drenched in a multi-colored, blissfully magical state.

"Sally!" David yelled at me.

I slowly looked round at him, then joined the group as we gathered for Secret Santa. I tried to position myself as far away from David as I could, but he just kept looking over at me. Wrapped packages of various sizes were then handed out by the MD, who wore a fluffy Santa hat and joked with the female employees about them "sitting on his lap and him getting what he really wanted for Christmas." He tried this line with every one of us. It was borderline sexual harass-ment, which was giggled and blushed at, respectively. When he called my name, he hugged me, slipped me the line, and kissed my cheek. He smelled of stale aftershave and sweat. I felt cold where he'd touched me and I recoiled from him a little, which in turn made David laugh. I scurried back to a dark corner of the office, my small, ill-wrapped box clutched in my hands.

I desperately didn't want to open my present in front of everyone. The whole point of Secret Santa was that you weren't supposed to know who got you the crap gift. With the possible gift giver watching your reaction, you had to fake a smile and act like it was some long-lost treasure that had been eternally missing from your life. I'd had some bad experiences of getting terrible presents at Christmas—I never truly got what I wanted.

"Open yours, Sally," David said.

I reluctantly scrapped my fingernails across the wrapping paper and tore it away to find a small box of cheap chocolates. I'm diabetic.

"Every girl loves chocolates," David exclaimed with a grin.

It had been him. He had been my Secret Santa; no one else was watching me like he was. He wanted to suck out all my ideas, pass them off as his own, and then kill me with tasteless confectionary! The chocolate box in my lap began to shake and I noticed I was now shivering. I reached down into my handbag and pulled out my pill box. I struggled to pick them up, so I took a deep breath and then focused on getting just one of the little blue pills out at a time and down my throat.

"What's wrong with you?" David pointed at me as I swallowed my second pill.

I looked away. Murmurs spread around the office like a roaring fire of Chinese whispers.

"Well, Merry Christmas everyone!" boomed the MD. "Take the rest of the day off and see you in the New Year."

I whispered, "Happy Christmas," back to everyone, then escaped into the office kitchen. A fat, iced fruit cake sat on the counter with a sharp knife stuck in it. You could see the cake was dry, as its raisins had begun to lose their purchase on the crumbs and were now tumbling out to freedom.

"Let me cut you a slice," David said, coming up behind me. "My wife made it."

"No, thank you."

He cut me a slice anyway.

"You know that you can come to me if you're not happy here, Sally." He put his hand on my elbow and held me in front of him. His breath smelled of coffee and he had a stray raisin trying to escape his tightly packed teeth.

"Merry Christmas," I whispered, trying to move from under his grasp. I picked up the knife and pretended to cut another slice of dry Christmas cake.

"When *I* do well, *we* all do well," he said.

His grip had become painful, and suddenly I felt faint. I was used to dizzy spells; I'd had them since I was little. I had a doctor that helped me with them, Dr. Ryan; I wished he was there to catch me, and I breathed out his name as I slid onto the kitchen floor, the knife handle painfully wedged into my palm.

❄ ❄ ❄

I blocked out the rest. Silly really, I know. Dr. Ryan says I don't have control over my mind sometimes, and that's why I have periods of not remembering the things that happen. The next time I really remembered was Christmas Eve. I was in bed, all warm and cozy, snuggled into a duck down duvet and listening to the natural sounds of my house creaking around me.

Christmas morning was bright and cold and I awoke feeling refreshed. The New Year was looming, and I'd decided to leave Storm Marketing and apply for another job, a ritual I'd performed many times before. I tiptoed from my bed and down the stairs to my living room. I stared at my pine Christmas tree for a moment and then focused on the mass of presents beneath it. Presents I hadn't bought. Santa! After all these years, he'd done it; he'd finally left me the gifts I deserved! I scrambled to pick up the first one. I read the label aloud, "To Sally." No name of the giver was included. I shrugged and tore into the red foil wrapping to find an old office printer box. I opened it up and inside, covered with stained tissue paper, was a... hand, a human hand. I dropped the box and scurried backwards. Blood was on my fingers, on the cuffs of my night gown, and smeared up my arms.

The hand had tumbled from the box and was now on my living room carpet. It was a man's stubby hand and had a gold wedding ring; a left hand.

I sucked in a deep breath and began opening the rest of the boxes: feet with broken and mangled toes, strips of stringy sinew and flesh, a flask of congealed blood, hair and nail clippings, a still heart that was now grey and turgid. The last box, the biggest box, the one wedged right under the tree, the spot reserved for the best present, was the last I opened...

I reached for my blue pills and took out a handful. I was shaking so much that I only swallowed one. I grabbed at my mobile and dialled Dr. Ryan. I explained that it had happened all over again and he said that he'd be over soon. Good ol' Dr. Ryan, it took him a matter of minutes to be at my front door. He hugged me closely; he smelled of fresh aftershave and expensive coffee.

"Don't worry, Sally. We'll fix this together," he said.

I knew he would; he always did. He'd always been there for me, ever since I was a little girl and woke to find a pile of presents under the tree filled with the corpses of my parents; the smell of freshly exposed human meat, mingled with sage and onion stuffing ripe in the air. I'd been sectioned on New Year's Day, apparently Christmas is a busy time for the police and it had taken the neighbors longer than usual to report my parent's disappearance. I'd met Dr. Ryan at the asylum, and under his watchful eye I'd gotten better, had fewer memory lapses. He had given me my blue pills that made me calm and sleepy.

"There, there, Sally, I'm here now. David won't bother you again."

"What?" I looked up at my doctor. "What has David got to do with this mess?"

"Why, you killed him of course, just like you killed your parents and a few other choice individuals along the way."

My eyes focused on that big box. I'd opened it just enough to see a mop of blood-encrusted hair poking out. I hadn't the stomach to lift it to see who I had killed this time.

"How did you know that was David?" I backed away from him.

"You told me, on the telephone, just now," he replied, hands out, palms up.

"I didn't say his name. I didn't know it was him. It might not even be him," I whispered, staggering toward the big box again. I opened it slowly and forced myself to grip the hair. I pulled the head out of the box in one heavy, wet motion. It had been David. He still had a raisin stuck in between his teeth.

The blue pill I'd swallowed began to kick in and I started to feel dreamy again.

"Sally, how many pills did you take?"

"One," I replied, dropping David's head so that it rolled amongst the other scattered body parts.

"Silly Sally, let's get another one down you so you can go to sleep."

"What?" I stumbled backward.

"You're having another one of your episodes. We need to get you under control."

I tripped on one of David's thighs and fell amongst by bloody presents.

"Sally, please be careful, you'll hurt yourself." Dr. Ryan bent to crouch next to me.

"Did you kill my parents?" I asked.

"Of course not, Sally. I didn't even know you then. Don't you remember when they brought you to me? Such a frightened little girl, matted with her mum and dad's blood. What was it you said, that they didn't buy you the princess dress you wanted."

"What?"

"You remember, right?"

I closed my eyes in an attempt to force my memory to open up and show me what was inside. I remembered being told that Santa only brought presents for good girls. I had been bad that year, yet still I'd gotten my presents. Not the one I wanted, but I had still been rewarded heavily by the man in red. Realizing that it didn't matter if you were bad, I'd taken a knife from my kitchen and, while my parents dozed off in a post-Christmas dinner haze, I'd sliced them open so that their guts had tumbled free, their stomachs breaking open to reveal turkey meat and raisins from mum's stuffing. I hated raisins. I'd gotten scared then, and tried to force my parent's intestines back into their gapping cavities using soiled ribbons and festive sticky tape liberally littered with little pine needles. But still they stared at me. I found mum's stash of Christmas wrapping paper and covered them both head to toe in it, then heaved them back under the tree. Santa would take them back. But he didn't. Instead, I was taken away and locked up. I spent years with Dr. Ryan. He was my friend.

"I'm sorry, Doctor Ryan," I said.

"It's all right, Sally, but please put down that knife."

I looked at my hand. I hadn't even realized I'd picked one up or even where it had come from. I placed it carefully on the floor and looked up at my doctor.

"You're struggling on your own. How about we work together for a little longer?"

"That's for the best," I replied.

He held out his hand and I took it. It was then that I noticed the dried blood under his finger nails. He nodded at my discovery and wrinkled his nose. "You really weren't ready, Sally. You're so timid that you let that David just walk all over you. You kept telling me over and over that he was stealing your ideas and bullying you. I had to do something. You see, many years ago, you taught me a very valuable lesson," he said through a kind smile.

"What did I teach you?"

"Why, that being bad was good, and of course," he grinned and looked around, "that Christmas is that wonderful time of the year when the police are stretched thin and people are too wrapped up in their own lives to notice much."

"So you killed David?"

"A little, although you helped. You're so much more fun when you're lucid."

"What about his wife? She'll notice."

"No, she won't. I left her under someone else's tree." He grinned.

I narrowed my eyes and tried to remember how many people I'd killed. So far I'd had a lot of Christmases on the outside. I opened my mouth to ask Dr. Ryan, but he gently put a finger to my lips. It smelled like blood.

"Sally, don't worry. I told you Christmas is so busy for the emergency services. We'll be long gone before they realize we did it again."

I nodded.

"Here, take another pill. You'll feel better then. More like old yourself." He pulled out an old pill box from his jacket pocket and handed it to me.

The box was cold in my hand, and before I knew what I was doing, I had a small pill to my mouth and it was tumbling down my throat—like Alice down that familiar hole.

"So am I a murderer, Doctor?" I asked. I could remember the smell of blood and torn flesh, but just not recall spilling or slashing it.

Dr. Ryan smiled and put his hands lightly on my shoulders. They felt warm and familiar, and I noticed that he was wearing a tie with mistletoe on it.

"Of course, Sally. And I've told you before... I'm not really a doctor."

KRAMPUSNACHT

Ben McElroy

Scott glanced in his rearview mirror at the green and red Dodge SUV that had been following him since he left his house. The other driver was tailgating him, keeping only about a foot away from his rear bumper. He resisted the urge to slam on the brakes and teach the jerk a lesson. No sense totaling his practically new car.

Granted, Scott had ignored the yield sign back at the intersection of Routes 49 and 9 in Spencer when he'd forced his Civic into the eastbound traffic. As a result, he'd cut off the Dodge, but whatever.

Tough luck, he'd thought at the time. *Don't get in my way next time.*

Ever since then, the gaudy SUV had been practically up his ass.

Did the fool think he could terrorize Scott with such pathetic scare tactics? Nobody intimidated him. Never had.

Never would. Scott Mason did what he wanted, when he wanted, and how he wanted.

A short time later, Scott's car idled at the stop sign at the end of Meadow Road. Several fat snowflakes tumbled onto the windshield. Although frozen precipitation was possible on December 5th in Massachusetts, it still irked him that he'd have to drive in it. He waited until there were several vehicles coming at him from both directions before turning left onto Route 31. He'd get rid of that stupid-looking Dodge yet.

After making the turn, Scott sped up and used his side-view mirror to check things out behind him. The driver of the SUV was riding his ass again. *How the hell did that happen*? There hadn't been enough room for the Dodge to make the turn without causing an accident.

That didn't matter, though. Scott's nerves would not be frayed by such a juvenile show of force. He continued to drive as if his was the only car on the road.

When he finally made it to the center of Paxton, Scott had to wait for the traffic light to change from red to green. The SUV crept by his Civic on the right. The sunglass-wearing, gray-bearded driver looked over at Scott, who grinned and waved at the dude. When the other man offered an open-mouthed smile, Scott's arm went limp and fell onto his lap.

The guy's gums and compacted teeth belonged in a goat's mouth. And those weren't sunglasses he was wearing; they were his coal-black eyes that stretched around to the sides of his head. Scott's winter jacket seemed to tighten around his chest, stifling his breathing, so he unzipped it partway.

An impatient horn honked long and loud. Scott jumped and cried out. The light had turned green, so he accelerated across the intersection. He kept looking behind him to be sure that the Dodge went a different way. It did.

What he'd just seen... no, what he *thought* he'd just seen was nothing more than his tired brain trying to make sense of a very normal and very mundane situation.

Due to the relative darkness of this early winter morning, coupled with the fact that he'd stayed up wicked late last night watching a West Coast Celtics game against the Lakers, Scott knew that his perceptions must be a little off today.

Because just like Santa Claus, goat-men *did not* exist.

When he got to work in Worcester about twenty minutes later, Scott parked in his usual spot and slumped into his seat without turning off the engine. He did silence the radio, however, just before leaning his head back and closing his eyes.

A series of knocks on the driver's side window pulled him from the slumber he'd fallen into without realizing it. His heart thudded in time to each rap of the person's fist on the glass. Scott opened his eyes and peered to his left.

He cringed at the sight of the goat-man, which now looked more like a demonic hircine humanoid than a person. It crouched down to glare in at Scott, who shifted the Honda into "drive." Before he could take his foot off the brake pedal, the engine died. He depressed the lock button and started to climb into the backseat, thinking for some reason that he'd be safer back there.

The goat-man ripped the driver's side door off of the Civic and flung it aside. It then latched onto his ankles. Scott ground his teeth against the scream ballooning in his chest as the creature pulled him out into the cold morning.

Scott grabbed onto the console, but his sweaty fingers slipped away almost immediately. By the time his lower half was out of the car, he'd managed to grasp the steering wheel with his right hand. The goat-man released its hold on his ankles and wrapped an arm around his waist.

With little effort, the beast scooped Scott from the Civic and tossed him over its bony shoulder, nearly impaling him on the four tapered horns jutting from its shaggy, gray head. Scott sucked in as much frigid air as he could. Then he opened his mouth to holler for help.

But it was not to be.

Before a sound could escape past his lips, the goat-man's mangy tail jammed itself down his throat. He gagged, almost vomited, and forced himself to exert some sort of control over his body. Then it occurred to him to defend himself, so he bit down onto the leathery flesh that had invaded his mouth.

His captor responded by gouging his thigh with its clawed hands. Molten blood burned a path down his quivering leg. The stiff tail slithered out from between his lips. Scott experienced a coughing fit, further bruising the inner workings of his throat.

In the midst of this latest torture, the goat-man dropped Scott into a half-rotted wooden washtub attached to an old, rusty chain. A foul smell like burnt shit and moldy cheese encompassed him. He puked. Dry heaved. Then puked some more. All the while, the goat-man dragged the tub toward its SUV.

No matter how much he struggled, Scott was unable to escape from his small prison. Even sitting up was impossible. He had no choice but to lie back and try to come up with a way to get out of this mess.

The goat-man stopped when it got to the green and red Dodge. It opened the hatchback, then lifted the washtub, with Scott still inside it, and tossed it into the vehicle before easing the rear door shut.

One of the front doors opened and closed. The SUV shifted from side to side. Then the goat-man's face loomed over Scott. He gazed into his tormentor's strange, large eyes.

Leaning over the backseat, the creature extended its hand, and Scott noticed for the first time that each of its fingers ended with a filthy, pointed, hoof-like talon. It shoved one of these nasty protrusions into each of Scott's ears.

His body convulsed as his face sagged into something that resembled a pile of half-melted lard. Scott's thoughts dwindled to a monotonous drone. Though he could still see and hear, he couldn't move. Unrelenting terror consumed him.

At last, the goat-man removed itself from his field of vision. The SUV started up and drove out of the parking lot. The vibrations of the vehicle's tires on the road lulled Scott into a semi-conscious state.

He had no idea how far or how long they traveled, but cloud-filtered daylight still brightened the sky when they finally stopped moving.

The goat-man got out of the Dodge, then opened the back in order to carry its cargo into its lair. Scott didn't recognize the visible scenery they passed.

Pine trees coated with a thin layer of ice and snow jutted into the cloud-covered sky. The ground beneath him was uneven, and the bottom of the tub crunched as the goat-man dragged it toward its destination. In the distance, a flock of birds offered a series of mournful caws to whoever would listen to their lament.

All movement ceased. A door creaked open. The bird calls increased in volume.

No. Not bird calls. As Scott listened more closely he realized with ever-growing terror what they were.

It was the din of a thousand crying children.

Scott trembled as much as his paralysis would allow,

which wasn't a whole helluva lot. His muscles ached with their pent up energy. A few stray tears oozed out of his eyes.

After passing from the light into the darkness, the door crashed shut behind them and the children's wails built to a deafening crescendo that threatened to shatter Scott's already brittle mental state.

The goat-man passed its gnarled hands over his face, which sent his facial muscles into spasm. In fact, his whole body shook with a host of unpleasant sensations, and the fog lifted from his mind. He added his own shouts to those of the children as he discovered he was suddenly able to speak.

The goat-man remained as silent as it had been since this encounter had begun.

Realizing his cries for help were useless, Scott tried to relax. He looked at his captor. "Who are you? And why are you doing this to me?"

The goat-man offered a snaggle-toothed grin and a single shake of its overlarge head before turning away from Scott and lumbering over to a small table set against a wall on the far side of the cavernous, murky room.

Twin candles sparked to life. They revealed two bound scrolls hanging on the wall above the table. The goat-man unfurled the one on the left by a few inches and then held a candle up to it: Scott could see that the words *Santa's Nice Girl And Boy List* was gracefully printed at the top of the scroll.

The creature turned to face Scott. Again, it shook its head just once. Then it unrolled the second scroll.

An unsteady hand had written *Krampus's Naughty Girl And Boy List* across the top. This document was much shorter than Santa's list. Krampus drew the candle down the parchment's length until a section of text was illuminated, then beckoned for Scott to come forward. He complied.

As he stood next to the goat-man, Scott scanned the list of names that had been compiled by year, starting with the most recent and going back God only knew how long. About half way down, under the year Scott had turned eight, he noticed all the names had been crossed off. All, that is, except one: Mason, Scott.

And that was soon remedied.

The goat-man, which Scott was just realizing must be Krampus, scraped at the unmarked letters with its grotesque fingernail until an uneven line appeared through the name. When it was finished, it rolled up the list again and returned it to the wall. The goat-man nodded, a grim, satisfied smile etched across its features, and gathered Scott into its arms. It carried him toward a long line of cages, most of which contained one or two bawling children of various ages. There was one empty one, and Scott experienced a tightening in his gut the closer they got to it. *No way I'm going to fit in there*, he thought. A sober-faced teenage girl in the cage next to his said, "You shouldn't be here. You're an adult."

Krampus whipped its head around and glared at her. She cringed and slid backward into the far corner of her cell. Though her chin quivered, no tears fell.

The goat-man tossed Scott into the empty cage, then slammed the squeaky-hinged door and locked it. Scott landed hard and the wind was knocked out of him. As he lay there gasping, Krampus walked away.

The girl in the next cage scooted closer to the bars that separated her from Scott. "How'd you end up here?" she asked.

"That thing captured me this morning when I got to work," Scott said.

"I don't care about that. I want to know why."

"Why are you here? You're practically all grown up

yourself. You must be, what, about eighteen or so?"

The girl shrugged and looked away. Scott figured that she very well knew why Krampus had brought her here; she just wasn't willing to share the reason or reasons with him.

"I think you're here because you've been a naughty girl this year," he said with a forced smirk.

"Fuck off," she said, turning her back to him.

"See? It's because of stuff like that, I bet."

Without facing him, she said, "Okay, smart ass, you must've been naughty all year, too, then. What I don't get is why that monster took you now instead of when you were a kid."

Scott reflected on the girl's comment, going over in his head the year in question and wondering what had been so special about the year he had turned eight. He thought back to that winter and soon realized that his parents had surprised him and his siblings with a trip to Florida to spend the holidays with his maternal grandparents. It had been the old couple's first time down south after retiring, so it was supposed to have been this big deal.

Other memories flooded Scott's mind from that same time period. He had, indeed, been a very naughty boy that year. He grinned at the recollection of some of the stunts he'd pulled. As the memories replayed in his mind, his smile faded as he recalled some of the other things he had done, things that had been intentionally mean spirited.

"I went away with my parents at the last minute that Christmas," Scott said. "I guess Krampus couldn't track me down back then."

"He finally got around to it, though, didn't he," the girl said with a series of nasty giggles.

"That doesn't matter," Scott said between clenched teeth. "We have to figure out a way to escape before… well, before Krampus does whatever it is it does with naughty children."

"Good luck with that, asshole," the girl said.

"Hey!"

But she didn't say anything else, so Scott glanced around his compact enclosure. A slimy stone wall made up the back and right sides of his cage, and dingy metal bars made up the front and left sides. He grabbed onto a couple of the door's slippery bars.

The moment he made contact, there was a flash of bright blue light and a crackling sound not unlike those made by a bug light when an unsuspecting insect got too close. Scott yanked his hands away. His blackened palms sizzled and smoked. The teenage girl began to chuckle again as Scott bit back a scream.

Just then, Krampus returned with his washtub in tow. Boiling water filled it to the brim. Steam curled up toward the distant ceiling. Scott scooted to the rear of his cell, bringing his knees up to his chest and securing his arms around his shins.

The goat-man unlocked the rude girl's cage door before tearing it open. She shrieked and kicked, then scurried toward the rear of the cell and curled into a fetal ball. Krampus hunched over and reached in to retrieve the girl, dragging her like a rag doll across the dirty floor. As it drew her from the cramped space, she flew into a frenzy, kicking and punching at her captor to no effect. Back out in the open, Krampus lifted her high above its horned head and plopped her into the washtub.

At first, the girl was completely submerged. Then she bobbed to the surface of the bubbling water and opened her mouth to release an ear-shattering scream. Pulsing blisters dotted her crimson-skinned face and neck. Her eyes rolled up, and she sank back down. Meanwhile, Krampus rubbed its protruding belly and licked its sagging lips.

Scott turned away when the goat-man pulled the girl's body from the washtub. He gagged at the sounds of the creature relishing its bountiful feast. When bones started to crack, Scott leaned to the side and heaved. He would have vomited, but there was nothing left in his stomach.

His entire body quaked when Krampus opened the door to his own cage. The goat-man's claws once again penetrated the young man's ears. Complete paralysis ensued, but he was still aware of everything going on around him.

Krampus scooped him out of the miniscule cell and positioned him so he could take in the entire corridor of cages. Crouching before him, the goat-man plucked each of Scott's eyelids between a thumb and forefinger and ripped them off.

The pain was excruciating, but Scott was unable to give voice to it. Then Krampus licked Scott's eyes and the surrounding area. Intense heat seared the flesh wherever the creature's tongue touched. No blood trickled from the now-cauterized wounds.

The pressure of his unreleased scream tightened his chest until he thought his upper torso would explode. Unfortunately, that didn't happen, and he was forced to witness Krampus dining on all of the other naughty children whom it had collected this year.

Hours later, Scott still kneeled outside his open cage. The paralysis held him immobile despite the mental and physical exhaustion that had overtaken him quite some time ago. At last, Krampus returned from the far end of the lengthy row of cells.

The goat-man loomed over Scott. It opened wide its blood-drenched maw and pointed down into its stinking gullet. Apparently, it was time for dessert… And Scott was the only available item left on the night's menu.

With a wave of his tormentor's malformed hands, Scott's paralysis broke. He slumped forward. Off in the distance, sleigh bells jingled. Scott ignored the merry noise, mistaking it for something his defeated mind had conjured up to help distract him from his imminent demise.

A moment passed. Then another. Scott just wanted Krampus to get on with it. Never mind prolonging his fate.

When nothing happened, Scott found the fortitude to roll over. He struggled into a sitting position and was surprised to find himself alone. He looked around and found Krampus standing over by the *Naughty* and *Nice* lists. And the monster had company.

The visitor to Krampus' lair was none other than Santa Claus, and the two appeared to be deep in conversation, though only the guest spoke. The goat-man got its point across with various facial expressions and exaggerated body language.

Eventually, the portly man wearing a red velvet suit released a hearty, "Ho, ho, ho," and placed a hand on Krampus' bristly shoulder. It patted Santa's white-whiskered cheek. Then the two figures embraced.

Scott gaped at this peculiar exchange. "What the fuck."

At the sound of Scott's voice, Santa turned to the young man and frowned. The jolly old elf then shook his crooked forefinger at Scott, who croaked, "Help me."

"Oh, no, I won't," Santa said before laying a finger against the side of his nose.

With that, Saint Nick rose toward the distant ceiling, quickly disappearing from sight into the gloom. His sleigh bells jingled again just as faintly as they'd done before. Scott's desperate hope at being rescued by Santa winked out of existence like an ancient star at long last going cold.

Krampus returned to its place in front of Scott. The goat-man bent toward the young man and smirked, exposing its hideous fangs, which were jammed with strings of flesh.

Gathering his meager resolve and reminding himself that—until today—nothing could intimidate him, Scott thrust his arms up and grabbed onto two of the horns on the creature's head. He then used his upper body strength to lift himself from the cold stone floor.

Krampus grunted. Seconds later, both horns snapped off. Scott fell back to the floor. Before the goat-man could recover, Scott jabbed the sharp horns into its gleaming eyes. The creature roared and took several unsteady steps away from him.

Scott forced himself to his feet. With a running start, he rushed at Krampus and shoved the goat-man. It fell backward into the washtub. Scott whooped. Krampus either couldn't or chose not to extract itself from the tub.

Scott hurried over to the small table beneath the scrolls and took both candles from their resting place. Then he returned to Krampus and dropped the candles onto the jittering beast.

The small flames ignited the goat-man's tattered clothes and the fur beneath. It squirmed all the harder as its flesh smoldered, and then ignited. Reeking smoke plumed from the washtub.

As much as Scott wanted to witness the demise of this grotesque creature, self-preservation became his priority, so he fled into the frigid night.

The green and red SUV was still parked where Krampus had left it when they'd first arrived here. Scott approached the vehicle at a sprint. He whipped open the driver's side door and peeked at the ignition. A crumbling set of skeleton keys dangled from the steering wheel's twisted column.

Scott got into the vehicle and closed the door. To his surprise, he had no sooner settled into the seat when the engine kicked to life. Not one to question his good fortune, he shifted the transmission into "drive" and depressed the gas pedal to the floor. The Dodge lurched forward a couple of feet, then jerked to a halt, almost as though it sensed he was not who it had thought he was.

"Come on, you piece of shit. Move," Scott said, trying to urge the vehicle along.

When the SUV began to tremble as if in fright, Scott twisted around to look out of the back window and froze. Burnt quite badly with the horns still protruding from its eye sockets, Krampus gave him a grim smile that chilled him to the core. The goat-man lifted the back end of the Dodge, then tilted it toward the left.

Scott knew he had to get out before the SUV tipped over, so he scrambled over the console and opened the passenger side door. It immediately closed again.

While Scott glanced around the interior for something with which to break a window, Krampus succeeded in turning the vehicle onto its side. Scott slid down between the steering wheel and the driver's seat. He clambered for purchase, but was unable to extract himself from the tight space.

The passenger side door disappeared with a grating, metallic squeal. Shivering now, Scott's breath poured out of his mouth in dense clouds. The blinded goat-man stretched its arm into the passenger compartment. Its claws swiped at Scott, but missed him by an inch or two.

Shuddering, Krampus withdrew its arm as its body started to tremble. The convulsions strengthened until the creature was unable to support itself and it collapsed from view. Was this a trick designed to draw Scott out of the relative safety of the vehicle? Did it matter?

Of course, it did. Scott had no intention of succumbing to the goat-man. Today or ever. He would defeat it. He had to. There were no other viable options.

Sore from the day's tribulations, Scott climbed from the SUV. Perched on the edge, he peered down. Krampus laid there in a heap, unmoving.

Scott jumped from the vehicle. When he landed, he lost his balance and fell onto his side. Krampus remained still. Scott scrambled to his feet and ran to the edge of the pine forest in search of anything that could be used as a weapon.

Several inches of snow covered the ground and any object that may have been of some help to Scott. As frustration mounted, a large lump off to his left caught his eye. He brushed the snow away, revealing a rock bigger than his head.

He grabbed for it, his numb fingers scrabbled for purchase on the ice-slick surface. When he had a pretty good grip on it, Scott lifted it and carried it over to Krampus.

The goat-man had managed to roll over onto its stomach and crawl a few yards away from the overturned SUV.

"You're not getting away from me, fucker," Scott said.

Krampus turned its head at the sound of Scott's voice. The young man approached the weakened beast and collapsed next to it. He raised the rock over his head, then brought it down onto the goat-man's hideous face. The thing cried out, then tried to crawl away, so Scott brought the rock down again, summoning up what little strength he had left.

Krampus appeared to be unphased by the blow. Seeing this, Scott dropped the rock and struggled to his feet.

With a primal yell, he dropped down onto the beast, hoping to snap the creature's neck. He landed on his intended target, but Krampus continued to drag itself forward.

The goat-man rolled over onto its side, then reached over and wrapped its arm around Scott's midsection and pulled him close to its heaving chest. Scott wriggled to get out of the creature's grasp, but the thing only tightened its hold on him.

At one point, Krampus placed its leathery lips against the side of the young man's head and whispered a string of unintelligible words before inserting its pointed tongue into Scott's ear canal.

Though his vision blurred and severe vertigo spun him in lazy loops, there was no pain. After a final expulsion of breath, Krampus' body went limp.

Scott lay there for a long time. Fresh snow began to fall onto his upturned face. He closed his eyes against the gentle assault of the snowflakes.

Then sudden strength and vitality infused his every muscle. Scott jumped up and started to walk away from this evil place and its deceased inhabitant. Because he had no idea where he was, he followed his inner compass, which had been very effective in the past.

Into the night he roamed, turning this way or that, not sure of where he was going, but confident he was heading in the right direction.

When the darkness of night gave way to the pale light of dawn, Scott realized that the cold no longer bothered him. The panic that had gripped him earlier had vanished sometime during the course of the night. Didn't that usually mean hypothermia had set in and death was near?

In an attempt to stave off these disturbing thoughts, Scott rubbed his arms with his hands. Something felt a bit off underneath the sleeves of his coat. He removed the bulky garment and rolled up his shirt sleeve.

Coarse, gray fur covered his skin. He felt along the top

of his head, where four tender horn buds protruded. His tongue licked at fangs that had replaced the human teeth in his narrowed jaws.

Scott opened his mouth to scream...

... and bleated like a goat.

Lots of Love, Uncle Billy
Adam Millard

The Carsons sat beside the tree, surrounded by torn paper and colorful boxes. In the background, Frank Sinatra was crooning in his own imitable fashion. The smile stretching across Ivie Carson's face was perhaps the best gift Roger and Donna Carson could have hoped for; the way in which she'd hurriedly rent the paper from her gifts — the magic still there, at least for her — had brought smiles to their own faces.

"Well, that was fun, wasn't it?" Roger said, pushing himself onto his haunches; his knees cracked beneath him, a reminder that he wasn't as young as he used to be.

"Daddy, there's one more," Ivie said, pulling a flat gift wrapped in plain brown paper from beneath the tree.

For a second, Roger stared at it as if it was liable to bite their daughter. "Ah, yes. The *mystery* gift," he said, remembering how it had arrived almost a month before. The delivery man had almost given up trying to deliver it, such was the scruffy handwriting scribbled across its front. If Roger hadn't been able to make out Ivie's middle name on the label, and confirm it with her passport, the courier would most certainly have taken it away; a regular Scrooge.

"Who is it from?" Ivie asked, brightening once again.

Roger and Donna exchanged a glance; neither of them knew. For all they knew, it was a big ol' box of anthrax; the only present at Christmas for which you had a right to keep the receipt.

"Can I open it?" Ivie asked, excitedly clapping her hands together.

Roger wished he'd had the gumption to open it beforehand. It had been sitting on top of the wardrobe in their bedroom for three weeks. It would have taken very little effort to grab it down, check it for suspicious substances, and rewrap it in time for the big day. He hadn't done any of that, though, and now here they were, staring at the box, at their daughter, at each other, not sure what to do.

"It is addressed to *her*," Donna said, almost pleading with Roger. "It's probably something from one of our distant relatives."

"Do you *have* any?" Roger asked. "Most of my family have access to a store that sells Christmas paper. This… This looks like something the Taliban leave next to an airport."

Ivie wasn't listening; she had already taken the paper off the box's corner, and was picking at the tape that held the rest in place.

"What the hell," Roger said, nestling back onto his ass. "Go on, Ivie. It's been driving me crazy this past month, anyway."

She tore the paper free, tossing it across to where the cat had, until that moment, been sleeping.

"It's a board game," Ivie said. "I love board games! Can we play it? Can we, can we?"

Roger didn't hear her words, as frantic as they were; he was too busy trying to piece together how the Ouija Board had come to arrive at his house, improperly wrapped, and addressed to their daughter, who saw no harm in the game. To Ivie—who knew nothing of the occult, and Roger intended to keep it that way—the box sitting in front of her contained nothing more dangerous than, say, *Jenga* or *Hungry, Hungry Hippos*.

"Who would send this?" Donna asked, searching the discarded paper for clues. The cat, nestled beneath the brown paper, gave up the ghost and retired to the kitchen.

"Anything?" Roger said. Whether it was the fatherly gene in him, or something else, he pulled Ivie away from the box; she continued to kick and struggle in an effort to get at her new toy.

"Daddy, I want to play with the..." She ceased kicking and read the box, slowly and deliberately. "... The Ooooja Board."

"It's not for children," Roger said, ready for the barrage of questions that would surely follow.

"But it was addressed to *me*," she said. "It had my name on it, and it's just a game."

She continued to talk, but Roger turned the volume down on her. He turned his attention to Donna; she was standing next to the tree holding up a small, brown envelope. Scrawled on its front, in almost incomprehensible script, was their daughter's name.

Roger released Ivie, who lunged for the game box, turning it over to read the back. He took the envelope from Donna and opened it.

A single, textured square of paper. Roger pulled his

reading glasses from his pajama shirt pocket and pushed them up onto the bridge of his nose. He read in silence; there was no need for Ivie to know of the box's origins.

Ivie,

I didn't know what to get you. I never do, but then I had a fantastic idea. This game will help you and I to keep in touch. Merry Christmas, Sweetheart.

Lots of Love, Uncle Billy

XXXXXXXXX

Roger read it again, and then a third time just to make sure he wasn't going insane.

"What does it say?" Donna said. How many times had she asked? Her irritated tone suggested it had been more than once, yet Roger was speechless. He simply handed the square of paper across to his wife and allowed her to read it for herself.

In front of them, innocently sitting on the hearth, hugging the box as if it were a doll or stuffed bear, their daughter remained oblivious.

❄ ❄ ❄

Donna stood in front of the mirror, going through her usual bedtime routine. Roger entered, removed his wedding ring, and placed it on the table next to his side of the bed. The subject of Billy's gift had not yet been broached; the day had been busy, what with Donna's parents driving all the way from Kent for dinner, but Roger had spent the day thinking about it. About how his brother had planned it all in advance, arranged for the box to be delivered at Christmas time, how he'd written that note back when he'd been...

"You okay, honey?"

Roger started. No, he wasn't okay. He'd practically had a meeting with the Ghost of Christmas Past.

"Why do you think he did it?" he asked. "I mean, I knew him better than anyone else, but I never expected him to be so... so *insensitive*."

Donna sat on the bed, still running the brush through her hair. "You know what Billy was like," she said. "He was never the most tactful person in the room. And he was going through a lot those last few months. You can't blame him for... for trying to keep in touch."

"Yeah, but a *Ouija* Board. *Fuck*, Donna, a nice letter for Ivie would have been enough. She's too young to know about death. Things like that can ruin a kid."

Donna sighed, placed the brush—thick with wispy blonde hair—on the bed. "Look, he didn't think like you. To him, this was probably a nice gesture. And come on, he knew we would never let Ivie play with the board. Billy meant no harm."

Be that as it may, his dead brother had sent their daughter a Ouija Board so she could keep in touch. Roger had a right to be angry.

Donna touched his hand. "You miss him, don't you?"

He dry swallowed. It had taken six months to get to a place where he'd made peace with his brother's death, to where he'd vanquished the memory of Billy's emaciated figure lying on that hospital bed, the jaundice a constant reminder he wouldn't be making a recovery. Not this time.

"I just didn't expect to hear from him again," Roger said, choking back tears that threatened to erupt. "And not like *this*."

Pulling him into a warm embrace, Donna said, "I know. If you think about it another way, he just wanted to be able to speak with his niece. He never got a chance to say goodbye."

She kissed his neck, and before Roger could object, she was running her warm, slippery tongue along his throat. He felt himself respond. Was it considered blasphemy to fuck on Christmas Day?

What the hell, he thought. It had been a long and tortuous day. Lying back, he welcomed his wife's weight on top of him, and yet he couldn't forget the words scrawled on that little square of paper.

Lots of Love, Uncle Billy.

❄ ❄ ❄

The next morning, Roger left Donna in bed and made his way downstairs to create some sort of breakfast. The scent of Christmas dinner still filled the kitchen, and there were still wine glasses on the countertop that needed to be washed. Donna and her mother had seen off the best part of two bottles the previous day. Roger couldn't help wonder if that was why his wife had been so willing to please him last night; they seldom made love anymore, and when they did, it was more of a chore than a pleasure. His wife would roll her eyes, pull her knickers to the side, grunt and moan as if from a Hollywood script. But not last night. Last night had been real, passionate, spontaneous, and fun.

Upstairs, Ivie was playing with her new toys. Roger could

hear some child-friendly DVD playing in the background.

Collecting eggs and bacon from the refrigerator, he set everything to cook, which was when he realized something that caused bile to rise in his throat.

Last night, before bed, he'd specifically placed the Ouija Board on the kitchen countertop, our of Ivie's reach. She'd taken her new toys up to her room, leaving behind Uncle Billy's gift. Roger dared to hope that she'd forgotten all about it. It was obvious she hadn't.

One of the kitchen chairs had been pushed up to the countertop, and the board was missing. He turned, enraged and disappointed in Ivie. She must have crept down in the night or the early hours of the morning and taken the game.

"I don't like you, Daddy."

Roger snapped his head around to find Ivie standing in the kitchen doorway. Still wearing her nightgown, she looked cherubic, and yet her words betrayed her.

"What did you say?" he finally managed. "By the way, young lady, I'm not pleased with you. When I tell you that something's not for children, I mean—"

Her scream cut him off. Roger panicked as her mouth fell open, so wide he could see her tonsils vibrating. He rushed across the kitchen, plucked her up from the floor, and began to comfort her the way he had when she'd fallen over as a toddler, soothing her with whispers and—more often than not—bribery.

Her scream faded, leaving Roger with a ringing in his ear as though he'd been stricken with tinnitus. "Shhhhh," he whispered. "What's the matter, sweetie?"

"What's happened?" Donna asked, rushing into the kitchen wearing nothing but white knickers. Her breasts bounced as she covered the distance to Roger and their daughter. Her eyes implored Roger to answer, but he didn't *know.*

"She just started *screaming*," he said. "I was making breakfast. I thought she was playing upstairs..." He trailed off as Donna pulled Ivie from Roger's shoulder and hugged her in that special way that only mothers knew how to do.

"Well, was she sleepwalking?" Donna asked, more than a hint of irritation in her tone.

"I... I don't *know*. I think she was awake. Her eyes were open."

To Ivie, she said, "It's okay, baby. Let's take you back upstairs."

And with that, they were both gone, leaving Roger standing in the kitchen, heart racing as if he was about to suffer something acute. *That's funny. I don't remember asking for a Christmas coronary...* And just like that, breakfast was off the menu. Roger sat at the kitchen table, incredulous, and more than a little frightened. His daughter's words—Had he heard right? Was she capable of such vitriol?—played over and over.

"I don't like you, Daddy."

❋ ❋ ❋

As soon as Donna entered Ivie's bedroom, she saw the board. It was laid out on the floor, one of the pillows from Ivie's bed next to it. On the TV, colorful characters were performing a song and dance about brushing teeth.

She placed Ivie on the bed, not taking her eyes from the Ouija Board. "Honey, what did we tell you about that?" she said, trying not to allow the annoyance to creep into her voice. Ivie was distressed enough.

"Just a game..."

"It's *not* a game," Donna said. "It's not for children to

play with. Perhaps when you're older, you'll understand—"

"Daddy *fucked* Aunty Glenis."

For a moment, Donna was too shocked to speak. It was as if she'd been slapped, very hard, by something extremely sharp. She grabbed Ivie by the arm, squeezing until she felt it burn. "Don't you ever use that word!" she said, struggling to moderate her tone. "That's a terrible word, Ivie Carson, and I never want to hear you say it again."

But then the rest of what her daughter said sank in and she realized that word wasn't the worst part about the sentence.

"Why would you say that?" she whispered. A single tear rolled down her cheek, though she didn't know whether it was from sorrow or anger.

Ivie pulled herself free of Donna's slackened grip, pushed herself to the edge of the bed, and pointed at the board on the floor. "Uncle Billy told me," she said. Just four words. Four terrifying, unsettling, grotesque words that made Donna want to run from the room, screaming, not stopping until she reached the car.

Instead, she sighed and wiped the elusive tear from her cheek. "That's not what happened," she said. "Don't lie to Mommy, Sweetie. I promise I won't be angry. Just tell me—"

"He *did*, Mommy. I'm not lying. Look, I wrote it all down." She leapt from the bed and produced a flowery notepad from beneath the board. Handing it to Donna, she smiled a toothless grin that would have been cute under normal circumstances. She perched herself on the edge of the bed, imploring her mother to read. "We were talking last night, and he told me all sorts of things about Daddy."

Donna closed her eyes. This was too much to take. It felt like a dream—a nightmare—and she silently prayed that she would waken before reading the childish, and almost illegible, writing on the flowery notepad.

She opened her eyes, saddened at the image of the pad in her tremulous hand. She began to read.

Hello Ivie,

Sorry. Dead. Cancer. Evil.

Never said Goodbye.

Still Sad.

Daddy Evil.

Daddy Fucked Aunty Glenis

Broke Billy Heart

Affair Three Years

Cheating Daddy

Tell Mommy

Please

For Uncle Billy

Love You

Ivie

Be Good

When she was finished—and it took a while due to Ivie's untrained hand—Donna glanced down at the notepad in silence. Her heart raced as gooseflesh rose on the nape of her neck, on her arms, and on her exposed breasts. The room suddenly felt cold, as if a window had been left open, and yet there was no draught; the central heating had been on since five o'clock.

Donna sniffed and placed the notepad down on the bed.

"Do you want me to show you how to talk to Billy?" Ivie asked. Her excitement at the prospect of revealing something unknown to her mother was palpable. Perhaps, if she knew what it might mean, what she would be doing by letting her mother speak with Billy, she wouldn't have been so eager.

"That would be nice," Donna said, lowering herself from the bed to the carpeted floor. "Show me how to talk to Billy."

"Yay!" Ivie said. "Uncle Billy knows things."

※ ※ ※

Roger finished pouring two mugs of coffee. He tossed out the food intended for breakfast, figuring instead that they would have an early dinner. There was plenty of turkey left over from the previous day's dinner, and the fridge was stacked with cold cuts and pickles. The Boxing Day spread was, he thought, more enjoyable than Christmas dinner. Sausage rolls, pork pies, beetroot, pickled onions, black pudding, potato salad... What's *not* to like?

He was sitting at the kitchen table, flicking through the TV guide to see what bullshit reruns were on over the festive period, when he heard something thumping down the stairs. He straightened, expecting Donna to appear, perhaps dragging the vacuum cleaner. She was a stickler for tidiness, and Christmas had left the house in all kinds of disarray. Honestly, Roger was surprised she'd lasted this long without retrieving the dustpan and brush, or mopping the kitchen floor.

But when she appeared in the doorway, she wasn't dragging the vacuum cleaner. Standing beside her, Ivie solemnly waved, as if they were going somewhere. Behind them were two suitcases. Ivie's was covered with stickers from whatever psychedelic cartoons kids were into these days.

"What's all this, then?" Roger asked, confused, but not concerned. They often played little games together, especially when Ivie needed distraction. That little screaming fit had obviously warranted a bit of role-play from Mommy, but Donna's face read otherwise; it was the epitome of seriousness, and Roger could see the glistening streaks upon her cheeks, remnants of tears. Her lips quivered as she attempted to speak, but nothing would come.

"We're going to stay with Grandma for a while," Ivie said, that toothless grin no longer cute and endearing. Donna squeezed her shoulder as if to silence her.

"What? Why? Is this some sort of *joke*?" Roger stood, suddenly aware that something—Lord only knew what— terrible had happened. "Is everything okay, Donna? Your mom, is she—"

"My mother's *fine*," Donna suddenly yelped. "I'm taking Ivie with me. I'll be back later for some things, clothes, bank stuff—"

"I don't understand," said Roger. "Have I done something wrong? What is this?"

"Daddy fucked Aunty Glenis," Ivie blurted.

Donna squeezed her shoulder again. "What have I told you about using that word?"

"Sorry, Mom."

Roger couldn't breathe. How? It made no sense. That had been years ago, an affair that had fizzled out long before

Ivie had even been born. How did they know?

Then it hit him like a ton of bricks. The Ouija Board. It had to be. Billy's parting gift from beyond, one final bit of revenge for ruining Billy's relationship, for causing his divorce. Billy had known all along, and yet he'd kept it all pent up, saving it for one Christmas when Roger's life couldn't get any sweeter.

"If you want to talk to him,…" Donna said, turning and pulling her suitcase through the hallway. Ivie mirrored her. "… he's on the floor in Ivie's bedroom." She opened the door and walked through it, out into the wintry Boxing Day morning, their daughter still waving at him as if they were merely off to the shops.

Y͙ou'd B̊etter W͙atch ͙Out

Mark Onspaugh

December 24, 2033

Santa woke up cursing.

He did that every morning these days.

Each night, he'd blow out the burners on the stove and turn up the gas, take a lethal dose of barbiturates, then open his wrists and carotid with a straight razor.

And every freaking morning he'd wake up to find his wounds healed and his health in the pink. He was beginning to think he could have one of the remaining elves cut off his head and he'd find it reattached in the morning.

Suicide was not an option for one of the Immortals.

Of course, nobody died these days, did they? Not really. The scientists of Earth had seen to that, unleashing some bioengineered bacteria that were supposed to eat discarded plastics and generate useful energy.

Nice idea.

Pure poetry.

Nobel Prize thinking, for sure.

Too bad the stuff mutated, went from chomping on plastics to brains. Any brains would do.

Yep, eating them and then reanimating the bodies, only now with a bacteria colony to do the thinking up in the old skull cavity... as in: SEEK OUT AND DEVOUR MORE BRAINS.

He'd lost all his reindeer to the plague thirty Christmases ago, and it had been Rudolph who had come looking for him... Eyes glowing like marsh gas, that silly red nose flickering like the filament was about shot.

Yeah, little Rudolph was hoping for a big bowl of Kringle gray matter... A little off the top, Santa, and maybe some of your hippocampus or medulla oblongata for dessert, hokay?

In those days, Santa figured humanity would triumph, so he had fought Rudolph, finally slaying him with a vorpal sword and slicing him open from glow-nose to toy-sac.

Writhing in an open slay.

Had Santa known how quickly the world was going to degenerate into *merde*, he might have volunteered his noggin for the noshing.

Sigh.

So, here it was, Christmas Eve, and he was still alive. And so, bound by the covenant he had made with the Calendar Lord, he had to deliver presents to any child not on the "Naughty" list...

Trouble was, most kids were now part of the huge herd of roving undead that worked its way from one end of their respective continent to the other, ceaselessly moaning and wailing because the lack of brains was more agonizing than the worst drug withdrawal, apparently. Was such a kid naughty or nice? Might as well try to apply that same question to a black widow spider, or a scorpion, or a rattlesnake.

Ugly? Oh yeah.

Deadly? For sure.

Efficient predators? Yep.

But nice or naughty, good or bad? How to tell?

They just did what was in their natures, no matter how unnatural.

Oh, there were little pockets of survivors, but not enough to prevail, Santa thought, unless there was some miracle. Not from him, of course. He could only deliver gifts, quickly and discreetly to good children, living or undead.

There's a secret, though, that no one ever divulges: magic folk have their own needs.

Tinkerbell needs believers.

Leprechauns need their gold.

And Santa needs joy. Childlike joy, unfettered and undaunted.

Not too much of that going around in these troubled times, and it hurt. Hurt bad, like his nerves were rubbed raw with sandpaper and then sautéed in a vat of needles and razorblades dipped in Tabasco and sulfuric acid while a flamenco dancer did a *zapateado* on his testicles.

Agony of the first order, and really a bitch to live with. Death would have been welcome, a respite, a kindness, but there was just enough joy in the world to keep him alive, keep him going.

And because of that, he was forced into this painful, pathetic existence, one with little resemblance to his heyday, the halcyon days of his glorious youth when he was celebrated by Coca Cola and TV specials, and the radios played songs about his exploits and he was more beloved than the Beatles or Jesus.

Sigh.

Being Santa sucked.

And so, being at the end of his wits, he decided five years ago to try and inspire fear and loathing rather than joy. He had no say over the gifts, that was part of the covenant. But his appearance, his mode of transport, that was up to him, so his visage took a decidedly darker turn.

Now he dressed in black velvet, his hat a black and pointed sorcerer's chapeau with a tiny skull at its point. More skulls for his belt, his beard and mustache painted red with blood.

His sleigh was the same, though now it was pulled by a team of eighteen zombies, all former gridiron stars with plenty of strength and stamina. And hanging out in front of them, the proverbial carrot: a newborn babe in a cage, dangling just out of reach.

The minute that kid cried, the pus-bags really moved into high gear.

To make sure he got his point across, that he was a harbinger of death, a Horseman most foul, a thing to be reviled and cursed, he had two signs over the baby's cage.

"Baby Jesus" going out, "Baby New Year" coming back.

※ ※ ※

It was fast approaching midnight, and he had thousands of cloned brains from the elf labs to distribute to zombie children. To the uninfected, the usual complement of dolls, bicycles, and sports equipment. Puppies and kittens were no longer the happy gifts they had once been.

The brains and toys were loaded, and Santa, now in his 1,687th year, cracked the whip over his undead team.

"On Peyton, on Tom, on Brian, on Sean…"

❄ ❄ ❄

He returned just after dawn, the melting polar ice cap glimmering in the morning sun. On his route, he had heard a little girl in the Australian Underground Enclave ask God to bless him, and a kid in the UN Eastern Fortress left out some homemade cookies (terrible) and milk (powdered).

It was enough to keep him going another year.

Merry freaking Christmas.

S*anta C*laws is C*oming to T*own
Rob Ferreri

The chill arctic wind whistles through the snow-covered mountains of the North Pole as the full moon shines down and reflects off of the snow, making it easier to see in the pitch darkness of the night. A familiar figure is seen riding a sleigh being pulled by eight reindeer. His red and white coat and hat give him warmth, and at times like these you can understand exactly why he has such a long beard. Santa seems to be following a set of tracks in the snow, which are being quickly obscured by the harsh weather conditions. The tracks appear to be human, yet smaller, most likely belonging to one of his elves.

As the tracks become too faint to follow any longer, Santa reluctantly signals the reindeer to stop with a tug on their reins. He surveys the area, trying to determine which way his wayward elf went when a scream echoes through the mountains. He gauges the general direction of the scream, disembarks from his sleigh, and heads towards it as swiftly as his legs can carry him.

"Hello?" Santa calls out as he trudges in what he hopes is the right direction.

No reply can be heard, but Santa sees something a short distance away. Unsure if it is his lost elf, he makes his way towards the unknown object. As he gets closer, he is able to make out more details and sees that it is indeed the missing elf. When he finally reaches his destination, he finds himself standing over the elf's badly mutilated body.

"Oh my God! What in the world did this to you?" Santa mumbles, shocked by grisly murder scene before him.

There is not much time for confused pondering, as a bone chilling howl interrupts Santa's thoughts and a grim foreboding overtakes him. The howl sounds close, and more than likely belongs to whatever butchered his poor elf. He looks back in the direction from which he came and tries to estimate the distance to his sleigh, but the snow and wind make it impossible to see that far. With his safety undeniably in jeopardy, he decides to try and make his way back to the sleigh with extreme haste and attempt to flee back to his workshop. Santa kneels down and picks up the elf's corpse.

"Don't worry, little buddy. I'm not leaving you here. I'll get you back home. I promise," Santa vows as he cradles his fallen comrade.

The winds that hindered him earlier are now at his back, but that is little compensation for the heavy load he now carries as he retraces his steps. Santa's breathing is heavy and labored as he trudges towards the sleigh, which finally comes into view a short distance away, and he breathes a sigh of relief at the mere sight of it.

"We're almost there," he whispers to the elf. He knows the elf is beyond caring, but he speaks the words out loud to ease his own nervousness.

When he arrives at the sleigh, he sets the elf down in the back, a place that is usually reserved for his magical sack of presents on Christmas Eve. As he is about to climb onboard, he hears a low guttural growl coming from directly behind him, causing him to pause as a feeling a dread washes over him. Slowly, he turns to face the source of the sound, but he is unprepared for what he sees.

The creature before him is not quite a man, and not fully a beast, but a strange hybrid of the two. It resembles a white wolf, but stands erect on two long, furry legs. Drool drips from its canine snout as it bears its teeth at Santa. Despite being a man whose daily life is filled with magic and wonder, finding himself in the presence of such a legendary creature is enough to freeze him in fear.

"Dear God in heaven."

The two stand facing each other for what feels like an eternity. Santa stands as still as he can, going so far as to breathe in only short, shallow breaths, fearing that any movement might cause the beast to attack. Moving just his eyes, he gazes toward the sleigh, hoping to spy something he could use to defend himself against the creature. He spies his walking stick in the front of the sleigh, which is made from oak and has a silver handle shaped like a Christmas ornament. Hoping the legends are true, that silver is one of the few things that could kill a werewolf, Santa decides that going for the cane is his only chance to escape meeting the same fate that befell the elf.

With no other options, Santa quickly turns and reaches for the cane, and as he does so, the creature charges. Santa grabs the cane, but before he can swing it at the creature, he feels a sharp pain in his right shoulder as the beast's powerful jaws lock onto him. Then the creature has him, and

Santa screams in agony as the thing's claws rake across his chest. Fighting through the searing pain, Santa makes one final, desperate attempt to save himself. He thrusts the cane behind him, and not being able to see, he hopes it strikes home.

The werewolf stumbles back, and Santa whirls, happy to see smoke rising from the creature's chest. The legends were true. Before the beast can recover, he leaps forward and drives the silver orb into its open mouth, forcing it down the werewolf's throat. Unable to breath, the mighty beast clutches at its throat, tears at its own flesh, but the damage is done. It collapses to the ground, and as it struggles to take its final breath, it starts to transforms back into its human form.

Unable to support himself any longer, Santa collapses weakly against the sleigh. Pain and blood loss are making him dizzy. He stumbles and falls into the sleigh. Consciousness is slipping away, but he manages to grab the reins and summon the strength to utter a single word to his reindeer before the world goes dark.

"Home."

The reindeer, whose loyalty kept them from bolting without their master when the werewolf attacked, now rush off as swiftly as they can to spirit him back to his workshop in the hopes that all is not lost and his life can be saved.

As the sleigh nears the workshop, a few of the elves taking a break outside notice it approaching and rush to meet it. The sleigh skids to a halt, and they see Santa's bloody, unconscious form in the front, and in the back, their mutilated comrade.

"Quickly, get Santa inside!" commands one of the elves.

"But what about…" starts another elf.

"There is nothing we can do for him," the first elf interrupts. "We have to help Santa. Someone go and get

Missus Claus."

Most of the elves quickly grab their master and carry him inside while one of them runs off to find Santa's wife.

One month later, Christmas Eve

Santa Claus awakens with a start and sits bolt upright, sweating and out of breath. He reaches for his shoulder, fully healed now, which is why he can't understand why it is suddenly spasming and burning. Mrs. Claus, hearing her husband's anguished cry, hurries into the room. Her face is worn with worry.

"I wish you would listen to me about tonight," she says, her voice full of concern.

"I'm fine," Santa reassures her as he tries to ease the tension in his shoulder. "Besides... I can't let all those children down. They depend on me to brighten their Christmas mornings."

"I don't see why the elves can't take care of it just this once," Mrs. Claus counters. "Under the circumstances, I think it would be okay."

"There's no reason I can't deliver the toys myself. My wounds healed quickly, all that remains are a few scars."

Mrs. Claus, knowing there's no point in arguing, shakes her head disapprovingly as Santa gets out of bed and begins to don his traditional Christmas attire. Even though she knows the futility of it, she feels the need to try again. "What about the nightmares? You've had them every night since you were attacked, and they've only gotten much worse these last few days. Please reconsider."

Santa finishes dressing and walks to his wife. "I can't shirk my duties because of a few bad dreams. I'll be fine. I promise." He kisses her on the forehead, then moves toward the door. He pauses before taking his leave, and looks back at his worried wife. He flashes her an energetic smile meant to soothe her nerves, then leaves the room.

"Stubborn old fool," Mrs. Claus mumbles to herself as the door closes behind Santa.

The elves snap to attention as Santa enters the workshop.

"Today is the big day, boys. Let's get ready!" Santa declares as he goes to his desk and sits down. He takes out his list and checks it over, then checks it over again, making sure he knows exactly which children have been naughty and which have been nice. Elves scurry around the workshop putting the finishing touches on presents and placing them in Santa's seemingly bottomless sack. There's still so much work to be done and the hours fly.

Once their tasks have been completed, the elves load the magical sack onto Santa's sleigh. A few of the elves open the double doors leading to the outside and push the sleigh out to a clearing where the reindeer had already been lead. The animals are hitched to the sleigh and await their master. Santa comes outside and approaches his sleigh team with a bowl filled with grain that's been mixed with a little magic dust. The reindeer pep up at his approach. Santa feeds each reindeer some of the magical feed and their hooves begin to glow slightly. Santa boards the sleigh, tugs on the reins, and issues those words made famous by a well-known holiday poem.

"Now, Dasher! Now, Dancer! Now, Prancer and Vixen! On, Comet! On, Cupid! On, Donner and Blitzen!"

The reindeer take off, pulling the sleigh toward the first stop on his long journey. They fly at an incredible speed, faster than the fastest jet.

"Ho, Ho, Ho!" Santa bellows as the reindeer near the first of many cities they are to visit that night.

The sun has set and the moon has risen, and Santa

begins to feel odd. A wave of nausea washes over him. His head begins to pound and his muscles feel like they are on fire. The reindeer sense something is amiss, and their nervousness shows; their flight pattern becomes erratic as they fight the urge to abandon Santa and flee to safety. Santa hands begin to itch and he looks down at them. Slipping off his gloves, he discovers that white hair has sprouted and covers most of his exposed flesh. As he looks on, his fingers elongate and his fingernails begin to grow. Santa lets out an anguished scream as the pain of his transformation sets in. The cry spooks the reindeer; they try to flee, but they are harnessed to the sleigh, prisoners, and they have no choice but to guide the sleigh down, and the ride is anything but smooth. Wracked with pain, Santa is unable to secure himself, and he is thrown from his seat. Without a pilot to guide them, the frightened reindeer are free to flee, and they head back home to the North Pole.

As Santa hurtles towards the ground, he's able to summon up enough of his own elven magic to slow his descent. The pain is intense, and he feels his face stretching, taking on a more canine shape.

Santa plunges into the snow bank, and for a few tense moments it's questionable if he has survived the fall, but then the mound of snow starts to shift, showing signs of something moving beneath it. What emerges from the pile of snow no longer resembles Santa. The werewolf throws back its head and howls at the moon shining full and bright through the clouds.

A homeless man sitting in the alley near where Santa fell questions his sanity when he sees the werewolf dressed in a tattered red Santa suit standing atop the snow mound. He rubs his eyes and takes a second look, but his eyes have not betrayed him. Unfortunately for him, the monster has noticed him, too, and heads in his direction. Frozen in fear, the man is unable to move.

"Please. No. Please," the vagrant begs as the creature reaches him.

Unlike its human form, the werewolf has no concept of mercy or kindness and growls angrily at the man, who promptly pisses his pants.

The homeless man flinches when the creature swipes at him with its razor sharp claws, slicing open his stomach. The beast drools as his intestines spill out onto the street. The werewolf then lunges forward and clamps its powerful jaws onto the dying man's neck, shakes its head savagely, then tears out his throat. It's all happens so fast, the man doesn't have time to scream, and now, as life leaves his body, all he can do is gurgle helplessly. The werewolf howls triumphantly before starting to feast, but then something... a noise... a smell... draws its attention. If leaves the body behind and follows the scent of live prey out of the alley and onto the crowded city streets.

Having lost their master, the reindeer return to the North Pole. The senior elf is in the workshop, cleaning up from all the last-minute work. He hears the sleigh bells and knows that something is amiss, as the sleigh should not have returned for several more hours. As he makes his way outside, he sees Mrs. Claus hurrying to meet the sleigh, her face a mask of concern.

"I told him not to go," says Mrs. Claus.

"Nothing you could have said would have convinced him not to go," the elf says, falling into step beside her. "The children mean too much to him."

They reach the sleigh and see that Santa is not aboard.

"Oh, my God. Where is he? Why would they come back without him? Something terrible must have happened." The words flow from Mrs. Claus in a rush as she imagines the worst.

"We don't know that," the elf says in an attempt to soothe her, but he, too, fears the worst. He climbs aboard the sleigh. "But there's only one way to find out."

Mrs. Claus quickly climbs in next to the elf and takes the reins. "Take us to Santa," she says, snapping the reigns, signaling that the reindeers should take off.

The reindeer obey and launch into the sky, pulling the sleigh behind them. Without needing any further instruction, they head for the spot where Santa fell from the sleigh.

Hoping to comfort Mrs. Claus, the elf tries to reassure her. "I'm sure he's alright." There's a quaver to his voice, an indication of his own fears as to what they will find once they reach their destination, that he hopes she doesn't detect.

With the help of some elven magic, it's only a matter of minutes before Mrs. Claus and her companion arrive at the spot Santa landed. Nothing could have prepared them for the horror that greets them. Blood. So much blood.

Drawn by screams, Mrs. Claus, with the elf following at her heels, investigates, hoping to find Santa, but what she finds is chaos.

Mutilated bodies of men and women. People running through the streets screaming and crying. At the heart of it all is not the man she loves, but a massive beast wearing the tattered remnants of a Santa suit. Instead of filling everybody with the Christmas spirit, the wolfen Santa is striking fear into the hearts and minds of all who see him.

The police arrive on the scene and open fire on the werewolf, but their bullets prove ineffective against the creature. They only serve to anger the beast, and it turns its fury on the police officers, who scatter at its approach. The werewolf jumps atop one of the patrol cars, raises its head towards the sky, and howls.

Mrs. Claus and the elf retreat to the sleigh and guide the reindeer to the rooftops, where they can watch what unfolds in relative safety, unseen by the citizens. Standing on the edge of the roof, Mrs. Claus tries, but she cannot hold back tears as she looks down at what has become of her beloved. Next to her, the elf can offer no words to dampen the severity of the nightmare unfolding below.

"I knew something was wrong," Mrs. Claus says, "but I never expected this." "Neither did I," the elf says. "I thought something just spooked the reindeer while Santa was inside a house delivering presents."

While his loved ones look on from above, something catches the werewolf's attention. A young boy, having become separated from his parents in the panic, stands on the sidewalk. The boy stands glued to the spot, too terrified to move while everyone else scurries away like rats running from a cat. The beast jumps down from the police car and stalks towards the boy, who seems like easy prey.

Mrs. Claus can't believe what she is about to see. The elf knows that something must be done, and done quickly, or the boy's life will be lost.

"We have to do something!" he cries out.

Mrs. Claus does not answer or even acknowledge her comrade in any way. Knowing that time is of the essence, the elf runs to the sleigh and reaches into the magic sack. From the enchanted bag he pulls a revolver containing a single silver bullet, then runs back to the edge of the roof.

The werewolf reaches the boy, who has tears streaming down his face. The beast slowly raises a clawed hand and is about to swipe at the boy. The elf sees this moment as the point of no return and aims the gun at his master. Before the creature can bring down it paw and deliver its gift of death to the boy, the beast pauses, and a strange look comes over its face. It's almost as if some part of Santa is still inside and does not want to harm the child. The battle of wills can be seen in the creature's eyes.

The elf also pauses, hoping that this display of mercy is a sign that Santa is not beyond saving. The moment is short lived, however, as the beast reasserts its will and starts to bring its claw down. Mrs. Claus sees the child's life about to be taken and knows that Santa would rather die than cause harm to a child. She grabs the gun from the elf and fires at her husband. The bullet, as if guided by magic, finds its mark and strikes the heart of the beast.

Without a word, Mrs. Claus drops the gun, turns, and walks back to the sleigh. The elf silently follows her. The reindeer, as if sensing what has transpired, need no command, and they launch themselves skyward.

The police approach the fallen Santa with trepidation, unsure if the beast is truly dead. They watch as it takes its last breath and slowly transforms back into rotund little man with a white beard and hair.

"What do we put in the report?" asks a young officer, not believing what he is seeing.

Unable to take his eyes from the body, the senior officer says, "We say that a department store Santa got hopped up on PCP, went nuts, and started attacking people."

"But..." begins the younger officer.

"But nothing. That's going to be my version of the story, and unless you want to be bounced off the force for being a nut job, I suggest it be yours, too."

Reports of the incident are in every major newspaper on

Christmas morning, though no reputable reporter dared to print the truth: that a werewolf went on a rampage through the city streets on Christmas Eve. Instead, they all stick with the official story as issued by the police department, although none of them even considered the possibility that the beast was, indeed, the real Santa Claus. Not even when they woke up Christmas morning to find nothing from Santa beneath their trees.

RILEY AND THE BIG MAN
BC Jackson

It was exactly one week until Christmas, and there was only one thing Riley Manford knew for sure: It was going to be the worst Christmas ever.

"Riley!" His mother shouted from the end of the toy aisle. "Let's go now or..."

The rest was lost around the corner as his mother walked toward the front of the store. Riley put down the stuffed lion he had been looking at. As much as he liked it, he would never ask Santa Claus for one because it was a baby toy. It was a toy his little brother, who was four, would like, and one that his older brother, who was eleven, would make fun of endlessly were Riley to get it. He was eight, after all, and way too old for stuffed animals. He still liked it, though.

Reed, his older brother, was only one of the reasons this was going to be the worst Christmas ever. He had become a major d-bag since turning eleven in August, and Riley was the main target of his douche-baggery. He called him a baby all the time and liked to give red bellies and Indian burns until his little brother gave in. Giving in meant saying his older brother was the best at everything and he, Riley, was a little baby-pussy. He dreamed of the day when he would be as big as Reed and could pay him back. He also made himself a promise each time he gave in that he would never treat his little brother Evan the same way. It was a promise he could feel grow stronger each time.

The main reason this was going to be the worst Christmas ever was that their father had been laid-off from his job in the middle of November. He wasn't really sure what his father did when he left for work, only that he referred to his job as "Big Yellow" on good days, and as "Big Pisser" on bad ones. He had stopped talking about his job altogether by December and spent his days just staring at the television. Mom had yelled at him just about every night for a few weeks. They argued about more stuff that Riley really didn't understand. He had gathered that his father's unployment wasn't enough to pay the bills and that his father wasn't going anywhere else until them bastards called him back. Riley had hoped the call would come soon so things could go back to normal, but then his mom left.

She didn't leave the family; she just left before dinner one night. She put the food on the table, but instead of sitting down next to their father, she had put on her coat, said goodbye to her three boys, and walked out the door. Evan had started crying, and Riley had felt like crying, too, but wouldn't dare in front of Reed, who he could feel watching him. Their father had grabbed Evan by the shoulders and told him, quietly but firmly, to stop crying. He said she would be back later, after they were all asleep, and that she would be there in the morning. Then he had taken his plate of food to the living room and ate while he watched Sports Center.

She'd left them alone every night since.

This night at the mall, one week before Christmas, was the first night she had eaten dinner with them in two weeks. Afterward they had left while their father cleared the table of dinner, which had been nothing more than baked chicken and green beans. A good meal, Riley knew, better than a lot of people these days, but a far cry from the kind of dinners his mother used to cook.

Riley had noticed his parents weren't talking that much anymore. Not since mom began leaving at night. When they did speak to each other, they kept their voices low and the conversation short. He had learned from one of these that his mom was leaving at night to go work at Andy's Diner as what she called a server and his father called a waitress. He always spat the word out like it tasted bad just saying it. It was clear that he wasn't happy she was leaving at night. It was also clear that she wasn't happy leaving at night. The whole thing confused the hell out of Riley, and when he asked Reed what was going on, all he got for an answer was a sore arm and another lesson in humility.

He had also noticed that his mother had started talking to herself quite a bit. She would mutter under her breath while making dinner and breakfast, while cleaning the house, and even while driving to the mall. The only time she didn't mutter to herself, it seemed, was when she was around father. That silence made him wish she would mutter, though.

"Riley!"

His mother sounded like she was already at the front of the store, so he ran down the aisle. Part of his mind was still fantasizing about the stuffed lion when he reached the tall cage of giant bouncy balls at the end, otherwise he would have noticed the sneakered foot that stuck out at the last second. He went sprawling on the floor, pain flaring in his knees and elbows before exploding in his face. He hit the concrete floor hard with his nose and lips, instantly tasting blood. Tears welled up in his eyes, and just as he was about to start crying, he heard Reed laughing.

"Walk much, pussy?" Reed asked, still laughing.

Riley got to his feet as fast as his aching knees would allow. Everything was blurry with tears and rage as he balled up his fists and charged at his older brother. He knew there was nothing he could do to hurt his brother, who was nearly twice his size, but fury like his, which had been building for months, never listens to reason. He just wanted one good punch.

He threw it wildly toward his brother's face with the complete lack of grace that one would expect from a boy his size and age. Still, the astonished look on Reed's face made him think it was going to do some damage. He felt sure he had caught him off guard and was about to give him a bloody lip to match his own. That little bit of confidence made him swing a little bit harder and a little bit faster. So when his older brother easily stepped out of harm's way, that extra momentum sent Riley spinning back down to the concrete.

Before he could get up again, Reed was already running toward the front of the store shouting, "Mom! Riley tried to punch me! He tripped all on his own and then tried to punch me in the fa—"

"Get over here, both of you," mother shouted back. "Quit fooling around or we're going to miss Santa."

Riley was on his feet and running. Realizing that his

mother was done shopping and it was time to go see Santa, he barely noticed the pain in his split lip, his nose, his knees, or his elbows. He had been waiting to sit on the Big Man's lap since Thanksgiving, and he wasn't going to miss his one chance because of his jerk brother.

He wiped the blood from his chin and lip on his sleeve before his mother could see it. If she did, she would demand an explanation as to why her son was bleeding, and even though it meant Reed might get in trouble, it also meant they might miss Santa. Mother was very protective ever since she started muttering to herself, but all he wanted to do now was get to Santa's lap before it was too late.

As they rushed toward the little make-shift room in the mall court, Riley felt a tug at his sleeve. Evan was staring up at him with his big brown eyes showing worry. "You've got red on you," he said, pointing at Riley's bloody sleeve.

"Don't worry about it, twerp," he shot back, smiling. There was none of the taunting in his name calling that Reed had, only affection. "Don't say anything or we might miss Santa."

Evan smiled back at him and grabbed his hand. He skipped next to Riley as they hurried to keep up with Mother and Reed. Skipping was a baby thing to do, but Riley never would have dreamed of saying anything to his little brother about it. Even when Evan was eight and he was twelve, he told himself, if his little brother wanted to skip, then by God he could skip.

Santa's room, which had been repurposed from part of the Halloween Haunted House, was a big black box with a door on each side. Even with the tinsel and the Christmas trees and all the sparkling lights covering the box, it still looked a little scary to Riley, who could remember the bats and the spiders and the skeletons that had hung from the same hooks two months before. It wasn't scary enough to keep him from going in to see Santa, though, and by the time they reached the line going in, he felt nothing but excitement. He was minutes away from finally seeing the Big Man.

"Okay, listen up, boys," mother knelt down in front of them. "Reed saw Santa with his friends a few weeks ago, so he's not going in tonight. I'm going to pay for the pictures and I'll meet you two on the other side, okay?"

Evan's eyes grew wide when he realized he was going in alone, and Riley felt his grip tighten in his hand. "Don't worry, twerp. It's just Santa."

"Yeah," mother said, hugging him. "He's just a jolly, old, fat guy, remember?"

Evan nodded, but wasn't convinced. He still looked scared.

"How about I go in first, Evan?" Riley said. "If it's scary or there's anything weird in there, I'll come running back out the 'in' door and you won't have to go."

"But I wanna go," Evan whined. "Why can't mommy go with me?"

"I'll go ask, sweetie," mother said, and hustled away.

Riley looked down at his little brother and smiled. He meant it, that smile, but Evan saw something else in it. He pulled his hand from Riley's and squinted up at him. "I'm not a baby!"

"I know, little brother," Riley said, but Evan had already crossed his arms and put on his pouty face. There was no point in trying to talk to him now.

Mother didn't come back to them until they had reached the front of the line. Riley was next to go in when she stomped over with a smile on her face. It was a smile she only put on after she had fought a battle and won.

"Well… we got that settled!" she said, stepping in line behind Evan. "I'm going in with you, Ev, and not a person

236

here is going to have a problem with it!"

Evan smiled up at his savior and held her hand like he had held Riley's. A surge of jealousy hit Riley out of the blue. He wasn't sure if he was jealous of his brother because mother would be going in with him or of mother because of the way Evan was looking at her. Either way, he turned and faced the door before mother could see it on his face. She was so good at seeing what he felt.

Moments later it was his turn to go in. A grown woman dressed up as an elf opened the plywood door and grabbed his hand. He looked back at his mother and Evan, who was bouncing up and down with excitement, as he allowed himself to be pulled into the big black box. His mother was looking the other way, muttering.

Once she closed the door, the woman, who Riley was certain was not a real elf, pulled back a black curtain to reveal a room that was not at all what he was expecting. Usually Santa's room was brightly lit and decorated like the outside of the room, with fake snow, Christmas trees, and all the rest. This room looked more like something that would be in the haunted house. Instead of fake snow, there was fog rolling along the floor about knee high. The usual bright lights and Christmas decorations had been replaced by red and green strobe lights mounted in little balls that scattered the Christmas colors randomly around the dark room. Riley's first thought was that he wished his mother was with him, and if the elf-woman hadn't been pulling him deeper into the dark room, he would have turned around and asked her to come in.

He dropped that idea as soon as he saw the Big Man.

The one thing that hadn't changed inside the room was the Big Man and his chair. He was sitting a little to the back of center in the room, and he looked almost exactly as Riley remembered from the year before. His hat was a little crooked, he wore wire rimmed glasses above his big, bushy beard, and his red suit was perfectly accented with fluffy white trim and white gloves. Just beneath the rolling fog he could see the tops of his shiny black boots as well. The plush red velvet chair with gilded trim and fancy scroll work sat beneath him.

Halfway across the room he no longer needed to be pulled. He was running. "Santa!" he shouted as he jumped onto his lap.

"Oh ho ho," Santa grunted back, making Riley cringe because he knew he had gained some weight during the year and was heavier than Santa would have been expected. "Getting big, aren't you, Riley?"

The breath caught in his chest. Santa remembered his name! It was the first time he could remember not having to tell Santa his name. The absolute joy that little thing brought to him made up for the strange lights, the fog, the slightly sour smell on Santa's breath, and almost everything else that had happened leading up to that moment. It was a sign that the magic was real. The nagging thought that had been in the back of his mind, the one that said all of this stuff was baby stuff, baby-pussy stuff, was silent. There was no arguing now because Santa had remembered his name.

The thought never occurred to him, and never would after what was about to take place on the Big Man's lap, that his mother could have given Santa or the elf-woman his name before he came in. It was the most logical explanation, but the joy he felt, like the rage before, never listens to logic. He would know before he left the foggy room that magic—at least some kind of magic—was real, even if by then he wished it weren't.

"So tell me, little boy," Santa leaned in, "what is it that you want for Christmas?"

This was the moment. He stared into Santa's face, watching the colors of Christmas flicker in his glasses and admiring his full, thick beard, and tried to form the words perfectly in his mind so that there would be no mistaking what he wanted, no disappointment on Christmas morning. The only thing that could have made the moment perfect was if the Big Man had used his name again.

When the words felt right, he spewed them out in a rush of enthusiasm. "I want a boys' nineteen inch SFX Super Racer Dirt Track bicycle with black and red paint and skull decals on the handlebars and seat."

With it all out, said perfectly and precisely, he leaned back from Santa and smiled. He wondered if any of the other kids who had sat on his lap had been able to tell him so accurately, so down to the detail, what they wanted for Christmas. He felt proud and a little grown up, not a baby-pussy at all, that he had been able say it exactly right even though he was so excited. But Santa wasn't smiling. In fact, he was frowning.

Riley's smile faded and his pride shriveled up as Santa just stared back at him, stroking his beard like he did in the cartoons, and only made one sound. "Hmmm."

"What?" Riley asked, forgetting for a moment who he was talking to. "Did I get it wrong?" He thought back and felt confident he hadn't. "Is there something wrong, Santa?"

"No, no, no," Santa said, managing a smile. It wasn't real though. It was a fake adult smile like his mother sometimes put on. "I just thought maybe..."

Santa waved the words away before finishing, but Riley wasn't going to let that happen. "What? You thought what?"

"Well," Santa shifted in his seat before leaning forward again. "I just thought that maybe you'd want something a little different. Something bigger. Like your father to get his job back, or your mother to not have to work nights anymore. Something like that."

As the words sunk in, Riley slumped on Santa's lap. The Big Man was right. He felt completely like a little kid again, a little baby-pussy. Here he had the chance to ask Santa Claus for anything in the world, and he had selfishly asked for a bicycle when he could have asked for either of those things and made life better for his whole family. He felt stupid and childish and couldn't look Santa in the eye.

"Now, now," Santa brought Riley's chin up with a gloved hand. It was warm. "Don't feel too bad, Riley. Very few children ever ask for such big things. And besides, that bicycle will make your life better. You'll be able to leave when you want and go farther than you've ever gone alone. You could get in all kinds of trouble with a bike like that."

Riley already felt like he was in all kinds of trouble.

"You could outrun Reed, as well. He would never be able to give you another red belly or Indian burn as long as your bike was near, right?" Riley nodded. "And Reed is a bad little boy. That's the real reason he's not in here. He knows he is on the Naughty List and," Santa leaned closer and whispered, "I'll tell you a secret. He will always be on the naughty list."

Santa laughed and pressed the tip of Riley's nose with his warm, gloved finger. Riley couldn't help but smile back.

"Now that we know what you want," Santa leaned back again, "let's talk about what I want."

Riley smiled because he didn't know what else to do. "What—What you want?"

"Oh yes, yes," he said. "Times are tough, as you well know, and I can no longer hand out toys, especially fine ones like SFX Dirt Track bicycles, without something in return."

Riley's smile faded. This wasn't right, he could feel it.

He was suddenly aware once more of the strange fog rolling on the floor, the red and green strobe lights, and the elf-woman standing by the exit. She smiled at him, and there was nothing humorous in it. It was a "gotcha" smile that Reed often wore. He looked back at Santa, the flickering lights in the glasses blazing more red than green, and tried to speak, but couldn't.

"Well, come on," Santa finally said. His voice was stern even though he smiled. "You knew exactly what you wanted from me, down the very last detail. I was surprised at the skulls, but I guess boys will be boys. Now what will you give up for that bicycle?"

The skulls. Riley didn't really like them, but he wanted them because of Reed. They looked and felt to him like the exact opposite of a baby-pussy, and he thought that maybe Reed would back off if he had them on his bike. It sounded stupid when he thought about it like that. It sounded childish.

"I have an idea," Santa said. He motioned for the elf-woman to come over. As she walked through the strobe lights, it looked like her clothes kept changing. In one light she was half-naked, and in the next, fully clothed. "I don't like taking things, bartering for Christmas gifts. It doesn't seem right. So let's flip a coin."

The elf-woman, fully dressed once again, handed Santa something, and then stayed by his side, her hand draped over his shoulder. Her nails were long and painted red with gold stars. They looked sharp.

"This side is tails." Riley looked at the silver coin resting in Santa's white glove. On the side facing up was a picture of Santa's sleigh with all the reindeer out front. He flipped the coin over and Riley jumped back. There on the opposite side was a smiling skull with a Santa Claus hat sitting crooked on its head and menacing red eyes. Santa laughed. "I thought you liked skulls, my boy! That's heads!"

Riley hadn't said a word since things had taken their strange turn, and he couldn't find any now. It all seemed like a dream, like something that his father would watch on the late night scary shows sometimes. Nothing felt right anymore. He had been looking forward to this moment since Thanksgiving. Longer, actually. He had been looking forward to this since he had jumped down off Santa's lap more than a year ago. He felt tears welling up in his eyes, but he fought them back. Last year's Santa would have consoled him if he had started crying, but this Santa was different. He knew that if he started crying this Santa would call him a baby-pussy and maybe even give him an Indian burn.

"Are you ready to play?" Santa asked. The reflection dancing in his glasses was all red now. Riley still couldn't find his voice. "I'll take that as a yes."

The elf-woman laughed and it reminded Riley of the sound cats make when they play or fight. When he looked at her, she was half naked again.

"You call it in the air, Riley. If you win, you'll get your bicycle, skulls and all, and won't owe me a thing. If you lose," he leaned in closer, "you must give me something."

"What?" The word came from nowhere and shot out of his throat. Once out, he wasn't even sure if he had said it.

"Good question, my boy," Santa said, the elf-woman laughed again. "Well, let's see. I don't need money at the North Pole. I don't any of the baby stuff you have in your room. What, what, what could you have?" He snapped his fingers and smiled. "I got it!"

He leaned in close to Riley's face, closer than he had before. The lenses of his glasses were all red now, pulsing with the lights, and his breath was more acrid with the smell of sour milk. His smile was wide and his jagged teeth, which Riley hadn't noticed before, were all shades of brown and yellow.

"I need help, Riley," he said. "I need more elves to do my bidding. You are too young and much too good to do my kind of work. You don't even like skulls. Your father would do, though. You want to give him to me for your bicycle?"

Riley shook his head. As bad as things had been, he loved his father. He took him fishing and camping and swimming and all sorts of fun stuff. When things were good they had a good time, and he knew things would be good again soon.

"Your mother—" Riley was shaking his head before he could finish the word. "Of course not! She's not my type anyway."

Santa looked down and started rubbing his beard again, just like in the cartoons. He was only pretending to think hard, even Riley could see that. The Big Man knew what he wanted and Riley was pretty sure of it, too. The only question was if any of this was real. What if it was all a joke or some big prank? What if there was no magic? What if Reed was behind it all? It was something he would do, more involved than he usually did, but it was cruel enough to have come from his d-bag mind. If that were the case...

"Reed!" Santa shouted, smiling wide and pointing a finger in the air. "Give me your older brother if I win and we'll call it even. You don't really like him anyway, do you? And he's a naughty boy who is going to grow up into a naughty man. A very naughty man. You can stop that and get rid of one of the worst parts of this Christmas all at once. What do you say?"

If that were the case, then none of this would matter. If it was real, though, then the fact that Riley would even consider giving his brother to a deranged Santa Claus for a bicycle said more about how Reed treated him than about Riley himself. Right? It would be his fault, not Riley's. And it's not like he was going to be killed or anything; he was just going to go work for Santa until things got better. Why else would the Big Man need help?

And then there was the chance that he would win the toss and get the bike for free, like it should be.

"Okay," Riley said.

"What's that?" Santa asked, cupping a hand to his ear.

"I said 'okay.'"

"Call it in the air!"

Santa wasted no time once Riley had agreed, and he sent the coin flipping through the air. He and the elf-woman laughed as the red and green lights were deflected by the bright silver coin as it spun impossibly fast, creating a humming noise that grew louder by the second.

"Call it, boy!" Santa shouted.

"Heads!" He shouted over the wobbly hum of the spinning coin. He called heads because that was all he could see as the coin flipped, and as soon as the word was out of his mouth, the skull's red eyes flared and the coin dropped like a lead weight into the fog. The humming stopped.

All three of them looked down where the coin had disappeared in the rolling fog. Santa reached out a hand and waved it slowly from side to side. Though his hand was at least a foot above the fog, it parted to reveal the silver coin on the floor beneath.

It was tails.

The elf-woman picked up the coin and grabbed Riley by the arm. He was still looking at the spot on the floor where the coin had landed when she pulled him off of Santa's lap and headed for the exit.

"Wait!" Santa shouted. "One more thing."

The elf-woman stopped as Santa stepped down off of his throne. He pulled the white glove from his right hand. The hand beneath was old and brown, but not like any skin-tone brown Riley had ever seen. It looked more like something rotten and halfway returned to dirt. The tip of each finger ended in a yellow, pointed nail.

"A reminder of our deal." He pushed Riley's sleeve up to the crook of his elbow, and then pressed one of his yellow nails down into the flesh. There was a brief stinging pain followed by a burning sensation, then nothing. He took his hand away and there was a black triangle burned into Riley's skin. "A pleasure doing business with you, Riley."

"You won't hurt him, right?" he asked, desperation in his voice. "You'll take care of him at the North Pole and he'll be okay, right?"

Riley knew the answer before the Big Man, who was most certainly not Santa Claus, spoke.

"You silly little baby-pussy," Santa laughed. "I don't want him at the North Pole! But, if it makes you feel better, his death will not be too terribly painful, okay?"

The elf-woman pulled Riley to the exit and shoved him out into the light of the mall. There were crowds of people still moving from store to store as gates were pulled half-closed and a woman on the loud speakers reminded everyone that the mall closed in five minutes. All of the hustle and bustle around him was just background noise to the whirling thoughts in his head. He stared at the mark on his arm and tried to comprehend all that had happened. Had it been real? Yes, he had the mark to prove it. Did he give up his brother for a bicycle? Yes, he did. When would it all happen? When would his brother die? Did it matter when?

He had wandered all the way to the pretzel stand at the

other end of the mall before his mother finally found him. He didn't notice her until she was down on her knees screaming in his face. When he finally snapped out of it, all he could do was throw his arms around her and hug her. He still couldn't cry.

Everything inside the little Santa room had been different for Evan. He talked the whole way home about the awesome Christmas trees behind Santa's chair and all the wrapped boxes spread out on the floor. He would nudge Riley, sometimes hitting the mark on his arm, but it didn't hurt, and Riley would just nod along as if he had seen the same things. He tried to imagine that he had seen what his little brother saw inside the little black room, to forget the sour-breathed Santa and the fog and the red glasses, but he never could convince himself.

On Christmas morning Riley got his bicycle. In fact, all the kids got what they wanted most for Christmas. Including an announcement by father that Big Yellow had called him back and that mother would no longer be working nights. Mother called it a Christmas miracle. Riley hoped it was, too. He hoped that his parents had bought him the bike and that the deal he made had been unnecessary. He held onto that hope until he saw the smiling skull with the crooked Santa hat on the front fork of his new bicycle.

New Year's came and went without incident. Slowly, things went back to normal. School started up again and father went back to work. Mother was home every night like before and they did more family stuff together. As summer approached, they even began planning a week-long camping trip. Riley had started to hope that the sour-breathed Santa was never going to collect on his debt, though he never believed it. Reed still picked on him, worse than before, but if something happened to him, then things would not be normal ever again.

The teasing made it a little easier when Reed finally died. He had just shoved Riley off his bike, the one with the Santa skull on the front, and stole it. As he rode toward the street, Riley saw the eyes of the skull flare red just like the coin had done in the little Santa room. Less than a second later, Reed jumped the curb right in front of a passing truck that was going a little too fast for a residential street.

He lived for five agonizing minutes with a broken neck. Nothing was ever the same again.

❄RNAMENTS
Christopher Miron

"**m**an, this store has all sorts of crap," Janice whispered to Mary Beth. "Look at this." She pointed to a little black and white painted Santa ornament that was badly chipped. "No one would buy this shit. For one thing, it's too expensive, and for another, it looks like junk from another century." Her stomach gave an embarrassing gurgle and she looked about, red faced, to make sure nobody else had noticed. "God! I hate shopping so late in the evening. Wanna go eat?"

Mary Beth rolled her eyes. She hated shopping with Janice—all her roommate ever did was complain—but what else could she do? If it had been up to her, she would've come to The Christmas Village by herself, especially given how the other woman felt about the holiday, but Janice didn't have a car, and leaving her stranded at the apartment while she was out enjoying herself would have left her feeling guilty. So now she had a clean conscience, but miserable company. Mary Beth, on the other hand, loved Christmas and everything about the season. Christmas shopping for her was like an addiction; it gave her a high like you wouldn't believe, so naturally when she found out about the new antique store at the village this year, she knew exactly where to go for her next fix.

The "grand opening" of The Christmas Village each year, she found out, was the biggest event in Mt. Morris. The only holiday that came close in the eyes of the public was Halloween, and that was only because it meant that the store would soon be opening. It brought in tourists from all over, and that meant thousands of dollars poured back into the community. It started out as a small, one-man shop back in the 1950s, and over the years it gradually expanded until it encompassed a small warehouse. The interior of the shop was decorated to look like individual store fronts, and the aisles in between were covered with fake cobblestones. Holiday lights decorated the walkways and Christmas carols were filtered in through concealed speakers, lending a sense of magic to the enclosed space. It was literally like walking the streets of a small village. To add to the festive atmosphere, snow machines sent a flurry of small, man-made flakes into the air.

"This place truly is a winter wonderland," Mary Beth said to no one in particular as she took in the holiday charm. The white tree in the window caught her eye. Why, she didn't know, as there was nothing special about it; in fact, it was unusually drab, it's ghostly branches adorned with odd-shaped brown decorations, and maybe that was what snagged her attention. While all of the other trees were decked out in their holiday finest of twinkling lights and red and green ornaments, this one stood out in its blandness. Before she was even conscious of her actions, she was moving toward the tree.

As she drew closer, she saw that the limbs were decorated with some of the oddest ornaments she had ever seen. Elves. Every single ornament. Elves of various of shapes and sizes in an assortment of positions. She was fascinated with them. They were not the elves typically associated with Santa and Christmas; there were no colorful clothes or friendly smiles. No mischievous sparkle in their painted eyes. Instead, these elves had been painted in various shades of brown, but they bore no resemblance to the Keebler elves either, those of the ever-present cookie. There was nothing friendly what-soever about these little creatures, and Mary Beth thought for a moment that they might be Halloween leftovers because, if she was completely honest with herself, they were rather repulsive looking, with their sinister grins and coal-black eyes.

"See what I mean," Janice said, coming up behind her and pointing to one of the ornaments. She snapped her gum. "Just pieces of fucking handmade shit."

Ignoring her, Mary Beth reached out and took one between her fingers. The ornament was heavier than she expected it would be given its size. She turned it over, looking for a price. Not finding one, she gently released the ornament and reached for another, but there was no price sticker on that one either. She couldn't believe she was actually considering buying one of the ornaments; they were so ugly, so un-Christmassy that she couldn't picture it on the tree in their living room, but she continued to search for a price. Not that money was really an issue, not any more at least, but she didn't want to be frivolous either. Still, one indulgence…

She stepped back from the tree, now looking for a sign nearby that would tell her how much, but there was nothing.

Maybe they weren't for sale. Maybe they were only for decoration. She didn't know why, but that thought saddened her. Reluctantly, she continued to back away from the tree, fully intending to continue browsing the village, yet she found she could not turn away. She was held by the stare of those tiny black eyes.

"C'mon, Mary Beth, I'm hungry."

The sound of her roommate's voice broke the spell and at last she was able to put her back to the tree. "Just give me a few more minutes. I need to find a new ornament for the tree."

"Like you don't have enough already."

"It's tradition. I buy a new one every year."

As Mary Beth continued to look through the assortment of ornaments in the store, her gaze kept drifting back to that white tree and its ugly inhabitants. After fifteen minutes and a constant barrage of complaints from Janice, Mary Beth had decided she couldn't take any more and headed for the door. She was brought up short when a deep, raspy voice echoed in her head. "Buy one."

Despite Janice's protests, Mary Beth made her way back to the tree and snatched one of the elf ornaments from the prickly white branches. She started for the register, but was again brought up short by the same raspy voice whispering seductively in her ear. "Why not buy two? He needs a friend."

❉ ❉ ❉

"You really aren't going to put those fucking things on our tree, are you?" Janice whined as they pulled up to the front of their apartment complex.

"Why, not?" Mary Beth replied. "I think they're great.

251

Besides, they're antiques. And a hell of a lot cheaper than I thought they would be for the set."

"That's because that old man running the place said he hasn't sold any of them and just wanted to get rid of them," Janice snapped back. "If you ask me, he probably didn't want them around either. I mean, getting them from an estate sale, that's just creepy. Buying dead people's crap." She gave an exaggerated shudder as she eyed the bag on the seat between them. "Nasty looking things, they are."

"You don't even like Christmas," Mary Beth said defensively, "so why would you care what I put on the tree?"

Janice had the car door open and one foot on the street. She sighed dismissively and looked at Mary Beth. "You're right. I do hate Christmas. It's so fucking depressing, so do what you want." She struggled to extract herself from the seatbelt and got out of the car. "As for me, I am going in and getting shit faced." She slammed the door and made for the steps leading up to the front door of their unit.

Mary Beth watched her roommate climb the stairs and pause at the top to paw through her purse in search of the keys. She pulled something from the bag, and it was only after she tucked it beneath her chin so she could continue fumbling for her keys that Mary Beth saw what it was. A flask, which, she had to admit, was a bit of a surprise, and it shouldn't have been. She knew Janice drank—in fact, she couldn't recall a time when her roommate was completely sober—but she never thought Janice would risk drinking on the job. She sat there behind the wheel and could only shake her head. "Keep it up," she said to Janice, even though she knew her roommate couldn't hear her. "You'll get what's coming to you." Tucking some stray hair behind her ear, she caught sight of her reflection in the rearview mirror and was taken aback by what she saw. The spritely sparkle that everybody commented on had faded from her eyes to be replaced by a darkness that brought with it unpleasant memories. She quickly averted her gaze so she wouldn't be reminded of what they had done and turned her attention back to Janice just in time to see the other woman stumble into the darkness. Seconds later, the lights came on, filling their dark apartment with light and life. From where she sat, she could see the outline of the Christmas tree standing through the curtain-covered living room window. She smiled as her hand absently clutched at the bag on the seat.

Naughty.

"What the—?"

The word was a haunting whisper in her ear, and she shivered. It was the same voice she had heard earlier, the one that had convinced her to buy the ornaments.

Naughty.

She glanced around on the off chance that somebody might have followed them from The Christmas Village, but there was nobody on the street.

Shaking it off, she got out of the car, then reached into the back seat to grab her purse and the shopping bags before closing and locking the door and following her roommate inside.

Mary Beth made her way to the living room and dumped her purchases on the couch before crossing to a light switch on the far wall and giving it a flip. The Christmas tree came to life in an assortment of colored lights that reflected off the ornaments and garland adorning its branches and off the gold-painted tops of the popcorn tins beneath the tree. She shrugged out of her coat and tossed it among the bags, then turned her attention to the radio. She turned it on and the smooth sounds of Bing Crosby's *White Christmas* filtered through the speakers. It brought a smile to her face, but it was short lived when she heard a noise in the kitchen, followed shortly by the slamming of a door.

"Janice? Are you okay?" Mary Beth wandered out into the hall and stared down its dark length.

The apartment was large by today's standards: two bedrooms, a bathroom, the living room, and a small eat-in kitchen. The latter was dark, and a soft light flowed from beneath the door at the end of the hall. Janice had retired to her private sanctuary.

Probably already downed a fifth, Mary Beth thought bitterly as she went into the kitchen to get a Coke from the fridge.

Admiring the holiday design on the can, she returned to the living room and dropped down on the sofa. Once settled, she opened the can and took two long swallows, wincing as the carbonation burned the back of her dry throat. Settling back against the cushions, she admired the tree. The longer she stared at it, the more something began to bother her. Something was off, but what? It took a few moments, but then she realized what it was: there was a hole in the decorations. "Well, I can fix that now," she said, then turned to search through the pile of shopping bags, looking for the one from The Christmas Village. Where was it? She knew she brought it in with her... Or was it still in the car? When she finally found it—it had slipped between the cushions— she reached in...

"Ouch, damn it!"

...and jerked her hand back. Blood was oozing from a yet to be seen wound on her pinky finger. "What the... There must be something sharp on one of them I didn't notice." Throwing the bag aside, she got up and hurried to the bathroom so she could clean and bandage the wound.

Once she cleaned her finger, she was able to examine her

injury more closely. If she didn't know any better, it looked as though something had tried to take a bite from her finger. The wound consisted of two semicircles with evenly spaced pin pricks around the edges. "What could have done that?" There was nothing in the bag except the ornaments, and there were no sharp edges or points that could create the kind of wound she was looking at, so what could it have been? Thankfully it had already stopped bleeding; there was no need for a trip to the emergency room. She didn't even think it needed a bandage, but she wrapped a band aid around it just to be on the safe side. Then she headed back into the living room; she wanted to look in the bag for the source of the injury, but she stopped dead in her tracks when she saw it was missing from the sofa.

She glanced around the room, wondering where it could have disappeared to, when she spied it on the floor underneath the tree. "How did you get over there?"

Walking towards the tree, Mary Beth paused midstride when she noticed the decorations she had placed on the tree had been rearranged. A chill coursed up her spine and she shivered. She studied the tree from the bottom to the top, and when her gaze reached the upper branches, she couldn't believe what she was seeing. Near the top of the tree, almost at eye level, were the two elf ornaments sitting on the branches. In the twinkling light, it appeared as though the painted-on smiles had vanished and somebody had painted frowns in their place. And there was something about their heads, but she couldn't gather her thoughts enough to figure out what it was. She was too unnerved by their beady, black eyes… and the way they seemed to stare at her.

"No way," she stammered. "That's not possible. I'm not crazy. I know I didn't hang those there." Her thoughts strayed to Janice, but her roommate was probably passed out on her bed in an alcohol-induced coma; there was no way she could have put them on the tree. "What the hell is going on?" She looked down at the bag, but it was gone. When she looked back up at the tree, she took a staggering step backward. It was back to normal. All the decorations were back where she had placed them several day ago, and the elves... They were nowhere to be seen.

Turning away from the tree, she started for the sofa, but stumbled to a halt when she saw the bag exactly where she had tossed it before running to the bathroom.

"You're losing it, girl," she told herself, her voice shaky. She ran her fingers through her hair and turned to study the festive scene before her, but she no longer found comfort in the holiday decorations. She took in the tree, the lights, the ornaments, the tins beneath the tree, and suddenly she realized what was ruining the holiday for her.

Guilt. That's all it was. Plain and simple. But she had nothing to feel guilty about. All she and Janice had done was right the wrongs that had been imposed on them. There was nothing wrong with that, was there?

"Just go to bed," she told herself. "You're just tired. Stressed. You'll feel better after a good night's sleep."

❄ ❄ ❄

Naughty.

That one word echoed in her mind, growing louder with each repetition, until it eventually jolted her from a fitful sleep. Wiping the blur of sleep from her eyes, she looked to her bedside table. She could barely make out the red lights coming from her alarm clock. Her vision slowly came into focus and she saw it was 2:13 in the morning.

Adjusting herself in her bed, she sat up, wondering what

had awoken her. Was Janice stumbling drunkenly around the apartment? She held her breath, listening, and thought she could hear music coming from the living room. She got out of bed, moved to the door, and pressed her ear against the wooden panel. It was definitely music, and it was coming from the living room. Had she forgotten to turn off the radio before heading to bed?

She opened the door a crack and was able to make out the words, and a song she had once thought fun suddenly took on menacing tones.

> *You better watch out,*
> *You better not cry,*
> *You better not pout,*
> *I'm telling you why*

It seemed, though, that the DJ had fallen asleep because the song was stuck and kept repeating the same four lines.

Peering out through the space between the door and the frame, she could see the colorful lights flashing in the living room. The reds, greens, blues, and yellows danced on the wall like the reflections of a mirror ball at a disco. She opened the door a little wider and stuck her head into the hall. "Janice?" But she knew her roommate wouldn't be answering; once Janice passed out, she was out, and a cannon could go off beside her bed and she still wouldn't stir. But if it wasn't Janice, then who, because she knew she had turned off the tree lights before retiring for the night.

She opened the door wider and stepped into the hall, moving as quietly as she could.

The song was down to one line being repeated now, over and over again: *You better watch out, you better watch out.*

Mary Beth made her way down the hallway one

painfully slow step at a time, back pressed against the wall. She didn't stop until she was able to see the tree.

The decorations were all messed up again, and the lights were flickering, blinking off and on, faster and faster, until each bulb became like a tiny strobe light. Under the barrage of flashing light, she couldn't get her eyes to focus. She strained her ears, tried to move past the repeated warning: *You better watch out, you better watch out,...*

Scared, but curious, Mary Beth inched forward until she was standing in the doorway to the living room. It was only then that she saw that the top branches of the tree were bare, the needles gone. The lower branches rustled as though something small was moving from branch to branch. Mary Beth let loose a startled shriek and raced back down the hallway to the kitchen.

Opening the drawer, she pulled out a small paring knife. Her heart was thudding in her chest and her breathing was rapid and shallow. There was another rustle from the living room, followed by a glass ornament falling from the tree and shattering on the floor. With the knife in hand, she left the kitchen and slowly retraced her steps until she once again stood in the doorway to the living room.

"Naughty."

The voice sound like it was coming from the tree, and as she watched, the branches shifted as though a squirrel had been set loose. She took a cautious step toward the tree, afraid that whatever was hidden by the dense collection of branches might jump out at her, then took another.

When she finally stood before the tree, Mary Beth used the knife to poke around amongst the branches. The glare of the blinking lights made it difficult to focus, so she leaned in closer to get a better look.

And there was nothing there.

"Naughty."

The voice came from higher up this time.

Startled, she jumped back, her free hand going to her chest to make certain her heart didn't break through like it was threatening to do. She tried to follow the source of the sound, but she froze when she saw, on the same branch she had seen them on earlier, the two elf ornaments she'd bought at The Christmas Village.

You better watch out.

They were no longer the cute antiques she'd brought home. They were more sinister now, their festive faces displaced by deep frowns of disapproval. Their black eyes stared right at her. No, not at, but through her, and before them she felt naked, as though they could see every dark thing she'd ever done.

She stumbled backward, not once taking her eyes away from the loathsome little things. Nor did they look away; they just continued to stare into the depths of her soul.

"Janice!"

They only reply she received was that of the voice on the radio, warning her she'd better watch out.

"Janice, wake up!"

You better watch out.

She turned to look down the hall toward Janice's room. Gray light, like a morning mist, filtered out from beneath the door.

Turning her attention back to the tree, she retreated slowly, afraid that any sudden movement would incite the elves to attack.

"Janice?"

You better watch out.

At the door, she knocked, and when she still received no response, she took the doorknob in hand and gave it a twist.

"Janice?"

With the door open, Mary Beth could now hear the hushed voices from whatever movie her roommate had been watching before falling asleep. She pushed the door open and stepped inside.

The constantly shifting light from the television caste dancing shadows all about the room and she tried to focus on every movement. When she was certain that there was no one else in the room other than herself and Janice, she shifted her attention to the other woman's bed.

Too blitzed to bother turning off the television, Janice had pulled the blankets over her head to block out the light.

Mary Beth moved deeper into the room. "Janice, wake up."

The blankets shifted as Janice stirred, but still no sound rose from beneath the mound.

"Naughty."

It sounded as if the voice had come from Janice, from beneath the blankets, but it definitely wasn't her roommate's voice.

"Janice, wake the fuck up! Somebody's in the apartment."

Childish giggles filled the air, and that one word was repeated. "Naughty."

Mary Beth charged the bed and tore the blankets from her roommate's sleeping form. "Janice!"

She stumbled backward at the sight that greeted her, a scream lodged in her throat.

At first it looked as though one of the elf ornaments had grown, but then Mary Beth realized Janice's face had been carved up like a jack o'lantern—her mouth had been sliced to give the appearance of a menacing grin, and someone, or something, had taken her eyes, leaving behind gaping black holes that seemed to look right through Mary Beth. Too drunk to be bothered changing into her pajamas, Janice was still dressed in the clothes she'd worn yesterday, but they were now slashed and stained a rusty brown.

Mary Beth continued to back away from the bed until she hit the wall, and then all she could do was stare as tears rolled down her face.

Suddenly, Janice sat up and turned her deformed grin on Mary Beth. Pointing an accusatory finger at her, Janice said, "Naughty!" Blood flowed from her roommate's mouth.

With a scream, Mary Beth turned and fled as Janice's body collapsed back onto the bed.

Mary Beth raced down the hall. As soon as she hit the living room, the radio fell silent and the lights on the tree went out. The drapes had been closed, so the room was now in complete darkness. She needed to get help, but she didn't want to risk staying in the apartment long enough to call the police, so she started for the front door, feeling her way like a blind woman without her cane.

Something hit the wall and shattered. She flinched at the sound, but kept moving.

"Naughty."

Something else hit the wall and shattered, and she realized then that someone was throwing Christmas ornaments at her. She quickened her pace as she moved toward the door, but then jumped back with a cry as something bit into her bare foot.

Another ornament hit the wall and shattered, this one closer, and she could feel the bite of the glass shrapnel as it dug into her cheek.

Stifling a cry of pain, she reversed her course, deciding to chance going back to her room and calling the police, but before she could take a half a dozen steps, something rough snaked around her ankle and gave a jerk. Her feet, slick with blood from a dozen tiny wounds, slipped out from under her and she crashed to the floor.

"Naughty."

Something scurried across the room toward her.

Mary Beth rolled over and tried to get to her hands and knees, but something looped around her wrist and gave a jerk. She collapsed to the floor again, and before she could recover, she felt something slip around her neck. Her free hand came up to pull it away, and that's when she realized they were using the garland from the tree to bind her.

"Who are you? What do you want?"

"Naughty."

"Wha-why are-you doing this?" she managed to croak before the tinsel was pulled tight, cutting off her words.

"Naughty."

Hearing them moving to either side of her, she renewed her struggles. It was only cheap garland, she should be able to snap it easily enough, but she soon found it was stronger than she had expected. She screamed her frustration and fear, but the sound was no louder than a croak. She couldn't even give voice to the pain when she felt that first slice around her mouth, and all she could do was whimper when they started to work on her eyes.

With each cut, the elves laughed and said, "Naughty," as if they were listing the crimes for which she was being punished, but she knew of only one that would warrant this type of punishment.

The last thing she heard before life fled was their gleeful laughter and that one word echoing in her mind.

"Naughty!"

❄ ❄ ❄

"It's the weirdest thing," the officer said as he waited for the landlord to unlock the door. "Her boss called this morning saying she hasn't heard from her in a few days. Since before Christmas. She didn't thinking anything of it until she didn't show up for charity event she helped organize. That's when she started to worry."

"Really?" the old man replied, pushing the door open. "Maybe she just took off for the holidays. Visiting family or friends." He looked at the officer. "Maybe she's shacked up with a boyfriend somewhere, getting her fireplace poked, if you know what I mean."

The cop ignored the innuendo and stepped inside.

Everything looked normal; there was no sign of a struggle. It was like a scene from *The Night Before Christmas*: one of the most beautifully decorated trees he had ever seen took up one corner of the room near the window, and decorations had been hung with care all around the room. The lights on the tree blinked festively, reflecting off the colorful array of glass ornaments.

"Hello," the officer called out. "Anyone home?"

Both men stepped into the living room. "Wait here," the officer said. "I'm going to check out the rest of the apartment."

Nothing seemed to be amiss, and he returned to the living room. That was when he noticed the piece of paper nestled amongst the branches of the tree. He stepped closer to get a better look.

It was a neatly written note. A confession.

To Whom It May Concern,

I'm sorry. My roommate and I embezzled over $50,000.00 from a charity event I helped organize. It's under the tree. It was a very naughty thing to *do, and we are truly sorry.*

Sincerely,

A Very Naughty Girl

The officer took a step back and looked under the tree. The only thing there was a couple of large, festive, metal popcorn tins. Dropping to one knee, he pulled one close and popped the lid. It was filled with money. He gave a whistle. From behind him, the landlord said, "Oh, shit."

The officer pulled out the second tin and opened it, only to find more cash. "You can say that again. Wherever they are, they don't want to be found."

"Yeah, but why go and leave all that?"

The cop shrugged. "Beats me. Guilty conscience maybe?" Standing up and starting for the door, he said, "I gotta call this in." He paused a moment and took another look around the room to make sure he hadn't missed anything. Before heading out to his patrol car, he said to the landlord, "Don't touch anything."

The instant he was left alone, the landlord hurried to the window and looked outside just as the officer hit the sidewalk. He waited until the man slid behind the wheel and picked up the radio mic before turning his gaze upon the open tins.

"Hmmm... Back rent, security deposit..." He ran through the list of monies these two broads owed him. No one would be the wiser. Before he could talk himself out of what he was about to do, he bent over and grabbed two stacks of bills and stuffed them in the pockets of his coat, then hurried back to the doorway of the living room just as the officer returned.

"Alright," he said. "You have to clear out so I can secure

this place. It's a crime scene now.

"Alright. If you need anything, you know where to find me."

The cop followed him out.

❄ ❄ ❄

As the landlord was locking the door and turning over the set of keys to the cop, the branches on the tree began to shake. Four elf ornaments, two male and two female, stepped into view. Settling down on the branch, they looked at each other and giggled. Then as one, they turned their black eyes toward the front door and grinned their evil grins.

"Naughty."

Holiday Icon
Michael Thomas-Knight

Two boxes of shiny decorations sat upon the withering lawn. Balls of red, green, blue, and silver were nestled among strands of metallic-looking garland of assorted colors and reflected the late afternoon light.

Elise had on her warm coat, Versace Winter Wear for children, and was bundled up to her neck. It wasn't cold enough to wear it yet, but she liked the expensive garment and had insisted she be allowed to put it on.

Her mother, Kirstie, brought out a box of lights and set it down next to the others.

"Momma, tell me about when you were a little girl and you used to decorate trees."

"Oh, Elise, I've told you that so many times already."

Elise looked up to her mom with the saddest of puppy dog eyes. Kirstie dropped to her knees beside her daughter. "How about I tell you while we work?" she asked while rummaging through the box of ornaments and pulling out a plastic bag filled with fish hooks. "You want to help mommy?"

Elise shook her head enthusiastically.

"Okay, just be careful with these, they're sharp. Watch out for the barbs."

"I will, Mommy."

Elise began to attach hooks to ornaments and placed them neatly in a line on the lawn in front of her. Kirstie stood and began draping the lengths of lights upon their traditional Christmas icon.

"When I was a little girl," Kirstie began, "there were many more trees than there are today. *My* mommy, Grandma Rose, would buy a tree, and we would set it up in the house and decorate it."

"In the house?" Elise giggled. "A tree? In the house?"

Even though she'd heard the story numerous times, Elise always responded to the tale in the same manner. Just the idea of a tree in the house was funny to her, and she laughed.

"Yes, in the house. We would decorate the tree with white garland and colorful ornaments. We'd place all of our Christmas presents under the tree. The fireplace would crackle with flames, heating the living room. Hot cider scented the air with traces of ginger and cinnamon. Grandma would bake cookies and make hot cocoa while holiday music filled the house with joy. *White Christmas* was Grandma's favorite. Did you ever hear that song?"

"No, Mommy, I don't think I remember that."

"I'll have to play it for you when we get back inside."

Kirstie stepped back to look at the placement of the lights. Satisfied, she retrieved another strand from the box. She continued with her decorating and her story.

"But then," Kirstie said, "they passed some dumb law and we weren't allowed to cut down trees anymore. Besides, they were messy and they littered the carpet with broken needles. The maid would spend days vacuuming and still wouldn't get them all up."

"Tell me where the zombies came from?"

Kirstie chewed anxiously at her lower lip. She knew the question was coming; it was inevitable, as it was always the next question, but she had to be careful how she answered it. She knew Elise would draw her own conclusions, but how much should Kirstie tell her, and how could she guide her to the right conclusions.

"Well... a long time ago, there were people that didn't want to work, lazy people with no money. The government would take some of our money and give it to them. They even tried to force your daddy to hire them. Can you imagine? Pay someone to do work that a machine could do, or that we could get children in other countries to do for hardly any money?"

"That sounds crazy, Mommy."

"I know, love, it was crazy. They even took money from us to pay for their doctor bills. It took many years, but your daddy finally helped convince the government to change the laws. Now we get to keep all of our money."

"But what about the zombies?"

"I'm getting to that, my dear. My, you sure are impatient. What happened was, when the laws changed, these people still didn't have jobs and couldn't pay for doctors. They all got sick with a virus, and in just a few years, they all turned to zombies. At first we used them as cheap labor in coal mines and construction sites, but then the government passed laws against using them for manual labor. In protest, people would catch zombies and tie them to posts on their front lawns.

One year, some folks began decorating their zombies and it was shown on the news. The idea really caught on after that."

"Because there were no more trees to use?"

"Exactly."

Kirstie tried to gauge her daughter's reaction, wondering how she was affected by this story. She couldn't tell, so she decided to end the story before more questions arose.

"The good thing is, now when people turn into zombies, we get to buy the zombies for $25 each and we can use them as decorations," Kirstie explained.

"You mean that all the zombies were people like you and me once?"

"Well, not *exactly* like you and me. They weren't important or from important families, but they were people... once."

Elise stood, holding in her fingers a two-inch fish hook with a glossy red ball hanging from it. "Can I start now, Momma?"

"Okay, love, go ahead," Kirstie said.

Elise swung the hook down; it caught in the flesh and ripped a hole between two ribs. The downward trajectory was brought to a halt when the hook came in contact with bone. She released her hold on the ornament and smiled as it rolled gently against the pink skin. Elise took a step back the way momma often did so she could look at her handiwork. The zombie, nailed to a giant wooden cross, tried to move its head, but had too little "life" left to elicit a response. It wore a small loincloth over its private parts, but was otherwise naked. Elise gouged another decoration into the zombie's left thigh.

"Mommy, why do *we* hang a zombie-man on the lawn and decorate it for Christmas?"

Kirstie glanced at her daughter. She wished Elise would stop calling it a zombie-man. It was a symbol of their religion and a testament to their faith. She darted a hook with a silver ball into the flesh under its outstretched arm.

"To show we are good Christians, dear."

Kirstie jabbed metal hooks into the tender flesh beneath the arms, hanging balls in a symmetrical line and repeating the color pattern. There was little blood. Kirstie had made sure she purchased one that was drained, and she'd double-checked for drain sites in the inner thigh and wrists when it had been delivered. The last thing she wanted was for the holiday decoration to get a sudden burst of energy and scare her daughter.

"Momma, I want to put some up high," Elise said.

Kirstie unfolded a lawn chair and held her daughter's hand as she stepped upon it. Elise looked into the face of the zombie. It had a C-shaped scar in its forehead.

"Momma, what's this mark on its head?"

"That's nothing, dear. They just have to *prep* them before we can buy them. We call that its Crown of Thorns."

Elise looked into the distant blue eyes of the man. She looked at the light mustache. She noticed a tattoo on his upper right arm, a heart with a girl's name under it, *Belinda*. There was an earring hole in his left ear, and he had wavy, shoulder-length hair.

"Momma? Who was this man? Before."

"That's not important, honey. You just have to know that he was a *nobody*. He had *nothing* to offer society; he was *useless* and *insignificant*."

Elise studied the face more intently. She hesitated, holding the hook, the ornament poised in the air above her head. Her eyes narrowed and her brow furrowed.

Kirstie watched her daughter, and she darted nervous

glances between Elise and the vacant face of the Holiday Icon. Elise had to know that there was a difference. She had to know that they were in a separate class from this vagabond, that not all humans were created equal. Kirstie didn't want to lose her daughter to silly virtues that had no place in the success of the family. Elise had to know that she was privileged. With privilege came certain expectations from society.

After several moments, Elise let her brow relax, as if she had come to a conclusion. Suddenly, she slammed a hook into the zombie's right cheek, dragging the flesh on its face downward. There was a slight flinch in the zombie's head, a miniscule snarl of the nose, nothing more. Kirstie blew out the breath she'd been holding. She sighed and smiled proudly at her daughter.

When they were done, they admired their work. The colored bulbs lit up the icon as it stood on the front lawn in its Jesus pose. On cue, a light snow began to fall just as sunset gave way to night. Elise ran across the front lawn in revelry of the season's first snow. Headlights bounced along the quiet road, coming toward the house. Jonas pulled his Lexus into the driveway, got out of the car, and came to stand by his wife. He kissed her on the cheek and put his arm around her.

"That's beautiful. You did a wonderful job," Jonas said to his wife.

"Daddy," Elise yelled, hearing his voice. She ran up to embrace him. He squatted down and kissed her on the cheek.

"Did you help mommy with the decorating?" he asked.

"Yes, I did," Elise said.

"You did a wonderful job, too!"

"You know what else? I can catch snowflakes on my tongue."

Elise ran off, twirling in circles and catching snowflakes. Kirstie leaned into her husband and he once again slipped his arm around her.

"How did the meetings go today?" Kirstie asked.

"It was a battle on Capitol Hill," he replied, "but we were able to keep the mandatory lobotomy laws in place. I'm afraid that one day they will be overturned."

"We give these dregs a useful purpose in society and all we get is protests. They should be happy with the wonderful gift we've given them."

"At least there are no complaints from this year's Holiday Icon," Jonas said.

Large snowflakes began accumulating on the front lawn. The colored lights shimmered in the snow collecting upon the Holiday Icon. Kirstie brushed the flakes from her husband's shoulder. She could sense that something was bothering him. She studied him, asking with her eyes what was wrong. He might not want to risk Elise overhearing.

After a moment, he said, "I got a call from Doctor Banister today. He said he had observed some strange behavior from the hordes during the last month that might be cause for concern."

"You mean something stranger than walking around randomly and bumping into each other? I can't imagine," Kirstie said with a snicker.

Jonas continued without acknowledging his wife's comment. "He saw them lining up at the gates to the city. He also observed them in the forest in small groups, all facing the same direction and walking in unison. He attributes it to perhaps a latent instinct, like ducks flying in formation or worker bees in a hive."

"*Is* there a reason for concern?"

"No, I wouldn't think so. The lobotomies leave no awareness of self or notion of self-preservation. The only thing I'm concerned with is Reggie's endorsement of the program. When a scientist begins questioning, they'll often find a reason to suspend common practice so they can do *further studies*. He's the biggest proponent of the program. I'd hate to lose his support."

"I'm sure Reggie believes in the program and wouldn't want it changed," Kirstie said. After a pause, she added, "We're on holiday now. Why don't you leave all the worrying until after vacation."

"Yeah, you're right," he said. "It's time to count our blessings and be thankful for what God has given us."

He kissed his wife on the cheek.

"Let's go in," she said. "I'll make some hot cider before dinner."

"That sounds wonderful."

The couple headed to the front door. Elise lingered a moment, pausing to look at the zombie-man again. She studied the lifeless face, sunken cheeks, and colorless lips. Suddenly, its icy blue eyes darted down to look at her. A knowing smile creased its pale face, exposing jagged brown teeth. The young lady's smile vanished. She swallowed hard and her arms fell limp to her sides.

"Elise," Kirstie called. "Come on, love. It's time for dinner."

Elise ran to the house and up the front steps. She turned to take one last look at the Jesus figure, but only saw the back of its head. It was not moving. Then she looked beyond her property to the other houses on the street. A dozen figures hung from crosses on the front lawns of the neighboring homes. Lights twinkled and sparkled, variations of red, white, and green against the new-fallen snow. They tinted the pale faces of the Jesus zombie-men. All at once, the

Jesus figures turned to Elise and smiled.

Elise retreated into the house and slammed the door behind her.

CHRISTMAS IN THE SNOW
Rose Blackthorn

Bonnie stood on the threadbare rag rug, first on one foot, then the other. The cold from the linoleum floor bleached through the rug and the two pairs of socks she wore and chilled her feet. She clutched her robe more closely around her, hands shoved under her arms for warmth, as she waited for the coffee pot to finish brewing.

She turned her head, green eyes peering past the loose red hair hanging over her forehead. The four-paned window above the sink was partially obscured by frost, and outside the snow had transformed the yard into an unrecognizable landscape of odd humps and rolls all the way to the wall of dark tree trunks.

The coffee pot gurgled and burped, letting out a tired hiss with a last wisp of escaping steam. Then it beeped twice and fell silent. She didn't waste any time, but quickly picked up the glass carafe and filled the two mugs waiting on the peeling

Formica countertop. She used a spoon to stir one cup, the cream and sugar that had been waiting at the bottom turning the coffee into a sweet, blond taste of heaven. The other cup remained black, just the way her husband, Jeff, preferred it.

Bonnie took a mug in each hand and headed back toward the bedroom. She hurried her steps, wanting to crawl back under the warm quilts, and sighed when she heard the heater kick on. Not that it would do much good. The house was old and in sorry shape, and the ancient heater did little more than keep the pipes from freezing.

"Coffee's done already?" Jeff was still cozy under the blankets and quilts, a couple of pillows stuffed behind him as he sat up in bed, reading a book.

"Already?" She couldn't keep the sharp tone from her voice as goose bumps crawled up her bare legs. She set the cup of black coffee on the shelf next to her husband, then scurried around to her own side of the bed. With no waste of motion, she set her cup down, stripped off her robe, and dove back under the heavy covers without bothering to take off her socks.

"Wha—" Jeff sucked in a shocked breath when she snuggled up against him. "Did you go out and roll around in the snow before coming back?"

"Didn't need to," she replied, sighing as she began to get warm.

"You're the one who said you wanted to spend Christmas in the snow."

"Mmm… I was hoping not to freeze to death, though."

"Sorry, hon," he said into her hair, and dropped a kiss on the crown of her head. "Old house, old heater."

"Single-paned glass, no insulation," she added, then pulled back a little to look up into his scruffy morning face and smiled. "An adventure, right?"

"I guess we can stay in bed until spring," he offered.

"Well, other than starving, that sounds pretty good," she said, moving her hand over his chest and stomach beneath the pile of quilts.

The book slid off the bed with a muffled thump, and the coffee quickly became cold, but neither of them cared.

❄ ❄ ❄

Eventually they got out of bed. Jeff dressed in thermals and jeans, t-shirt and sweatshirt, and wool socks with his winter boots. He pulled on a ski parka and a pair of heavy gloves, then headed outside to clear snow off the car.

"How deep is it?" Bonnie called before closing the door.

"Deep enough," he said as he trudged through a foot of fresh powder.

"Brr," she said, and shivered. She fixed herself a fresh cup of coffee, then went into the bedroom to put on her own cold-weather clothing.

Once dressed, she paused to look out the bedroom window. Like all the windows in the old house, it was made of several small panes separated by wooden mullions, and like all the other windows, it was currently obscured by frost. She leaned forward and wiped her fingertips across the center glass in the nine-paned window. Their room was at the back of the house, so the view was of the snow-covered clearing that stretched from the house and dilapidated outbuildings to the circling wall of lodgepole pines. The snow wasn't falling right now, but the world had been reduced to shades of black and white, stark, and yet somehow beautiful. This view could not have been any different from the reds and golds of the desert she had lived in all her life. Finally, she made herself turn away and went out front to help her husband.

Between the two of them, they cleared the heavy, wet snow off their small SUV, as well as a walkway around the parked vehicle and a path from the front door to the wood shed. They had made a list the night before, and intended to drive into town this morning to stock up on whatever supplies they would need to keep them through the holidays. Because the ancient furnace seemed to be laboring to put out any heat, Jeff had decided to get a new filter, hoping that would help. He also intended to fill up their plastic five-gallon gas can; if the furnace couldn't do the job, he would just have to use the chainsaw and make sure they had enough wood for the fireplace. Bonnie had lived all of her life in a warm climate, but he had grown up here and knew just how dangerously cold it could get.

"Okay, let's get going," Jeff said. "I want to get back before it starts snowing again." Bonnie climbed into the passenger side of the SUV, leaving the chore of driving in the snow to her husband. Jeff got in and started down the long driveway. The fresh powder muted the sound of the tires, and he felt as though they were gliding through cotton candy.

Bonnie watched out the side window, gazing through the endless black trunks of the lodgepole pines while Christmas music played softly on the stereo. The Carson family property, on which the old house stood, included acres of forest, and their nearest neighbor was over a mile away on the road. The sky that showed through the breaks in the trees was the color of pearls, and even with the cloud cover, it was bright enough to make brilliant kaleidoscope swirls in her vision. Her eyes began to water, and she closed them tightly against the sting of tears. Stark against the darkness of her eyelids, she saw the negative impression of what looked like a slender figure between the trees. She opened her eyes again, blinking rapidly as she tried to clear her vision, but whatever she thought she might have seen was gone.

"Are you okay?" Jeff asked.

Bonnie nodded, pulling off her gloves to wipe at her eyes. "Yeah, it's just really bright. Makes my eyes burn."

"Snow-blindness is a real thing. Check the glove box for some sunglasses. They'll help."

She rummaged through the small compartment, finally finding a plastic case with sunglasses inside. She put them on and looked back out her side window, wiping away her condensed breath. All she could see was snow and more snow, slashed by the black trunks of the pines. But in her mind's eye, there was a white negative image against black snow of a slender figure with wide eyes and long fingers splayed against a tree trunk.

❄ ❄ ❄

The nearest bit of civilization was a small resort town named Union Creek, which was less than thirty miles from Crater Lake, and just over five miles from the old house. In the heavy snow on the winding unplowed road, it took them the better part of an hour to get there. The small general store stood just off the main road. White Christmas lights ran along the eaves and three immature pines planted out front had been decorated with glass and brass ornaments. Strangely, there was a small black bird perched in the branches of each of the trees, carved from wood with shining bead eyes that glinted in the twinkling lights. Half a dozen vehicles were already parked in the small lot, and Jeff carefully nosed in between an old Chevy pickup and a late-model Land Rover.

"Got the list?" he asked as he shut off the engine.

Bonnie nodded and got out of the car, being extra careful as the blacktop was still patchy with ice and scattered rock salt.

Inside, they got a cart and quickly checked off the items on their list. Bonnie had made a point of noting perishables, and they stocked up on milk, eggs, and bread. When they finished with the necessities, Jeff opted for a six-pack of beer, and Bonnie chose a bottle of blackberry wine. It only took them a few minutes to check out, and the cashier wished them a Merry Christmas and safe travels back home before the coming storm. When they carried their purchases out, Bonnie gazed askance at the bird ornaments. Doves or cardinals she would expect, but ravens? Not a likely Christmas display, in her opinion.

They stowed everything in the back of the SUV, then drove half a mile along the main street to the gas station. While Jeff filled the gas tank and the spare gas can he'd brought for the chain saw, Bonnie went inside the station to get some hot coffee. She waited while Jeff finished fueling so she could pay for everything. Idly, she scanned through the rather tacky display of maps and pamphlets displayed near the counter.

"What's that?" Jeff asked when she climbed back into the vehicle, noting the glossy paper pamphlets and a thin paperback she held in one hand with the paper coffee cup.

She handed him the other cup she carried, then pulled her door shut. "Just some info on the area. Did you know it's supposed to be haunted?"

Jeff took a cautious sip, grimacing when he burnt his tongue on the hot, black coffee. "Yeah, I've heard the stories. The natives used to sacrifice virgins to the volcano, or some such."

"Very funny," Bonnie snorted. "I'm serious. There's all

kinds of stuff here about dark spirits in the winter woods, and people disappearing."

"When did you start believing in spooks?"

She shrugged uneasily, remembering the figure she'd seen in the trees. "Not everything can be explained by science. Some things are still mysteries."

Jeff was quiet for a moment, remembering stories he'd heard when he was young. He remembered Poppa warning him never to threaten the ravens that visited the house in winter, and to never follow anyone into the woods. "There are all kinds of old superstitions whispered around here, mostly by the older folks. But that's all they are. Old stories to tell around the fire to scare the gullible," he finally said, and pulled out onto the road to head back to the house.

"You said you grew up here with your grandparents. Did they scare you with these old stories?" she asked.

He didn't answer, making a point of concentrating on the snowy road instead. The drive back to the house was uneventful, although the sky had darkened and light flurries of snow began to drift down. When they reached the house, it took two trips to unload the car. Bonnie stripped off her gloves and coat, then started putting the groceries away. Jeff went into the little bare closet off the back porch where the furnace was located with a flashlight and the new filter.

When he reappeared in the kitchen, Bonnie had put all the perishables away, and was placing canned and boxed items in the cupboards.

"I'm going to go out and get some wood cut. I'd appreciate some help stacking it under the lean-to," he said.

"Let me finish putting this stuff away and I'll be out in a few minutes." She watched as he went out the front door, chewing on her bottom lip while she thought about their odd conversation in the car. She hadn't brought it up again, but she was more than curious about what kinds of stories he had been told when he was young. When Jeff inherited this old house and the surrounding property from his grandfather, Nollaig Carson, she had been the one to suggest they move here. Financially, it just made sense—why not live in a house that was paid for instead of paying rent? There was enough money in his inheritance to keep them comfortable for several years if they were frugal, and getting out of the rat-race in the city had appealed to them both. But now she had to wonder if he had been as willing as she to come here. He had just gone along with her the way he always did, but she wondered now if she had missed some subtle sign that he really didn't want to come back. Were there dark stories from his childhood that he'd never shared?

❅ ❅ ❅

Bonnie sat on the floor before the fireplace, a glass of blackberry wine in her hand. She had put some pillows and quilts on the floor to protect her from the cold, and luxuriated in the warmth coming from the crackling fire Jeff had built. In her lap was the slender book she'd picked up at the gas station. It had been written and self-published by a local resident, and she was alternately fascinated and horrified by the historical accounts of unsolved disappearances dating back as early as 1853.

Jeff sat on the couch, another quilt pulled around his shoulders while he read his novel.

"Jeff, did your grandparents know any of these people?" she asked, turning to look at him.

"Hmm?" After a moment, he pulled his eyes from the page. "What did you say?"

She held up the book and asked again, "Did your grandparents know any of these people that went missing? You said they lived here for over fifty years, isn't that right?"

He glanced at his novel, then set it down and rubbed his eyes. "They talked about it sometimes when someone was reported missing up around the Lake, or in the surrounding forests. I don't know that they knew any of them personally."

"It must have been scary, hearing about this when you were just a boy."

He shrugged, wishing she would get over her fascination with it. He hadn't thought about any of this since his teens, and didn't want to now. Other than whispers traded between the locals who lived in the area full time, no one ever talked about the odd traditions and beliefs that survived in the area, some brought by the early settlers and some left over from the original Native tribes. The disappearances had been attributed to everything from animal attacks to alien abductions, and everything in between. "It wasn't scary, hon. Like you said, my grandparents lived here for more than fifty years, and they didn't mysteriously disappear. But living in a place like this, you have to take precautions."

She raised one eyebrow at his phrasing, and waited for him to continue.

Jeff grinned at her, his eyes twinkling. "You don't go hiking alone without a map or a compass, unless you're begging to get lost." He dropped the smile when he added, "People come out here completely unprepared, and unfortunately, they pay for their ignorance with their lives."

"I'm going to get another glass of wine," Bonnie said finally, when it was clear he had no more to say. "Would you like another beer?"

He shook his head and picked up his book again. "No

thanks, hon."

"Okay." Away from the hearth, it was doubly cold, and goose bumps crawled up her arms when she opened the refrigerator to get the wine. When she filled her goblet and had replaced the bottle in the fridge, something moved in her peripheral vision. She glanced at the window above the kitchen sink. A pair of silver-white eyes glinted outside the glass.

"Shit!" The goblet, set too close to the edge of the counter, tipped and tumbled to the floor. Dark wine sprayed across the kitchen when the delicate glass shattered.

"Are you all right?" Jeff asked, tossing his book aside.

Bonnie jerked her eyes back to the window, but there was nothing there except the glaze of ice from the deep cold. "Fine, just clumsy. Turn on the light so I can see where the broken glass went."

With the lights on, it only took a few minutes to pick up the shards of the goblet and clean up the spilled wine. Bonnie kept glancing at the blank window. It had probably just been a reflection from the lamp, she told herself, but she kept remembering the strange slender figure that she'd glimpsed out in the snow among the trees. Had its eyes been silver?

"Let me get you another glass," Jeff offered when everything was set to rights again.

Bonnie shook her head, stepping forward to put her arms around him for a moment, her head resting against his shoulder. "I changed my mind. No more wine tonight." She hadn't drunk enough to hallucinate, but she didn't want to become inebriated. "I think I'll just camp out in front of the fire. Unless you're done reading?"

"I'd like to at least finish this chapter..."

"I know what that means," she teased, and lifted her

face to kiss him. "Wake me up when you finish the book."

He protested, but not too strenuously. When she lay down on her pile of pillows and blankets before the hearth, he took his place on the couch and lost himself in the story again.

Bonnie gazed at her paperback for a moment, but decided to leave it alone. Instead, she watched the flames licking at the darkness, the soft crackle and murmur like a language she had once known. The warmth and soft susurration lulled her to sleep, and into ephemeral dreams filled with black tree trunks that went on forever and odd carved ravens with glinting bead eyes.

❄ ❄ ❄

The next day was Christmas Eve. After coffee and a late breakfast, they bundled up and headed outside. Jeff pulled an old wooden sled with metal runners from one of the outbuildings. He strapped the chainsaw to the deck, and they walked laboriously through new snow to the younger pine trees at the edge of the forest.

Bonnie struggled more than Jeff to get through the snow. She had no happy childhood memories of snowball fights or building snowmen like Jeff did, and she had quickly come to learn that while beautiful, snow was not an easy thing to deal with. It was cold, wet, and heavy, and just walking through it could be exhausting, so she made no complaint when Jeff went first, breaking the trail and pulling the sled behind him.

"How about this one?" Jeff asked.

She looked up at the tree he was pointing at and shook her head. "Something a little fuller, maybe?"

He glanced around at the multitude of pines. "That one?"

Bonnie shook her head again. "It's shaped funny. With all these trees to choose from, we should be able to find one that's just right."

Jeff walked a little farther, leaving the sled behind while he looked for a tree that would please his wife.

Bonnie went the other way, struggling through the deep, soft snow, breath puffing out in front of her face in clouds of mist that obscured her vision. She stopped every couple of steps to look up at the trees, still hoping to find the right one.

"How about this one?" Jeff called, and she turned to look where he pointed.

Immediately, she smiled. "Perfect!" Something moved at the corner of her eye, and she turned her head, her latest exhale hiding everything for a moment. When the mist cleared, she saw a large black bird perched on a low branch just a few feet away, staring directly at her. For a second, it reminded her of the carved and painted ornaments on the trees in town, but this bird had heavy talons gripping the bark and a ruff of coarse feathers circling its neck. It opened its beak, but made no sound.

"Shit," she said, heart pounding and a chill raising the hair on the back of her neck. She bent slowly to gather a handful of snow.

"Come and help me with this," Jeff said, leaning down to catch the rope tied to the sled.

Bonnie threw the snow, not even packed into a ball, toward the tree where the raven glared at her. With a rough call that echoed between the trees, it launched into the air and took flight.

"Bonnie!"

She grinned as the bird disappeared among the trees, calling, "Chicken!" When she turned back to her husband, she was surprised by the dismay on his face.

"What did you do that for?"

"It startled me," she said, having no better reason to give. The way the bird just sat there and stared at her, it had given her the creeps. "I didn't hit it. Didn't even come close."

Jeff shook his head, searching through the trees with his eyes. The raven was gone. In his memory, he heard Poppa's voice saying, *"Don't ever threaten the ravens, son. They're guardians and messengers, and you don't want their ire."*

"Jeff?" she asked, confused by his reaction. "I didn't hurt it."

He shrugged, trying to push away the old memories. "Just don't mess with them, hon. It's like bad karma." Then he pulled the chainsaw off the sled and prepared to cut down the tree they had chosen. By the time they dragged the tree back to the house, it had begun to snow again, and Bonnie groaned.

Jeff smiled and said, "You'll get used to it." But the smile seemed forced, and Bonnie worried that she'd done something to offend him.

Inside, they placed the trunk into an old metal tree stand Jeff had found in the attic along with his grandparents' antique decorations. When he brought the boxes of Christmas décor into the living room, Bonnie had the fire going again. Even though they'd both warmed up considerably during their excursion outside, it was quite chilly inside the house. Changing the filter hadn't seemed to make much of a difference in the heat output of the furnace.

"What have we got here?" she asked as Jeff opened the first box.

They pulled out garlands strung with pine cones sprinkled with glitter, boxes of glass ornaments that looked as though they'd been hand-blown, strings of beads, and a beautifully embroidered tree skirt. In the next box, Jeff found the old wooden train set his grandfather had carved, with the track that would go around the tree outside of the tree skirt. This box also contained the carved wooden ornaments that Jeff remembered from his childhood, made by his grandfather and painted by his grandmother. There were nutcrackers and wooden soldiers, rocking horses and angels with gilt wings. In the last box were strings of lights, the old kind with multiple wires and bubble-lights or the large frosted bulbs as big as Jeff's thumb. He had already decided not to use any of the ancient lights because he worried they would be a fire hazard.

When they finished decorating the tree with the old-fashioned ornaments and several strands of contemporary lights, Jeff plugged it in with a flourish. Bonnie turned out the lamps, and with only the flickering firelight, they admired their first real Christmas tree.

"Oh, I almost forgot," Jeff said, and pulled one more thing out of an open box. Bonnie watched while he un-wrapped and carefully placed the last decoration. When he stood back, she expected to see an angel, or maybe a glass star. Instead, what she saw was a kind of stylized version of a bird covered in real feathers. It was like the strange bird decorations she'd seen at the general store in town. Its beak was painted black, and the feathers were black as well. A blank frosty eye made of glass seemed to stare back at her. Just like earlier on the edge of the woods, she felt a chill scamper up her spine.

"What is that?" she asked softly.

"It's Poppa's winter raven. He made it himself, and it guarded the tree every year."

She crossed her arms, holding herself as though the cold had deepened, wishing he would take it down, wrap it up again, and put it back in the box. "What do ravens have to do with Christmas?" she finally asked.

At his perplexed look, she added, "There were raven ornaments on the trees in front of the general store. Didn't you notice them?"

Jeff shrugged. "Everyone around here has raven decorations. It's a tradition."

"Really," she said. "Why is that, I wonder?"

"One of those old stories Poppa used to tell," he said, glancing back at the ornament. "The Winter Woman with her ravens, who roams the forest and the rim of the Lake. Whatever you do, don't threaten the ravens. And never follow anyone into the woods."

Bonnie shivered, then turned to the fireplace to put another log onto the flames. "What kind of story is that to be telling children?" The warmth from the fire washed over her, smoothing away her chill and relaxing taut muscles. At last she sat back on her heels and took a deep breath. "Maybe all those people who went missing followed her into the woods," she whispered, remembering once more the strange figure among the trees.

Jeff went to join Bonnie by the fireplace. "Maybe so. I don't know. All I know is that Poppa lived here all of his life, and Gran from the time they were married until she passed away, and they were happy here."

She said nothing, just leaned against him in the fire's warmth. Outside the mullioned windows, the snow was falling again, and shadows grew between the trees.

❄ ❄ ❄

Bonnie awoke sometime in the middle of the night. The house was quiet, and she grimaced in the dark when she realized the furnace wasn't running. Quietly, she climbed out of bed, shivering in the cold, and pulled on her robe. She made her way out of the bedroom, lit only by the glow of the clock's backlit numbers. Chills rippled up her spine, and she thought about going back to find her slippers.

"Just check the damned thermostat and go back to bed," she whispered to herself. She hurried down the short hall on the balls of her feet, trying to keep as little of her skin as possible from touching the icy floor. She flipped on the light switch to check the old-fashioned dial thermostat. It was set at seventy degrees, and said the internal temperature was seventy degrees.

"Seventy degrees my ass," she hissed, and tapped the dial with the heel of her hand. "Merry Christmas, and try not to freeze to death." Warm light flickered from around the corner, and she heard a muffled pop. In the living room, the fire was burning down into a bed of smoldering embers. Bonnie went in and crouched next to the screened opening, holding her hands out to the warmth. *Maybe we should sleep out here by the fire*, she thought.

The gas-station booklet was still lying by the hearth. She picked it up and slowly flipped through the flimsy pages. Toward the back was a list of names, and the dates and areas where they went missing. She skimmed the columns, wondering how so many could disappear and not make headlines. Toward the bottom of the page, her eye caught on a particular name. Thea Carson, reported missing in December 1987.

A board creaked, and she started, turning to see if Jeff had followed her out of the bedroom, but there was no one there. The tree they had decorated was dark and fragrant, with little glints and sparkles as the glass and glitter reflected the lowering flames. Her eyes were drawn to the handmade bird, which seemed to stare back at her with one frosty silver-white eye.

Bonnie caught her breath, feeling for a moment as though everything stopped—her heart, the flickering of the fire, maybe even the rotation of the earth itself. Jeff had told her once that his mother died when he was two years old, so he had been raised by his grandparents. He had not said how, only that he had been too young to really remember her, and Bonnie had not asked any more questions, as it seemed the subject was painful for him. "Did you follow a stranger into the woods?" she whispered.

There was another creak, this one coming from the direction of the kitchen. Bonnie slowly stood, reaching out to take the wooden bird off the tree. She held it against her chest, stroking it gently as though to comfort it—as though trying to prove her good intentions. Cold air flowed across the floor, almost negating the warmth of the fire behind her, and she realized that the kitchen window was wide open, swung back on its rusty hinges as far as it could go. Flowing into the house on the breath of winter, the color of frost and black winter tree bark, was the figure Bonnie had glimpsed in the woods on their drive into town. She was tall and slender, with long, black, tangled hair and moonstone eyes. When she reached the edge of the firelight, the stylized bird in Bonnie's hands twisted like a living thing, freed itself from her grasp, and flew out the open window.

Bonnie opened her mouth, to call the bird back or to scream, but her voice was locked and she couldn't move. The bitter cold of winter stole into her, through the soles of her bare feet, and into her open mouth. Her vision blurred, like frost building on the mullioned windows, and a corset of ice closed around her ribs. Soft black feathers fluttered, brushing her cheek, and claws scrabbled at the shoulder of her robe. Behind her, the fire collapsed into cold, grey ash.

❄ ❄ ❄

Jeff opened his eyes to pearl-colored light coming through an opening in the curtains on the window above the bed. He was burrowed under the covers, just the top of his head exposed. He took a deep breath, pulling the quilts down a little, and exhaled a puff of mist. He turned to wake Bonnie, but she wasn't in the bed beside him.

"Bonnie?" he called, wondering why she had gotten up so early. The clock on the shelf beside him said 7:34 am. It occurred to him then that it was Christmas morning, and he smiled, wondering if she was hiding presents under the tree. "Hon, have you started the coffee yet?"

The house was silent, not even the furnace running, and he frowned. "Damn, did the pilot light go out?" he groused softly, and tossed the covers aside. The icy air made him hiss, and he hurried to pull on the jeans and sweatshirt he'd left crumpled on the chair beside the bed.

He minced down the hallway, toes curling up in an attempt to stay off the cold floor, and checked the thermostat. It had been turned all the way down to the lowest setting of fifty-four degrees. Jeff turned the dial back up to seventy, hopping from foot to foot in an attempt to keep warm. When he heard the heater kick on, he went in search of his wife.

"Honey, why did you turn the furnace down?" he asked, turning the corner into the living room. The Christmas tree lights were on, twinkling points of color the only illumination. The fire had burned out in the fireplace. A fresh draught of icy air flowed into the room, and he turned to see that the kitchen window was wide open.

"Bonnie?" he called, worried now. Why would she turn the heater down and open the window?

He crossed the kitchen and pulled the window shut, turning the thumb-lock with shaking hands. Something cold grazed the back of his neck and he flinched, turning quickly.

The front door was open a couple of inches, letting more frozen air into the old house. He walked toward it, moving a little more slowly now. The morning had taken on a dream-like quality, and he was starting to wonder if he was still sleeping. But if this was a dream, why was it so cold?

Lying discarded on the floor was the book Bonnie had been reading, its pages open to a list of names. His mother's name seemed to jump out among all the rest, and tears welled and spilled before he could stop them. An old memory, his very first and long repressed, came back to him—a tall slender woman with long black hair and a huge black bird on her shoulder, leading his stumbling mother into the trees...

Jeff grasped the edge of the front door and pulled it all the way open, checking for footprints. The new-fallen snow was unmarked as far as he could see. Something flickered, catching the corner of his eye, and he turned his head, desperately wiping away freezing tears. In the trees, a figure moved, slender and dark between the trunks, with what might have been a flash of red hair, but it was soon lost to sight. When a raven dropped from its perch in the higher branches to follow the shadow, Jeff straightened. He ran to the bedroom to pull on socks and boots, snatched his parka from the closet. There was no time to call for help. There was no time to lose.

"Bonnie!" he yelled, heading out into the virgin snow. "Bonnie, wait!" He left the door open behind him, and followed the flicker of ravens' wings into the endless expanse of winter.

S☃ILENT N❄IGHT
Liam Hogan

It was the night that all was silent.

In homes across the country, people cowered beneath their Christmas trees. Only real ones would do, the pine scent masking their fear. The trees groaned with brightly colored baubles, the more the better to try and confuse Santa's sensors. It used to be said that he knew if you were naughty or nice, and that he'd come for you if you had been bad, but the truth was much simpler. Any noise, any movement, *anything* that gave away your hiding place, and that would be that.

In one living room, made double the height by the collapse of the floor above, there were, unusually, two such trees. Under the larger, a family huddled. The youngest was a mere four years old, small for her age, and the only one among them who would be safe this night. But the sooner she learned the dangers of this night, the better off she'd be. Her sister, eighteen months older, had her by the hand and snuggled close. The night was cold and the small fire eating away at the dampened Yule log offered little in the way of either heat or light.

Under the other tree, the eldest child, Tommy, lay listening to the wind howl, his grandpa beside him. He'd begged and cajoled to be allowed this privilege. Earlier, Gramps had ruined the traditional telling of the holiday tale and had been in disgrace ever since, but as the long night dragged on and the danger lurked ever closer, Mother and Father had finally relented. Besides, Tommy was getting bigger every year, and there really wasn't that much space under either tree.

"Gramps?" Tommy said.

Gramps started, and fearfully checked his watch. It was still early—Santa wasn't due for another hour. He let out his breath in a plume of vapor. "Yes Tommy?" he said, just above a whisper.

"That story you told. Is it true?"

Gramps sighed. He'd already gotten into a heap of trouble on that account. And yet, he was the oldest person in the village. At 43, he was perhaps the oldest for miles around. It was hard to tell because travelling wasn't as easy as it had once been. And when his time came, which could very well be tonight, who then would know the truth? "About the presents? Yes, Tommy, it's true."

Tommy took a moment to digest the full horror of this. His parents had passed it off as a sick joke, but he'd known that wasn't the sort of thing that Gramps did, which was why he had been so eager to leave the family tree for the first time and join Gramps under his.

"What sort of presents?" he asked.

Gramps blinked. Truth be told, he could hardly remember.

He'd been younger than Tommy was now, that first year it had all changed.

"Oh..." he muttered. "Wonderful things. Magical things. Games that made moving pictures and sounds, make believe worlds of bright colors, toy cars..."

Tommy knew cars, but couldn't understand why you'd want to make a toy out of them. They were dull, uninteresting things, and only good for hiding in or sheltering from the rain.

"Why..." Tommy gulped, "Why did he ... it ... change?"

Gramps thought for a moment. This was the crux of it, and he wished he understood it better, but he'd been so young. On that first night, very few kids his age or older had survived; those who by luck had taken shelter beneath the Christmas tree, amongst the presents that would never be opened.

"There was a war..." he began tentatively. Of this, he was quite sure. He remembered one of the toys he'd gotten the year before—a tank—and how his mother had not approved of the way he'd lined it up against his other toys, the foam shells knocking them over one by one to the sound of electronic explosions, while his dad looked on beaming.

"There was a war." he said, more strongly. "A war in distant lands, a war won by drones. There were no prisoners, no wounded, and no civilian casualties. I mean, nobody who wasn't a terrorist, wasn't a baddie. The drones went from house to house looking for hidden weapons, seeking out and killing the enemy. And that was that. The war that had seemed to last forever came to an end in a single fortnight."

It was amazing how it all came back. For almost 40 years, he'd hardly thought of it; he'd been too busy surviving. They all had. After the adults had gone...

But he was getting ahead of himself.

"It was the first Christmas after. The celebrations were

barely over, and everyone was happy, everyone was joyous. You know that word? I haven't used it in a long while. Joyous. We all went to bed that Christmas Eve, certain that there were only good things in our future."

"Under the Christmas tree?" asked Tommy.

"What?" Gramps said, a moment of confusion. "No... This was before all of that. We slept in our normal beds, but with stockings hung on the bedposts, and a plate of mince pies and carrots put out for Santa."

Tommy looked at him disbelieving. "Carrots? For Santa?"

Gramps laughed, a muffled exhalation that shook the broken red bauble nearest his head. "No, not for Santa. For the reindeers! Donner and Blitzen. And, of course, good ol' Rudolph!"

Tommy bit his lip. So many things that he didn't understand. It was like a nonsense poem—like the battered copy of *Alice in Wonderland* that Gramps used to read to them, until one of the wild dogs had ripped it apart. *Was this all made up as well*, he wondered.

Gramps shook his head, slowly. "But the reindeer didn't come that year, or ever again. Nor did Santa. Not the Santa I remember. The *real* one. Not these *killing* ones." He patted Tommy's head lightly, and fell silent.

Tommy waited for a moment, then another. "What... happened?" he nervously asked.

Gramps took a deep breath. "I awoke to the sound of screams, of guns. I didn't know where I was for a moment, and then the bedroom door was flung open and a dark figure stood in the doorway. "Hide!" my father said. "Quick! They're coming! Hide! For God's sake, hide!" It was the last I ever saw of him—alive. I hid under the bed with my brother. I heard more shouts, my mom screaming at my dad for the combination to the gun safe, my dad telling her not to be stupid, that guns wouldn't help, not against them. My dad was in the army, before the drones, so I guess he knew. The front door slammed open, or perhaps shut, and there were a couple of loud bangs, and then... and then there was silence. We could still hear shots and screams, but they were distant, and growing more so. I was trembling and desperately needed to use the bathroom, so I edged out from under the bed while my brother hissed at me to stay put. I crept downstairs. The front room flickered with colored lights from the tree, and as I looked about me, wondering where my parents were, something red flitted past the window, a strange humming noise that suddenly stopped."

Gramps ran his worn hands over his face. "I dived under the Christmas tree just as the door was blown off its hinges, just as my brother was creeping down the stairs to see where I had got to. I... I like to think it was quick for him, but from what everyone who survived said, he wouldn't have been safe anyway. But I sometimes think I should have stayed under that bed and shared my brother's fate, whatever it was to be." There was a tremor in Gramps voice, and something hot and wet splashed onto Tommy's hand.

"You see, in those days, there were so many targets, they didn't check as closely as they do now. I even pushed aside a branch and saw the damned thing hovering over a lifeless body. You don't do that anymore. You see it, it sees you, end of story. But somehow I survived. It was a drone, of course, dressed in a red cloak. Someone's sick idea of a Santa."

Tommy gasped. "But... I thought you said you'd won the war?"

"We did." Gramps said grimly. "All the drones were ours. They were brought home and put into storage. We don't know for sure what happened next, but smarter boys than I have guessed, and it makes a strange kind of sense."

Gramps levered himself up slightly so he could look Tommy straight in the face. "Some idiot down the depot gets bored of standing guard over a warehouse of tin soldiers, maybe he's had a Christmas drink or two, and suddenly decides to reprogram them. Decides to turn them into the military's very own Santas, delivering presents to the whole country. Only, he didn't do a very good job of it. We guess he managed to remove most of the safeguards and retargeted the drones on the civilians—the children, the adults. Everyone, in fact, except the very young. Thank God he left that one in! The least capable of hiding, of staying quiet—they're the only ones who turned out to be safe. He probably tried to disable the weapon systems as well, but... Did they re-arm themselves? Or did he just mess up?"

"I hope he was their first victim, when they awoke as programmed that first Christmas Eve," Gramps said bitterly, shaking his head. "When I think of my parents, my brother, and all the others... I hope he was the first." He was silent a moment. And then wearily he finished his story.

"We survivors didn't know then that Santa would be back. That he would be an annual event. We lost a lot of people that second year—all those who laughed at the childish fears of the more timid kids, or were simply too busy looking after all the little babies to count the days. We lost more the year we thought we were grown up enough to attack the depot. I was there, on the fringes. We thought, since it wasn't Christmas, they'd be defenseless. We were wrong. We did manage to kill a few of them, though, and more have fallen by the wayside since. There's no one to repair them, after all. Perhaps, one day, they'll all be dead. Perhaps even in your lifetime. Until then... thank God they weren't programmed to cope with Christmas trees!"

"Gramps?" whispered Tommy. "What was Santa like—before?"

"Before? Oh, he was a big, jolly man. Dressed in red, just like the drones, but with a flowing white beard and a hearty laugh. He had a sack of presents slung over his shoulder, and everywhere he went, he used to call out, 'Peace and goodwill to all men.' He used to say, 'Peace—'" Gramps fell abruptly silent and held his roughened finger against Tommy's lips. In the distance, the first of the shots rang out in the cold night air. Santa had arrived.

S*PECIAL D*ELIVERY
Simon Bradley

The Devil is a sniveling, bitter, miserable prick with a giant ego and a history of mostly tiny accomplishments. He smells like a dirty ashtray. Pointy nose, sharp knees and elbows, always looking like he hasn't eaten in a week. Yeah, it's true that he has horns, and it's also true that he has cloven hooves, but they cause him so much grief that he has to wear orthotic shoes, which make him look ridiculous. Fucked-up feet couldn't have happened to a more deserving guy. He gets no sympathy from me.

He ditched the pitchfork ages ago. The only thing he carries with him these days is a smartphone, pimped out in one of those gaudy cases with the sparkling costume jewelry. He uses it to send bogus emails advising people to stock up on ammo because some thug from the United Nations will soon be knocking on the door, coming to take away all the guns. Every once in a while he manages to dupe some moron into wiring money straight into one of Hell's accounts by claiming to be an unfortunate friend, recently robbed while on vacation in Italy. Mostly, though, he's just stirring the shit, collecting souls to fuel the furnaces, making sure the power stays on and keeping it toasty down there. Small-time stuff. You know.

Credit where credit's due, though. He started off strong. He had potential. That whole bit with the apple, you would have thought big things were ahead and the Boss might have had a little competition. Satan was like one of those minor call-ups who knock it out of the park on their first at-bat. You know the story: the crowd gets excited; the local press writes them up as the Next Big Thing; ruby-lipped, pink-nippled starlets start calling them up for dates. They think they're getting the million-dollar endorsement deal from Nike and their name on a fat contract; there'll be a Ferrari in the driveway and they'll think the future's all set. It hardly ever works out that way, though. The next time they're at the plate, it's Whiff City, and before they know it, they're back on a stinky bus somewhere between Timbuktu and Buttfuck, Idaho, wondering how it all went wrong.

Bah. I exaggerate. It hasn't been *that* bad for Satan, I guess. He lucks out now and then when he whispers in the right ear. He had some success with Hitler, who was unstable to begin with on account of being born short one testicle. That was his last time around the bases, though. It's been mostly singles and foul-outs since then. The score isn't even close.

Personally, I think the Boss only set the game up to give himself some entertainment. He's probably pretty disappointed in the result. You won't have been to Heaven yet, but it's not exactly a laugh riot over there. Whatever hobbies you enjoyed on Earth tend to lose their appeal when you're staring down the barrel of Eternity. Mind you, they've got one hell of a band, and the drinks are free. But still. There's a lot of time to fill.

I was pretty disillusioned in Heaven, let me tell you. Most of my time on Earth had been spent wandering around handing out gold coins, multiplying wheat and whatnot. I had a talent for making people happy, and I got a kick out of doing it. I was a busy guy. Sitting around playing cards with Jude the Apostle on a Friday night wasn't doing it for me. Looking for a way to keep myself occupied, I applied for a management position. After I died, I had been Sainted — which always looks good on a resume — and so the Boss put me in charge of distribution for the Western Democracies, by far the most lucrative territory. It also happens to be the same turf that Satan works.

I bumped into Satan at the last Annual General Meeting, which was being held in a swank hotel in Purgatory. I'd just finished giving my report about the ongoing negotiations with the Elves. We were due to start the collective bargaining process with the Toymaker's Local, and it was my job to get their tiny signatures on a reasonable contract. They can be stubborn little bastards, but I was pretty sure we would come to an agreement without a work stoppage. After my presentation, I headed down to the bar to have a tipple and take a load off. Satan was over in a dim corner with a few demons and some dodgy-looking whores, spouting off about how many souls he'd collected this year. I had a few doubles at the bar, figured what the hell, and strolled over to say hello.

"Good evening, Nicholas," he said. He had a way of speaking that suggested he was always suppressing a giggle. It was one of his many irritating affectations.

I pulled up a chair. "Hey, Lucifer," I said, knowing full well that he prefers to be called Satan — his Christian name.

"How goes the battle?"

He ignored my little dig at his poor showing against the Boss. "May I buy you a drink?" he asked, tittering. "Eggnog, perhaps?"

I waved the waiter over and ordered a scotch and soda. "I see you still have a wicked sense of humor."

"Ah, yes, well, it is a great virtue, wouldn't you agree?"

"Humor?"

"Wickedness."

I sighed. It was always like this with Satan. You couldn't just sit down and shoot the shit. It always had to be a battle of wits. Pathetic, really.

"What are you doing here, anyway?" I asked. "You're not on the agenda."

"No," he said, "I am not on the agenda. I am merely here to raise a glass. You see, my friends and I are celebrating, and there is no law against that, is there? At least, not yet."

More tittering. One of the whores leaned over and stuck a tongue in his pointy little ear.

I was mildly intrigued. "Oh yeah?" I said. "What's the occasion?"

He held up a red silk purse. "Can you guess what I have here, Nicholas, hmm?"

"Hitler's missing nut?"

He sneered. "Incorrect as usual, my fat friend. No. This bag contains a soul."

"Asshole?"

He stopped smiling. "Trust you to employ that old *chestnut*, Nicholas. Very droll."

"You think I should be impressed that you managed to con another poor sucker out of his soul?" I asked.

He began to answer, but I'd already heard enough. I cut him off. "Look," I said, "I've got two thousand Elves who tell me they're not going to work unless they get another week's vacation and better dental coverage. You ever seen an Elf's teeth? They've got the same amount as us, but in half the space. It's a mess. Every single one of them is going to need braces. Blitzen has been messing around again, and she's going to want maternity leave right in the middle of our busiest shipping period, and to top it all off, I've got that global warming sneaking up my ass. Sort all that out and I'll be impressed."

Was he pissed? You bet. Satan isn't what you'd call humble. He snarled and pointed a bony finger at my chest. Little sparks flew from his horns.

"Listen to me, fat man," he said. "Collecting souls is no small matter. It requires intelligence, cunning, dedication. A man does not give up his soul easily. One must be a master salesman. It is an art, and as such it requires the skill and talent of an *artist*. Of course, I do not expect a bearded, boorish pig who spends much of his time picking up reindeer excrement to appreciate the skill involved."

We were beginning to cause a scene. Over in the corner booth I could see the Easter Bunny giving us nervous glances from behind her salad. She's easily spooked, that one.

"Relax," I said. "Have another drink."

"You are an ignorant fool," he said. He stewed for a minute, and we sipped in uncomfortable silence. I was preparing to get up and go when he put his glass down and folded his arms across his chest. "Perhaps you'd like to find out just how difficult a task it is to convince a man to give up his soul."

Shit. I knew better than to deal with the Devil, but I was three drinks in and feeling pretty confident.

"What did you have in mind?"

He grinned. "A friendly wager? A gentleman's bet?"

"What's the bet?"

Satan rubbed the tip of his finger around the rim of his glass, producing a high-pitched whine. "You have one week to collect one soul. Should you fail to do so, you will deliver only coal to all those darling children this Christmas."

"And what if I get a soul?"

"Asshole?"

"Good one, Lucifer. Very original."

He giggled. "If you are successful in acquiring one soul within one week, I will agree to shut down the furnaces closest to the Pole. It will not solve your global warming problem, of course, but it may help slow it down for a while."

To be honest, I didn't care what was at stake. I just wanted to knock that bony bastard down a few notches.

"Okay," I said. "You're on."

We shook on it.

He giggled again. "You may find our wager more difficult than you imagined."

"How's that?"

"You know the law. The soul may not enter into a binding contract until age eighteen. There isn't an eighteen-year old in the world who still believes in Santa Claus."

Shit.

The Devil was right, of course. Adults don't believe in my existence, which suits me just fine. I have enough on my plate catering to the whims and demands of kids. Besides, Satan can offer things that adults really want; fame, ability, talent. People might say they will sell their soul for material goods, but when it comes down to putting a signature on the dotted line, they will invariably have a change of heart. Fame and talent and ability can be used to acquire all kinds of material gear. Why sell your soul for a flashy car when you can sell it for rock stardom and buy as many cars as you want, drive them to the finest restaurants, and leave with top-shelf pussy in the passenger seat?

Still. There might be a way to do it. I put my memory to work, and by the time I got back to the Pole, I had a candidate in mind.

All the lists and letters that are sent up north are sorted, catalogued, and archived. I sent one of the Elves to pull the file of a certain Jeffrey Peter Colley of Buffalo, New York. I hadn't heard from Jeffrey in seven years—not a peep since the year he'd turned eleven. Most kids quit writing earlier than that, but Jeffrey was one of those children whose imagination took a little longer to be squashed. His letters were a mess. Spelling errors, grammatical miscues... The earlier ones were completely unintelligible. In those years I just dropped off standard stuff—dinky cars, a bike, an air rifle—since I couldn't figure out what the hell he wanted from his lists. The last few were more readable. It was the final letter he sent before he stopped writing that I was after.

I pulled the letter from the file and read it again. My memory was correct. It took a while to decipher, but all Jeffrey Peter Colley of Buffalo, New York wanted for Christmas in 2005 was to live with his mom again. That wasn't going to happen. His mom had been flattened by a Piggly-Wiggly delivery truck and had been watching reruns of Growing Pains upstairs ever since.

The letter from Jeffrey ended with the promise of "warm mlik and a Niggerbread Man" if I popped by with his mom on Christmas morning.

Bingo.

It wasn't the last line of the letter that I recalled, though. It was the first.

"Dear Satan."

Stop me if you've heard this one: You know how to spot a dyslexic? He'll be the one at the toga party dressed like a goat.

Well, I had found my goat.

I drew up a simple contract stating that—in return for reunification with his mother—Jeffrey Peter Colley of Buffalo, New York, will hereby relinquish any and all claims upon his soul and transfer, upon death, ownership of said soul to Santa. I picked the ugliest Elf and had him dress in leather pants and a black t-shirt, gave him a few bucks to say he was one of the Devil's Imps and he'd come with an offer, and sent him down to Buffalo on Comet to deliver and witness the contract. Poor Jeffery was still pining for his mom, all these years later. He was apparently quite happy to sign. He didn't even pause long enough to ask why one of the Devil's Imps would show up on a reindeer. Easy peasy.

Satan just about lost his mind when I turned up with the contract.

"That is not a valid agreement!" Smoke billowed from his nostrils.

"How do you figure?"

"You have promised to return the mother of this man. This is beyond your ability. The contract was not signed in good faith!" He was fuming.

"Listen," I said, "What the hell do you know about *good faith*? I promised the lad I'd reunite him with his mother. That's what he wants more than anything in this world. My job is to give people what they want, and that's exactly what I intend to do. When Jeffrey Peter Colley of Buffalo, New York, dies—which will be pretty soon—I'll personally deliver his soul to Heaven, special-like."

Hell, I've already wrapped the bomb. I know when you've been naughty, I know when you've been nice, and I

know this: people will open anything you put under a
Christmas tree.

ABOUT THE AUTHORS

Richard Farren Barber was born in Nottingham in July 1970. After studying in London, he returned to the East Midlands. He lives with his wife and son and works as a Development Services Manager for a local university. He has written over 200 short stories and has had short stories published in *Alt-Dead*, *Alt-Zombie*, *Blood Oranges*, *Derby Scribes Anthology*, *Derby Telegraph*, *ePocalypse–Tales from the End*, *Gentle Reader*, *Murky Depths*, *Midnight Echo*, *Midnight Street*, *Morpheus Tales*, *MT Biopuink Special*, *MT Urban Horror Special*, *Night Terrors II*, *Siblings*, *The House of Horror*, *Trembles*, and broadcast on *BBC Radio Derby and Erewash Sound*. Richard was sponsored by *Writing East Midlands* to undertake a mentoring scheme in which he was supported in the development of his novel, *Bloodie Bones*. His novella, *The Power of Nothing*, will be published by Damnation Books in September 2013. His website is www.richardfarrenbarber.co.uk.

JP Behrens has been a storyteller most of his life. He has weaved an intricate web of bold faced lies, some of them in the form of stories. Everything in one's life is a learning experience, and he's tried to learn from both wondrous successes and miserable failures. Though JP has managed to fib less often, he still tells the occasional exaggerated tale here and there. Get updates at JPBehrensauthor.com.

Rose Blackthorn lives in the high mountain desert of Eastern Utah with her boyfriend and two dogs, an Australian Shepherd mix called Boo and a Yorkie named Shadow. She spends her time writing, reading, being crafty, and photographing the surrounding wilderness. An only child, she was lucky enough to have a mother who loved books, and has been surrounded by them her entire life. Thus instead of squabbling with siblings, she learned to be friends with her imagination and the voices in her head are still very much present. She is a member of the HWA and has been published online and in print with *Necon E-Books*, *Stupefying Stories*, *Cast of Wonders*, *Buzzy Mag* and the anthologies *The Ghost IS the Machine*, *A Quick Bite of Flesh*, *Fear the Abyss*, *From Beyond the Grave*, *Horrific History*, *Eulogies II: Tales from the Cellar*, *Cellar Door*, and *The Best of the Horror Society 2013*, among others. For more about Rose, you can follow her on Twitter @rose_blackthorn or visit her at her blog, http://roseblackthorn.wordpress.com/, or on Facebook, http://www.facebook.com/RoseBlackthorn.Author. To purchase her stories, visit her Amazon author page, http://amazon.com/author/roseblackthorn.

John Boden lives a stone's throw from Three Mile Island with his wonderful wife and sons. A baker by day, he spends his off time writing, working on Shock Totem, or watching rubbish on TV. He likes Diet Pepsi, cheeseburgers, heavy metal, and sports ferocious sideburns. While his output as a writer is fairly small, it has a bit of a reputation for being unique. His work has appeared in *52 Stitches*, *Everyday Weirdness*, *Metazen*, *Black Ink Horror*, *Weirdyear*, *NECON E-Books*, *Shock Totem*, the John Skipp edited *Psychos*, and the upcoming anthology *Once Upon an Apocalypse*. He just released *Dominoes*, a unique chapbook of surreal end-of-the-world horror presented as a children's book that is not for children.

Chantal Boudreau, an accountant/author/illustrator, lives in Nova Scotia, Canada. A Horror Writers Association member, she writes horror and fantasy, with several short stories published to date. She has released four novels in *Fervor*, her dystopian series, and three in her *Masters & Renegades* fantasy series. Find out more at http://chantellyb.wordpress.com.

Simon Bradley lives in Toronto with his wife and their stubborn French Bulldog. His work can be found in *Spark: A Creative Anthology Vol. II* and online at *Postcard Shorts* and *Chrome Baby*.

Jeff C. Carter lives in Venice, CA with two cats, a dog, and a human. His short stories appear in the anthologies *Cellar Door Volume 1*, *Song Stories: Blaze of Glory*, SUPER, TALES FROM THE BELL CLUB, SHORT SIPS Vol 2, AVENIR ECLECTIA Vol 1, SCIENCE GONE MAD and FRIGHTMARES as well as Trembles, Calliope and eFiction magazine. He is currently developing MECHAWEST, a steam punk RPG for Heroic Journey Publishing. Visit him at Jeffccarter.wordpress.com.

Matt Cowan's love for the horror genre stretches back beyond his earliest childhood memories. At a young age he stopped having nightmares after beginning to enjoy them too much. His primary literary influences are Ramsey Campbell, M.R. James, Algernon Blackwood, Fritz Leiber, and H.P. Lovecraft. "The Collective of Blaque Reach" was originally published in 2008 by Dead Letter Press as the bonus chap book story for the anthology *Bound for Evil: Curious Tales of Books Gone Bad*. It was also read on episode 90 of the Tales To Terrify podcast in 2013. His short story, "Here He Comes A Wandering," won the Pod of Horror Christmas Horror Story Contest in 2009 and was read on episode #58. He's had stories appear in *Indiana Horror Anthology 2011* and *Indiana Horror Anthology 2012*, as well as *Indiana Science Fiction Anthology 2011* and *Indiana Crime Review 2013*. In addition to writing fiction, Matt produces articles highlighting some of the legendary names in the field at his blog, *Horror Delve*, which can be found at mattcowanhorror.wordpress.com. He lives with his beautiful wife Lynne and stepson Brett in Lawrence, Indiana, where he works for the local water utility. He's currently crafting several more tales to fill the void left by his long lost nightmares. You can also find him on Facebook at https://www.facebook.com/mattcowanhorror.

Rob Ferreri is an award-winning writer and director born and raised on the Jersey Shore. He is the author of *People are Milk & I'm Lactose Intolerant*, a collection of comedic anecdotes, and has written and directed two feature films, *Camp Dead* and *Blood Feud*. He has also created several successful web series, including: *Not So Amazing*, *Outer Rim*, and *Geek vs. Geek*. Rob has also produced and directed several short films, music videos, and commercials, and has been known to act on occasion.

Raymond Gates is an Australian Aboriginal writer based on the Gold Coast, Australia, whose childhood crush with reading everything dark and disturbing evolved into an adult love affair with writing horror. He has published a number of short stories and, with the help of his muse, plans to drag the novel that lurks within him into the light. Delve into his mind at: www.raymondgates.com.

Catherine Grant is an Assignment Editor for Shock Totem Publications, office monkey for a Connecticut mental health and addictions non-profit, freelance journalist, bibliophile, gamer, and connoisseur of caffeine-laden beverages.

Liam Hogan was abandoned in a library at the tender age of 3, to reluctantly emerge blinking into the sunlight many years later, with a head full of words and an aversion to loud noises. His work has been performed by others at Liars' League and 'Are You Sitting Comfortably?', and you can find it in print in *London Lies* (Arachne Press), *FEAR: Vol II* (Crooked Cat), *In On The Tide* (AppleTree Writers), *Litro*, and *OpenPen*, as well as in various online magazines. He lives in London and dreams in Dewey Decimals. For more information, visit http://happyendingnotguaranteed.blogspot.co.uk/.

BC Jackson writes short, horrifying stories from his home in the Illinois Heartland. He does have an older brother who has survived well into adulthood. Contact BC at bc.jackson.9@gmail.com.

Randy Lindsay is a native of Arizona. From an early age, his mind traveled in new and unusual directions. His preoccupation with "what if" eventually led him to write speculative fiction. According to his wife everything is a story to Randy. And it is. His stories have been published in *Gentle Strength Quarterly*, *The City of the Gods: Mythic Tales*, *Penumbra eZine*, and *The Flash 500*. More of his stories will appear soon in the *Once Upon An*

Apocalypse anthology by Chaosium, the second *City of the Gods* anthology, and *HNR* (*Horror Novel Review*). His first novel, *The Gathering*, is scheduled for release in January of 2014.

Michael McCarty has been a professional writer since 1983 and the author of over thirty of fiction and nonfiction including *A Hell of Job, Liquid Diet & Midnight Snack: 2 Vampire Satires, Monster Behind The Wheel* (co-written with Mark McLaughlin), *Conversations with Kreskin* (co-written with The Amazing Kreskin), *I Kissed A Ghoul* and *Lost Girl of the Lake* (co-written with Joe McKinney). He is a five-time Bram Stoker Finalist and in 2008 David R. Collins' Literary Achievement Award from the Midwest Writing Center. He lives in Rock Island, Illinois with his wife, Cindy, and pet rabbit, Latte. He is on Twitter as michaelmccarty6. Facebook! Like him on his official page: http://www.facebook.com/michaelmccarty.horror. Or snail mail him at: Michael McCarty, Fan Mail, P.O. Box 4441, Rock Island, IL 61204-4441.

Ben McElroy is a full-time admissions representative for a Massachusetts state university and a part-time writer of horror fiction. Though his day job can be terrifying at times, his creative inspiration stems from far more bizarre and eclectic sources than that. Ben's almost one dozen published stories can be found in various print and online venues. If you're patient enough, you should be able to read more of his written works in the near future. He welcomes any comments or questions regarding his creative output at ben.mcelroy1978@gmail.com.

Mark McLaughlin's fiction, nonfiction, and poetry have appeared in more than 1,000 magazines, newspapers, websites, and anthologies, including *Galaxy, Fangoria, Living Dead 2, The Best of All Flesh, Writer's Digest, Cemetery Dance, Midnight Premiere, Dark Arts*, and two volumes each of *The Best of HorrorFind* and *The Year's Best Horror Stories* (DAW Books). His latest releases are the story collection, *Best Little Witch-House in Arkham*, and the two-author poetry collection, *Revenge of the Two-Headed Poetry Monster* (with Michael McCarty). Other recent works by McLaughlin include the story collection *Beach Blanket Zombie*, the collaborative collection *Partners in Slime* (with Michael McCarty), and the collaborative horror novel, *Monster Behind the Wheel* (with Michael McCarty). Also, he is the coauthor, with Rain Graves and David Niall Wilson, of *The Gossamer Eye*, which won the 2002 Bram Stoker Award for Superior Achievement in Poetry. Feel free to visit his Facebook page, www.facebook.com/markmclaughlinmedia.

Adam Millard is the author of fourteen novels, five novellas, and more than a hundred short stories, which can be found in various collections and anthologies. Probably best known for his post-apocalyptic fiction, Adam also writes fantasy/horror for children. He created the character *Peter Crombie, Teenage Zombie* just so he had something decent to read to his son at bedtime. Adam also writes Bizarro fiction for several publishers, who enjoy his tales of flesh-eating clown-beetles and rabies-infected derrieres so much that they keep printing them. His "Dead" series has been the filling in a Stephen King/Bram Stoker sandwich on Amazon's bestsellers chart, and the translation rights have recently sold to German publisher, Voodoo Press. Adam also writes for This Is Horror, whose columnists include Simon Bestwick, Jasper Bark and BC Furtney. Adam lives in the post-apocalyptic landscape known as Wolverhampton, England, with his wife, Zoe, and son, Phoenix.

Christopher Miron was born and raised in Michigan and moved to the Chattanooga are in 2008. He is married to Valerie and is an avid animal lover, with three dogs, two cats, a rabbit, and a bird. He enjoys horror movies and books, and his favorite time of the year is Halloween. In his spare time, he makes ornaments. "One day I cut myself on one, and that is how I ended up writing *Ornaments*."

Mark Onspaugh is a California native and the author of over fifty published short stories. He studied psychology at UCLA and worked with exotic animals in Moorpark College's Exotic Animal Training and Management program. He learned techniques of special effects makeup from artists like Thomas R. Burman, Rick Baker, and Rob Bottin, and studied improve comedy with the Groundlings. Mark has also written for television and film. His first novel, *The Faceless Ones*, has been published by Random House under its Hydra imprint. His second novel, *The Ravenous Dead*, is Book I of *The Thetis Plague Trilogy*, published by Severed Press. He currently lives in Cambria with his wife and three peculiar cats.

Nicky Peacock is an English author in the UK. She writes both YA and adult horror, paranormal romance, and urban fantasy. She's been published in 5 countries in over 35 books. You can find more details of her and her work on http://nickypeacockauthor.wordpress.com.

Michael Thomas-Knight haunts the local coffee shops of Long Island, NY, somewhere between a famous house in Amityville and Joel Rifkin's lovely home. His horror fiction has been published in *Twisted Dreams Magazine*, *Infernal Ink*, *SNM Horror Magazine,* and *Dark Eclipse*. Michael's fiction has also been published in several horror anthologies in 2013 including: *Shadow Masters, From Beyond The Grave, 100 Doors of Terror, Miseria's Chorale,* and *Cellar Door II.* You can find Michael at his blog, *Parlor of Horror*, which deals with all things horror—movies, books, and articles for the horror enthusiast (http://parlorofhorror.wordpress.com). You can check out Michael's latest publications at his Amazon Authors Page, https://www.amazon.com/author/michaelthomasknight, or you can join him on Facebook, https://www.facebook.com/michael.thomasknight.9.

D. Alexander Ward lives with his wife and daughter in Virginia on the farmland where he grew up and where his love for the people, passions, and legends of the South was nurtured. Over the years, his short fiction has appeared in multiple venues and anthologies, most notably including *Shifters* and *A Quick Bite of Flesh* from Hazardous Press, *Deadlines* from Comet Press, *The Midnight Diner 4: Wastelands Under the Sun*, and *Attack of the B-Movie Monsters: Night of the Gigantis* from Grinning Skull Press. His collection of stories, *A Feast of Buzzards* (due to be released in the fall/winter by Hazardous Press) will pair nicely with his novella, *After the Fire*, which is now available from Dark Hall Press.

Peter White spent most of his youth digesting as many horror movies and novels as he could get his hands on, but he only took up writing as a hobby a couple of years ago. He spends the rest of his spare time running, and will be competing in his fifth full Marathon early in 2014. He currently lives in London and works in the Pharmaceutical industry.

For some, death is not the end. There are those who are doomed to walk the earth for all eternity, those who are trapped between one plain of existence and the next, those who, for whatever reason, cannot or will not let go of the lives they left behind. These are the vengeful spirits, the tortured souls, the ghosts that haunt our realm. Welcome to FROM BEYOND THE GRAVE, a collection of 19 original ghost stories.

Available in print from Amazon.com and Barnes and Noble, and in digital formats from <u>Amazon.com</u>, Barnes and Noble, and Kobo books